NIGHT OF THE FREAKS

Book 1

DOMINIC R. DANIELS

Dedicated

to

All Rockers and Rock Stars. Long live Heavy Metal.

WGA Registered.
Dominic Rocky Daniels
Email: dominicdaniels777@gmail.com

EXT. LOUISIANA ROAD - NIGHT

A jet black van wickedly detailed with illustrations of demons and monsters passes through a small Cajun town. On the side is painted, in garish script, "THE METAL MACHINE".

The Metal Machine van leaves town and heads out on the dirt highway.

Suddenly, the van hits a dark figure with a sickening THUMP!

The van screeches to a halt.

ROXY, early 20s, the gothic queen of the night and talented pianist. The free spirited soul of the group, smart, witty and very pretty, and LISA, early 20s, blond bombshell knock out, the girl-next-door, bossy yet sweet and kind. She is the lead singer of the group, powerful vocalist like Doro Pesch. She peers out the passenger window.

> ROXY
> What was that? Did you see
> that?

The dark figure they hit quickly crawls under the van and to the other side of the road.

SWITCH, early 20s, buff, a metal head burnout dude with serious flare and a bad ass temper. He's the groups drummer. Behind the wheel, looks out the driver's window.

> SWITCH
> I don't see anything.
> LISA
> Let's go, there's nothing here.
> SWITCH
> Well, there was a minute ago, and we hit it.
> LISA
> It's not there now. Maybe it was a rock or branches.
> SWITCH
> I don't wanna know. Place gives me the creeps. Let's get the fuck out of here.

The women turn back from the windows. The van drives off.

By the side of the road, a dog lies, whining plaintively. A dark shape in the shadows rises out of the weeds behind it.

The shape falls onto the dog with great violence. We hear RIPPING flesh, SNAPPING bone. The sounds of someone, or some <u>thing</u>, eating hungrily.

INT. VAN - NIGHT

The van is stuffed with musical gear, and wallpapered with stickers of bands, instrument companies, and the like. Heavy metal music plays in a CD player.

Along one side wall, a large logo reads "THE MIDNIGHT FREAKS". Cartoons of the four here in the van are arrayed underneath. Clearly it's the name of their group.

                    SWITCH
          Hey babe, pass me the weed.

Roxy passes the joint to Switch. He tokes, then passes it back to RICKY, early 20s, Spiky haired punk and clown of the group. Laid back and chill. The band's lead guitarist.

Lisa kicks Ricky when he doesn't pass the joint over fast enough. He grins, surrenders it.

Roxy turns on a small light to read. Switch looks in the rear view mirror -- watches Roxy reading her book.

                    SWITCH
          How can you read that stuff?
                    ROXY
          This book has a cool history
          of our town. Besides, I love
          scary stories, they give me a
          thrill.
                    SWITCH
          What thrills me is how we
          kicked major ass at the gig
          last night.
                    RICKY
          Yeah man, people were whal-
          ing all over the place. It was
          crazy man -- few more shows
          like that and we'll be on our
          way with a record deal!
                    ROXY
          A few hundred grand in the
          bank and we won't have to
          live in the dorms any more.

Get a nice four-bedroom loft in the French Quarter and jam all we want.

LISA

(sarcastically)

Yeah and flying in a jumbo jet, eating bon bon's and smoking crack.

SWITCH

What the fuck is wrong with you. You missed your Prozac and early morning shit, today?

LISA

WAKE THE FUCK UP.

ROXY

Come on Lis, what about the show we did. It was great.

LISA

So great that, we got our asses thrown off the stage when Switch here puked during the show. They laughed at us like bunch of jokers.

SWITCH

Hey fuck you. I like getting wasted before a show, helps me play better.

LISA

Go play with your dick!

The whole group laughs. Even Switch.
Switch snickers.

      SWITCH
Okay, I won't do it again before a show. Deal.

Lisa smiles.

      LISA
Deal.
      RICKY
You guys still have to admit that it would be really
cool. To be a record label I
mean. Just think, no more
dealing with shitty room-
mates, no dorm inspections.
Total fucking freedom. We
could get drunk, smoke
weed, and throw parties every night.
      SWITCH
Sweet.
      LISA
Hey, Switch, we've been
on the road for almost two
hours.
      RICKY
Yeah, I'm starving, dude.
Let's stop to get something
to eat.
      LISA
    (annoyed)
Ricky, all you think about is
food.

Lisa peers into her compact and applies red lipstick.

> RICKY
> All you think about is your
> face.
> LISA
> Can I help it if I'm beautiful?

Lisa blows Ricky a teasing kiss.

> RICKY
> (laughs & smiles)
> What a babe! You're hot Lis,
> I'll give you that. But you're a
> prick tease.
> LISA
> No, I am not!
> RICKY
> (fondly)
> I'm just messin' witcha.

Ricky tries to move in and steal a kiss. She gives him a stripe of lipstick instead. Then she laughs and kisses it into his lips.

> SWITCH
> Hey, get a room!

Lisa breaks off, laughing -- he breaks off, panting. He's got wood.

> ROXY
> Yes, why don't we all get a
> room. And some eats. Let's
> grab a pizza.

> SWITCH
>
> Just relax you guys, we'll get something to eat when we head back into town. Right now we need to get this stupid project done.

(A beat)

> SWITCH
>
> Anyway, we should there in about an hour. Hell, the swamp is not too far from here. I think.

Switch lights up a cigarette casually, takes a drag, exhales a quick puff of smoke.

> ROXY
>
> This whole thing really sucks, we still have to do that stupid report for that stuck up bitch, Professor Bellflower.
>
> LISA
>
> Relax, Rox.
>
> ROXY
>
> It's just so lame. We could be having fun partying tonight, moshing at The Cobra Club. But instead were out here in the freakin' sticks being teacher's little bitch. It's Halloween, for god sakes! I

hate doing homework on holidays.

LISA

Sorry!

ROXY

You should be sorry! It was your idea! Volunteering us for this dumb ass project without even telling us?

LISA

I'm sorry, for the millionth time. Besides, you'll thank me when you graduate. With all the times we cut to go play gigs -- we need extra credit just to squeak by. You should thank me for saving your college career.

SWITCH

Homework and studying, blows balls.

LISA

It's true. But when we get this thing done it will be worth it and besides, The battle of the bands will be in town. We win that, we win it all or at least some respect. Which this band really needs.

SWITCH

We'll Nail'em.

RICKY

Chill out, you guys. If it doesn't work out, we'll get my brother to help us... fake something up with his visual FX stuff. The guy is a pro in the movie biz.

LISA

Bellflower's not a moron, she'd know.

RICKY

No, she's a bitch, and she's going to have us expelled if we don't ace this team project.

SWITCH

Hey she's a hot bitch, is what she is. I would not mind hitting that.

ROXY

SWITCH!

SWITCH

I'm just kidding.

RICKY

It's true, you can't deny that. Bellflower is one hot woman.

The girls look at both the guys. They roll their eyes: men.

LISA

Whatever, anything's better than being right now in town anyway. Who would want to be winding up the next victim of that hidden serial killer...

ROXY

I know! All the murders the news said were strange as hell, and the dumb ass cops don't even have a clue! From what I heard all the victims were drained of blood. It's pretty creepy when you think about it.

(A beat)

RICKY

I heard the bodies looked all dried up corpses when the cops found them. Who the fuck knows what killed them. Maybe it was a nut job from the local mental hospital.

SWITCH

Yeah like you're crazy dad.

RICKY

Hey shut up!

SWITCH

Does the word fuckhead, spelled on his face, mean anything to you. He's a prick.

RICKY

Can I help it if I got an asshole for an old man. He's always up tight.

LISA

Ricky, take it easy.

ROXY

Let's not talk about this stuff.
We all got enough problems
at home. Ricky's dad is a
drunk, my mom is a fucking
hippie, Switch's your folks
don't give a shit about you
and Lis, our dad is a bitter
assface. Why don't we listen
to some music. It's too de-
pressing to think about. Let's
put on some tunes.

SWITCH

You got it.

Switch pulls out a CD from the visor and inserts it into the CD player.
Instrumental heavy metal powers out of the speakers. Everybody starts head-
banging wildly.

SWITCH

Now let's see what this bad
girl can really do, yeah!!!

Roxy is amped up.

ROXY

Let's get this party started!
Whooo!

Switch floors the gas pedal as the van takes off speeding, in a chorus of banshee yells from the adrenaline-pumped friends.

EXT. LOUISIANA ROAD - NIGHT

The sun sets behind creepy trees. The van speeds past down a dirt road.

INT. VAN - NIGHT

The party is totally over. The four look tired and bummed.

ROXY

Dammit, where the hell are
we?

SWITCH

Relax, I'll get us there.

Suddenly, CHARLIE STEVENS, 70s, an old gray-haired white red neck hermit, appears in the middle of the road, carrying a lantern. A sly and nasty dog of a man. In better words a weasel. Slick and sneaky.

Switch slams on the brakes!

SWITCH

OH FUCK!

The van screeches and stops, missing Charlie by inches.

CHARLIE

(angry)
What the hell are you doing?
You damn kids trying to kill
me?

                    SWITCH
        You didn't wanna be killed,
        you shouldn't be in the mid-
        dle of the fucking road!
                    CHARLIE
        You young son-of-a-bitch!
        You see any sidewalks around
        here? Where else'm I sup-
        posed ta walk?

Charlie peers through the windshield.

                    CHARLIE
        What the hell are you kids
        doing out here any ways?
                    LISA
            (to Switch)
        Let me handle this.

EXT. VAN - NIGHT
Lisa and Roxy open the door and get out of the van.

                    LISA
        Listen we're sorry about our
        driver. We've been on the road
        for a few hours -- we've come
        out here to find ghosts to docu-
        ment. It's called spirit photog-
        raphy. We are doing a report
        for our comparative religion
        class on disembodied spirits
        and paranormal hauntings.

CHARLIE
Find ghosts heh?

LISA
We're college students. Figures right.

CHARLIE
Ah, city folks. From the uni-
versity up to the town, eh?

ROXY
Yeah, that's right.

Charlie thinks a bit. Lisa and Roxy exchange humorous glances.
Ricky and Switch exit the van and drift up to join the conversation.

CHARLIE
Hmmm. You know... I guess
maybe I could show y'all a
place... but it'll cost ya some
cash.

ROXY
Really. What are we talkin'
here?

Charlie gives them a good once-over, trying to decide how much he can
reasonably extort.

CHARLIE
What exactly are you looking
for? Ghosts, spirits, spooks...

LISA
Anything --
            (hold up camera)
-- long as we can get <u>proof</u>.

> CHARLIE
> Well... there's an old cemetery
> down near the swamp.

Ricky pulls out a road map. Charlie points to a location.

> RICKY
> Ain't on here.
> CHARLIE
> That's 'cause it's been aban-
> doned for years. Lucky you
> met an old man like me -- I'm
> the only one who remembers,
> all the stories that is. The
> townsfolk act like it never
> existed. Anyway, it ain't safe
> to go down there alone. So I
> don't.

Charlie sizes up the boys.

> CHARLIE
> But I could use the scratch.
> And you boys look like you
> can take care of yourselves.
> (to Switch)
> 'Specially you.
> (to group)
> A Hundred bucks.

The entire group scoffs.

SWITCH

You're crazy!

CHARLIE

Take it or leave it, boy! There ain't nobody else round here for twenty miles, and definitely nobody else knows exactly where that old graveyard is.

RICKY

Okay, band meeting!

Ricky takes the other three a few feet away.

RICKY

Let's just pay the guy. It's worth it, if we can pass this stupid class. We go down there, get some pictures, then maybe we can get back while there's still some Halloween left!

Everybody seems to agree.

SWITCH

(to Charlie)

Gives us a sec.

The group returns to the van. Charlie watches them. He hawks and spits. Sniffs. Fidgety. His eyes shine with greed.

The foursome return with the cash. Lisa forks it over.

                    LISA
          Okay here. That's a hundred
          bucks. If you screw us, we'll
          jack you up. Be cool about it,
          they'll be no problem.

Charlie crosses his heart.

                    CHARLIE
          Cross my heart and hope to
          die. I'm Charlie, by the way.
          Charlie Stevens.

Each of the group gives him their names, as they head back to the van.

                    LISA
          I'm Lisa...
                    ROXY
          Roxy...
                    RICKY
          Ricky...
                    SWITCH
          And I'm Switch. And we're
          the most kick ass thrash band
          you ever heard --

He indicates the sign visible inside the van.

                    SWITCH
          The Midnight Freaks!

Charlie grins at the group.

> CHARLIE
> Damn metal head punks. I guess you don't know any Hank Williams, do ya?
> RICKY
> (smiling)
> Don't count us out, old man. We may be metal head punks, but we still know our roots.
> SWITCH
> Alright, let's get a move on.

Everybody gets inside. Switch starts the van and they move off down the road.

EXT. CEMETERY FRONT GATE - EVENING

The van moves up an overgrown road. The headlights splash across some imposing gates, craggy with rust. Switch cuts the engine and the lights go out.

The swamp fog hugs the ground. A bright moon shines from behind a scud of dark night clouds. Toads, grasshoppers and crickets chorus all around.

The group gets out of the van to get their bags, cameras and flashlights. Charlie grabs his lantern and sees the cemetery front gate.

The wind blows the front gate open.

> CHARLIE
> Smack dab! And call me shit-less! Here we are. LaFayette Cemetery.

Ricky looks at the cemetery. Lightning strikes. A few moments later, thunder rolls.

RICKY

Awesome.

Switch pulls Roxy aside and whispers something into her ear. She gives him a coy, sexy smile.

ROXY

Hey you guys, listen -- you go ahead. There's some other, uh, "equipment" we gotta unload here.

The others snicker. They know. Charlie's clueless.

LISA

Um-hmm. Don't be too long. You don't want to get lost in there.

RICKY

Have fun you two.

Lisa, Ricky and Charlie enter the cemetery. Soon they and their light are swallowed up by the tombstones, the long wild grass, the old gnarled trees.

Roxy and Switch laugh. Switch lifts Roxy up, and sets her against the van's hood. They start to make out.

Roxy heats up fast. She yanks off her top, exposing her young full breasts. Switch stares -- then a NOISE behind causes him to whip his head around.

SWITCH'S P.O.V.

For a second, glowing red eyes appear in the bushes -- then just as quickly disappear.

BACK TO SCENE

Switch is freaked out more than he cares to admit.

SWITCH

What the hell was that!

ROXY

Baby, relax. They're just my boobs!

SWITCH

I just thought I saw a pair of red eyes.

ROXY

Are you for real? What is this, Scooby Doo?

SWITCH

(serious)

You think I'd make up something like this? I'm not lying.

ROXY

Switch, c'mon. Cut it out. This isn't funny.

SWITCH

(pissed)

Whatever.

He grabs her top and hands it back to her, distracted.

SWITCH

Look let's just go. Sooner we get the hell out of here, sooner we can get back home and get busy, or don't you?

Roxy stares back at him.

ROXY
(disappointed)
Okay, fine...

EXT. OLD CEMETERY - NIGHT
Charlie, Ricky and Lisa stand in a clearing, looking around.
They hear the CRASHING of BRUSH, and freak out for a second -- then
Roxy and Switch jog up.

LISA
That was fast... what's up?
SWITCH
Nothing. C'mon, let's go.

He moves past. Lisa eyes Roxy. Roxy shakes her head, irritated: don't ask.
The group moves on through the tombstones and bushes.

CHARLIE
You kids don't know about
the history about this place,
do ya?
ROXY
How would we?
RICKY
What history?
CHARLIE
(chuckles wickedly)
My granddaddy told me sto-
ries... 'bout what happened
here during the Civil War.
Infamous murderers and
thieves were buried here. No

one in the town of Labou
ever came here, not even
back then...

FLASHBACK - EXT. LABOU FIELDS - DAY
SUPER: "1984"
A fields of dead weeds, resembling wheat stalks, blows in the wind.

> CHARLIE (V.O.)
> The story goes back to 1984,
> when a local Creole tribes-
> man known as Kane Louis
> Williams, a vodun high priest
> was murdered and hanged
> here. They called him the
> "Voodoo Man".

An angry, armed mob of townspeople -- farmers, migrant workers, young
hick children -- moves through the field, hunting purposely for something.

Out front, a burly local sheriff with a tin star on his chest, and a dandy in a
top hat, the mayor, scan left and right, eyes full of concern.

INT. KANE'S HOUSE - NIGHT

A large black man kneels before a voodoo ritual altar. Wax candles light up
the dark room.

> CHARLIE (V.O.)
> It was said that he was a de-
> scendant of Marie Laveau,
> the famous voodoo queen
> of New Orleans. The local
> legends say that he would
> kidnap the infant children

from the town and sacrifice
them to his voodoo gods by
draining their blood and eating their flesh -- that is while
they was still alive. Color and
race never made no differ-
ence, so they say.

KANE LOUIS WILLIAMS gets up from his kneeling position. Late 40s,
he's a tall black man with eyes full of merciless hate and lust.

On the wall behind him, an oil painting of Voodoo god Baron Samedi
hangs, surrounded by occult symbols painted in what might be human
blood.

On the altar table stands a bowl of human ears, and another bowl of human
eyes. Voodoo dolls, human skulls and the other bloody relics of his religion surround him.

Kane places a black baby on the altar to prepare a sacrifice. He pulls out a
voodoo knife.

Kane slowly raises his voodoo dagger up high in the air and quickly thrusts
it down. His hand pulls back up -- the knife drips with blood.

EXT. OLD CEMETERY - NIGHT (BACK TO PRESENT)

The guys grin. The girls pull faces.

LISA
(disgusted)
That's terrible!

ROXY
(intrigued)
How did he die?

Charlie smiles, knowing he's got them hooked.

FLASHBACK - EXT. LABOU FIELDS - DAY

Kane breaks from cover and sprints for his life. The mob is faster -- they capture him. The sheriff binds his hands behind his back.

> CHARLIE (V.O.)
> The townsfolk eventually, caught up with him and gave him a good old-fashioned lynchin'.

Nearby rises a tree. The mob's got a rope, already fashioned into a hang noose.

> CHARLIE (V.O.)
> Course, they beat him half to death first, to soften him up.

They beat and kick Kane, harder as he goes down. They mock him and laugh at him -- they've having a good old time.

KANE'S POV

Through a red mist, Kane sees a specter wink into being behind the oblivious crowd. A black man wearing a high hat crowned with a red feather. BARON SAMEDI.

He grins a toothy grin down at Kane. Ceremonial fetish charms ring his neck, hanging down over a vest jacket. He wears black shorts and black sandals, and carries an old wooden staff with rune markings carved into it.

BACK TO SCENE

Kane smiles.

> CHARLIE (V.O.)
> Lotsa strange stories came up outta that day. They said he had strange powers. Offerings

would appear on his grave.
Only God knows where. You
wouldn't want to be out there
alone. Scary stuff.

Kane's lips move slowly, while the crazed townspeople continue their attack. Some see his lips moving and become afraid.

                    CHARLIE (V.O.)
          They say that just before he
          died, he said an incantation --
          and put a curse on the town...

The mayor puts a stop to it and they haul the bleeding, broken man to his feet. Kane's lips still move.

                    CHARLIE (V.O.)
          ...vowing he'd return from
          the grave and avenge his foul
          and unnatural death.

The mob throws the noose over a branch and hauls him upright.

                    KANE
          You'll all pay -- with the
          blood of your children!

Baron Samedi, looking on, smiles evilly.
The mob yanks the rope -- and stretches Kane's neck for him.
EXT. OLD CEMETERY - NIGHT (BACK TO PRESENT)
Charlie looks gravely around at the four kids.

CHARLIE

Needless to say, I don't like this place. Hence... the hundred bucks.

Switch scoffs.

SWITCH

(sarcastically)

The Voodoo Man, ooooo-ouuuh! Scary! Bunch of bullshit!

Charlie is annoyed then concerned.

CHARLIE

It ain't bullshit, boy, I'm tellin' ya. There's weird things in this cemetery and if I were you, I wouldn't hang around here too long. Heh, 'hang' around, get it?

(waits in vain for a laugh)

You really sure you kids want to go in here and take pictures and --

LISA

Look Charlie, we're here to do a project, find some spirits, take a few pictures, say a few bloody Mary's and get the hell out of here before sunrise.

The group fans out, looking for ghosts. All that's to be found around here are tombstones and dead grass.

> CHARLIE
> But what happens if you kids get into trouble or get hurt or something? I'd feel responsible.
> RICKY
> Don't worry, we'll be fine. We got Switch here to protect us.

Switch pulls out a switchblade knife. He flicks it open, and grins in a cocky way.

> SWITCH
> I can take care of these dipshits.

Roxy punches Switch hard in the arm, making him drop his knife.

> SWITCH
> (whiny)
> Ow, that hurts!
> ROXY
> Jerk.
> SWITCH
> I was just kidding around! Take a joke!

Switch drops to hands and knees, searching with his flashlight for his knife.

CHARLIE
Alright, tell you what. I'll go
wait in the van. Make sure no
spooks steal it from ya.

Switch gets up with his knife. He thinks a moment, then nods. He moves
toward Charlie.

SWITCH
Fine. You watch the van. We
come back and it's gone... I'll
hunt you down.

CHARLIE
Relax. That piece of junk
ain't worth my time. No real
man'd be caught dead drivin'
that. I wouldn't be able to
show my face.

Switch's eyes narrow. Insulting his van -- his baby -- is not allowed. He grabs
Charlie by the shoulder and shoves the knife within an inch of his throat.

SWITCH
Hey respect the wheels, you
old fart.

Switch lets go of Charlie.

CHARLIE
You really got a way with people, kid. Relax, I'll just catch me a nap.
(mutters)
Prick.

SWITCH

Say what?

Charlie irritated waves him off, true old man fashion. He heads out of the graveyard.

Lisa rolls up on Switch.

LISA

Way to go! What the hell's wrong with you? All you care about is that stupid van.

SWITCH

Hey, that's my baby back there! It took me all the money I saved up since I was a fucking kid for that ride!

RICKY

What the fuck. You said you fucked a kid. That's sick.

SWITCH

No dumb ass. I said since I was a fucking little kid. Damn. Listen fucker.

They laugh.

(A beat)

Roxy interrupts the dispute.

ROXY

I thought <u>I</u> was your baby.

> SWITCH
> You are, baby, but... my van is
> priceless.
> ROXY
> But what, I can be bought
> with a six-pack of beer and
> some cheap jewelry?

Switch puts the knife back into his pants pocket.

> SWITCH
> Aw, Rox. Come on babe, I
> didn't mean that.
> ROXY
> Sometimes you can be a real
> jerk you know.
> SWITCH
> Only sometimes. The rest
> of the time, I'm your dream
> man. Come here.

He cuddles her a little. She laughs, slaps him away. But you can see she won't stay mad for long.

EXT. OLD CEMETERY - LATER

It's later, it's dark, and it's raining. Thunder and lightning. Shivering, Roxy, Ricky and Switch sit next to a small mausoleum with large vines, sheltering from the rain.

Roxy wraps her arms around Switch to keep warm, while Switch holds her arms. Ricky shakes as he wraps his arms around his body from the cold.

Lisa still actively wanders the cemetery, watching for ghosts with her flashlight and camera. Finally, she gives up and returns to the group.

Switch checking his watch.

SWITCH

Guys, this is ridiculous. It's
nine o'clock. We've been here
two hours, and nothing.

ROXY

Switch is right. Let's go back
to town and come back to-
morrow. At least we know the
way now.

Ricky shivers and nods his head vigorously.

LISA

Yeah, alright, let's head out
then.

EXT. CEMETERY FRONT GATE - NIGHT

The group exits the cemetery with all their gear -- the van's gone. A trail of
tire marks on the muddy ground leads away.

Switch shouts in frustration and anger!

SWITCH

What the Fuck! AHHH!!!
This is fucking bullshit!!
Shit, the guy ripped us off.
The damn van is gone. Look,
it's not here. That dick head
stole it!

ROXY

Oh great. Just freaking great.
Not only did we lose our
money, now we lost our ride
home, thanks to you, Lisa!

Lisa falls back, guilty.

> LISA
>
> What the hell are you blam-
> ing me for? How was I sup-
> posed to know?

Switch jingles his keys wildly.

> SWITCH
>
> Fucking redneck! He musta
> hot-wired it, the bastard! I
> wonder how many other stu-
> pid idiots he's done this to!

Lisa pulls out her cell phone.

> LISA
>
> I'll call the cops and report it
> stolen.
>
> SWITCH
>
> Oh yeah, do that!
> (mocking voice)
> 'Hi, Ossifer, some old hillbil-
> ly hotwired our van! Please
> help us and by the way could
> you please give us a ride back
> to town?"
> (angrily)
> Yeah right, that'll go over
> real well. They hate my ass
> in town, you guys know that.

I got a previous criminal record. It's not like they'll be
<u>real</u> motivated to go find the
damn thing.

Lisa punches her phone, irritated.

LISA
Damn, I can't get a signal.

Roxy pulls out her cell phone.

ROXY
Here let me try, I'll text 'em.

Roxy punches keys, unsuccessfully.

ROXY
I can't get a signal either.
SWITCH
'That's cause we're in the
middle of nowhere in a damn
cemetery!

The rain is getting heavier. Puddles of water start to rise. Lightning strobes,
thunder flashes...

RICKY
(looks up)
Damn, it's pouring like hell!
Come on, we're gonna drown
out here!

                    LISA
We better find shelter until
the storm clears. This lighting is getting dangerous.
After the rain stops we can
hit the road and hitch a ride
back to the campus.
                    SWITCH
Hey fuck this, man, I'm not
catching pneumonia!

Switch separates from the group to find shelter. Ricky also separates in order to find shelter. Lisa and Roxy stick together to find shelter.

As they all move off, the dark silhouette -- the dog-eater -- appears in the bushes. Watching them.

EXT. OLD CEMETERY - NIGHT

Switch searches through the tombstones for a tree or bush or structure to keep the rain off. No luck.

His flashlight's batteries are running down. He hits it to get more light, but it fades away.

EXT. MAUSOLEUM - NIGHT

Ricky's returned to the mausoleum they sheltered under earlier. He opens the door and pokes his flashlight inside. Bare stone... one wooden coffin front and center.

                    RICKY
                 (shouting)
            Hey guys! Over here!

Lisa and Roxy appear from the bushes.

                    LISA
            Oh yeah. It's open?

RICKY

Yeah.

ROXY

(points to coffin)

What about that?

RICKY

He won't mind.

Ricky enters the mausoleum. Lisa follows.

ROXY

Wait, you guys...

(calls out)

Switch! Where are you?

Switch pops up from behind a tombstone!

SWITCH

Rawr!

Roxy screams. Switch dissolves in laughter, comes out, hugs her. She punches him some, but he kisses her and she relents.

Switch looks at the entrance of the stone mausoleum.

SWITCH

Cool.

Switch and Roxy head inside. Switch pulls the heavy door shut behind them.

INT. MAUSOLEUM - NIGHT

Darkness, silence. Everybody turns on their flashlights, except for Switch.

In the light, it's clear there's a lot more to the mausoleum than was initially visible. A number of different tombs occupy the space.

Lisa is amazed of the design of the tombs.

> LISA
> This place is amazing.
> SWITCH
> Yeah, totally badass, just like
> in the movies.
> (to Ricky; evilly)
> Muah ha ha!!!
> RICKY
> Quit screwing around.
> SWITCH
> Lighten up.

The group fans out, exploring. Everywhere, cobwebs, water damage and dust. Ricky finds candles. With his cigarette lighter, he lights them all up.

The increasing light reveals an altar chamber. An inscription is scrawled on the altar, in French. Including the words "Baron Samedi".

> RICKY
> How long do you think this
> place has been here?
> ROXY
> Who knows? For years maybe.

Roxy finds a black crystal Loa idol statue. It has a white painted skull face with a black top hat.

> ROXY
> Check it out -- look at this
> coffin there is a black crystal
> idol above it. It looks like its
> glowing.

Lisa picks up the idol and examines it.

                    LISA
It an African Loa idol. They're
used in tribal ceremonies and
rituals in vodun -- voodoo. I
read about them in world cul-
ture studies.
                    ROXY
Creepy. Hey, check it out.
There's something engraved
here.

Roxy points her flashlight at the altar and scans the inscriptions.

                    LISA
What does it say?
                    ROXY
It says: "Here lies, Kane
Louis Williams. 1940-1984.
Executed by the state of
Louisiana, approved under the
order of the governor. June 1st,
1984."
                    LISA
How can you read it?
                    ROXY
I speak French and Creole
fluently. I study. Remember?
                    LISA
Oh yeah, I forgot.

Roxy finds another inscription -- this one's scratched into the stone.

                    ROXY
          This is interesting. It's hand-
          written in French.
                    LISA
          What does it say?
                    ROXY
          "Burn in hell."
                    LISA
          Cute.

Lisa places the idol back to the shelf. She grabs her camera and takes photos of the mausoleum.

Switch looks at the old wooden coffin.

                    SWITCH
          So that old man was right af-
          ter all.

Switch tries to open the coffin.

                    RICKY
                (alarmed)
          Dude!

The coffin's nailed shut.

                    SWITCH
          What? You guys wanted to
          see ghosts and dead bodies,
          so let's see a dead body.
                    ROXY
          Might as well. That's why
          we're here. Besides it might

be fun. In a sort of creepy
way.

Switch finds a spade and pries open the casket. Dust puffs out in a cloud. The group coughs as they look into it:

There's Kane Louis Williams, aka the Voodoo Man. In the flesh. In the badly decomposed flesh, as it were. Maggots and worms crawl all over the corpse.

                    RICKY
          Oh, fuck!

Lisa, revolted, turns and spasmodically pukes.

                    SWITCH
          Shit! Lisa, You got barf on my
          shoes.

Lisa wipes her mouth with a handkerchief.

                    ROXY
             (to Lisa)
          You alright?
                    LISA
          I think I'm going to be sick.
                    SWITCH
          There's more? Stand back!
                    ROXY
             (to Lisa)
          Ah shit. Damn. You act like
          you never seen a dead body
          before?

> LISA
> Sure, at a funeral -- not all
> covered with worms and shit
> like this! Can we take the pic-
> tures and just go? This place
> is gross.
> ROXY
> Okay, hold on. Let me set
> the flash. Lucky this thing
> still works after being in the
> rain...

Roxy takes pictures of the body, despite the grotesque look of the rotted corpse.

Roxy notices a rune stone medallion and a staff buried with the body in the coffin.

> ROXY
> Hey, check it out -- looks like
> a medallion of some kind.
> And a staff...

Switch looks at the medallion. Bravely, he reaches in and pulls it out. He shakes off a maggot or two, wipes the slime off on his shirt, then shines his flashlight on it.

> SWITCH
> Well, hell -- maybe this is our
> lucky day after all! We could
> sell this medallion to the town
> museum. I bet this thing is
> worth some serious cash.

Roxy inspects the necklace. It's covered in gold and the red coral stone. Then, she finds an inscribed symbol in French.

ROXY

There's runish writing here.

SWITCH

What's it say?

ROXY

(reads)

"Born in blood. Life is in death. Eternity is but a dream."

The Loa idol glows brighter.
The ground quakes briefly, then stops.
The four stare, holding their breath. The Loa idol stops glowing.

LISA

Roxy, I don't think you should've done that.

ROXY

How was I supposed to know?

SWITCH

Oh, relax. It's nothing.

Switch leans down and looks closely at the corpse. Then, he touches and shakes it. He turns his head to the group.

SWITCH

See? We're perfectly safe--

The corpse's right hand SHOOTS UP and GRABS Switch by the neck! The girls scream like hell.

> SWITCH
> (gags)
> Get it off me!!!

Switch struggles to break free from the rotted hand. Ricky quickly grabs the spade and chops the corpse's forearm in half in one hit. Switch throws the arm on the ground.

The entire group darts out of the mausoleum leaving their belongings behind.

The reanimated corpse of Kane Louis Williams rises up from his coffin and roars in terror.

EXT. OLD CEMETERY - NIGHT

The rain has stopped, and the weather is misty and foggy. The four run flat out toward the front gate.

> KANE (O.S.)
> Nowhere to hide! Run, run
> and die.

VOICES, DEMONIC LAUGHTER, DISEMBODIED SCREAMS terrorize the group.

Lisa trips and tumbles to the ground.

> RICKY
> Lisa!

Roxy shoves the medallion in her pocket.

She and Ricky pull Lisa to her feet. They haul her along after and keep running.

The group finally reaches to the front gate.

The gate SLAMS shut by itself!

The wind starts to blow like a hurricane.

The group tries to budge the door, but it's sealed tight. Switch puts all his brute strength into it.

LISA

Open it!

SWITCH

I can't!!!

INT. MAUSOLEUM - NIGHT

Kane, still in his decomposed form, recites a magical spell in an indistinct language... and slowly regenerates.

KANE

Tulo Shonto Suta!

The Loa idol starts to glow.

EXT. MAUSOLEUM - NIGHT

Kane's skeletal hand appears from the mausoleum. He points his finger... and laughs maniacally.

EXT. OLD CEMETERY - NIGHT

Lightning strikes five gravestones.

A decomposed hand pops out of the ground.

The ground shifts, as the rotten head of a zombie arises.

Five slow zombies emerge from the ground and walk toward the group.

The girls scream like little girls. The guys stare, frozen, dumbfounded looks on their faces.

EXT. CEMETERY FRONT GATE - NIGHT

Badly decomposed, covered with slimy maggots, glistening green and black, the zombies gain on the foursome.

Switch looks around frantically. Through the swirling mist, he sees a large abandoned wooden shed with no windows.

>   SWITCH
>   Look! Over there! Run!

Switch leads the group, as they flee to the shed.

The zombies slowly track and turn their attention to the shed. They move toward it.

INT. CARETAKER'S SHED - NIGHT

Lisa, Roxy, Switch and Ricky lock themselves in the small caretaker's shed. Ricky and Lisa turn on the flashlights.

>   ROXY
>   Those are freaking zombies!
>   SWITCH
>   Zombies don't exist!
>   ROXY
>   Guess they do now! You saw
>   'em with your own eyes!
>   SWITCH
>   Okay -- you're the expert,
>   what the hell do we do now?
>   ROXY
>   Well... okay... in the mov-
>   ies zombies eat human flesh
>   and brains. They have the
>   strength of humans, but
>   they're not invincible --
>   you gotta go for the head.
>   Anyone who's played a video
>   game knows -- go for the
>   head.
>   SWITCH
>   This isn't a video game.

>   ROXY
>   Well, whatever! We got to de-
>   stroy their brains... one good
>   head shot will do it. Or burn
>   them with fire. I think.

>   RICKY
>   Hello! We don't have any-
>   thing to fight with!

Lisa steps up. Puts a hand on each of the frightened men.

>   LISA
>   Okay, look guys get it togeth-
>   er, we got to find something,
>   anything, that we can use as
>   weapons to fight with.

The zombies outside of the shed POUND on the door.
The group fans out, searching every inch of the shed.
Beneath a rusty metal bed with a beat-up old mattress, Switch finds an old footlocker. He opens it up.

>   SWITCH
>   Check it out.

Inside the footlocker: tools and weapons. A pickaxe, a hatchet axe, a Civil War confederate sword and a Civil War pistol with a small box of bullets.
Lisa quickly grabs the pistol and bullets.
Switch grabs the axe.
Roxy grabs the sword and pulls it out from its scabbard.
Ricky hefts the pickaxe... nearly falls over backward. Way too heavy!

RICKY

Better stick with the shovel.

Lisa opens the gun barrel and spins it.

LISA

This old gun probably doesn't
even work.

RICKY

Try it anyway.

ROXY

(to Lisa)

Lis, you know what you're
doing?

LISA

Did you forget that dad's a
cop. Besides I can shoot better than he does.

Suddenly, zombie hands punch through the shed in several places. They flail about, trying to grab the group.

The group huddles away from the grasping hands as Lisa frantically loads the gun.

Zombie hands grab Roxy -- Switch whirls and chops away. Roxy swings the sword. Zombie limbs go flying.

Zombies scream and moan as green and black blood sprays the shed and the group's clothes.

More zombies pound hard on the door, which splinters, about to give way...

Lisa still loads the gun, with dithering fingers.

SWITCH

Load the damn gun!

LISA

I'm trying! I'm trying!

The door explodes inward in a shower of pulverized wood. Two zombies appear and move slowly toward the group.

Finally, Lisa loads the gun -- BANG! BANG! SPLAT! She shoots the zombies in their foreheads!

Green and black blood sprays right in Lisa's face.

Lisa screams and wipes madly at the gore with her shirt.

LISA

Get it off me! Get it off me!

Ricky wipes her off with the bottom of his shirt.

The two zombies fall dead, but three zombies -- without arms and hands -- remain undead.

ROXY

It's not over!

Lisa, Roxy, Switch and Ricky run out of the shed.

EXT. OLD CEMETERY - NIGHT

The group confronts the three armless zombies, moving slowly toward them.

Roxy, Switch and Ricky attack in unison. Simultaneously, they decapitate the three zombies!

The zombies fall dead, blood gushing out their necks.

Everyone takes a breather. Except for Switch -- he maniacally chops up the zombie he killed into little pieces. Green and black blood splatters all over Switch, Ricky and Roxy.

Roxy grabs Switch and his axe.

                    ROXY
              Switch, it's dead!

Roxy restrains Switch as he finally calms down.
Lisa keeps her distance, freaked out by the blood.

                    ROXY
              Is everyone alright?

Ricky starts to bawl and gibber. He's losing it.
Switch slaps Ricky across the face.

                    SWITCH
              Snap out of it! Pull yourself
              together!

Ricky settles a bit.

                    RICKY
              Ah. Okay. Shit.
                   (breathes)
              That was kinda' cool. What
              a rush.

Tension relieved, the group all starts chuckling a little bit. It sure was an
adrenaline rush.
    All except Lisa. She's in shock. She lies down and covers her knees, trembles.
Roxy crosses to Lisa.

                    ROXY
              Relax, Lisa, it's over, we're
              okay.

Ricky and Switch walk up, concerned.

> SWITCH
> What's with her? I've never
> see her like this before.

Roxy hugs Lisa protectively.

> ROXY
> She's in shock. She's got a
> phobia about blood.
> (to Lisa)
> It's okay, Lisa. We're here, we're
> here, calm down, calm down!
> LISA
> Let's just get the hell out of
> this place.

EXT. CEMETERY FRONT GATE - NIGHT
The gate still won't budge. Switch whacks it with his axe. No luck.
Ricky tries to lever it open with his shovel. Nothing.

> SWITCH
> What the hell, man.

Lisa shoots the lock -- the bullet ricochets back at them, forcing them all to duck.
The lock, however, is undamaged.

> LISA
> (exasperated)
> Oh, great!

SWITCH
We'll find another way out.
There's gotta be some holes
in this old fence.
LISA
Split up!
ROXY
Screw that! We should stay
together!

Suddenly, out of the fog -- Kane arrives. Now fully regenerated into human form: a tall, African-American man.

The left half of his face is rotted half away, exposing jaw and teeth -- the right side is fresh human flesh.

KANE
Leaving so soon?

He exposes sharp rows of fanged demonic teeth and fingernails that are claws. His eyes glow a fiendish burning green.

RICKY
What the fuck!
SWITCH
Run!

The group bugs out in all directions.

Kane laughs indulgently. Then he abruptly disappears in a flash of green light.

INT. MAUSOLEUM - NIGHT

The Kane appears at the altar, and kneels.

KANE

Lost kin of the damned, angels of the undead – rise from
your sleep and serve your
master, I command you!

The idol glows. Lightning flashes, inside the mausoleum.

Seven coffins within the mausoleum burst open. A group of devilish vampires emerges from the coffins.

KANE

Awake from your graves and
serve me. Now. By the god
Baron Samedi, I summon
you, arise!

The five male vampires are hideous, demonic beings with hellish red eyes.
They wear stylish clothing and sport sharp curved fingernail claws.

The two female vampires are beautiful, sexy and evil. All the vampires'
clothes are frayed, decayed... and out of style!

Kane surveys his charges.

KANE

Form a line! Elias, Anton,
Xerxes, Emilio, Jacob,
Lucille, Felicia, Nicholas...

The vampires line up.

KANE

Nicholas?
(calls out)

Nicholas! Where the hell are
you?!

NICHOLAS (O.S.)
Interesting choice of words.

The dark silhouetted figure we've seen twice before appears. This is
NICHOLAS, the leader of the vampires. Smart ass and mysterious. A man of
many secrets and allure.

Dashing, in black leather rocker clothing, he stands next to the entrance
holding a dripping dog's leg like a drumstick.

KANE
(angrily)
Where have you been?

NICHOLAS
Having a bite.

Nicholas walks into the mausoleum. Kane abruptly knocks the drumstick
out of his hand.

KANE
Next time, tell me when you
go out of the field to feed.

NICHOLAS
(sarcastic)
I'm sorry. I was hungry.

Nicholas curls his lip... but bows his head submissively to his master. He
joins the others.

Kane walks down the line.

KANE
Elias... Anton... Jacob...

ELIAS, an arrogant pale-skinned male vampire, sneers. ANTON, a muscle-bound vampire, flexes his guns. JACOB, a boyish skinny vampire, giggles demonically in a clownish way.

> KANE
> Emilio, Xerxes...

EMILIO, a teenage punk vampire with a mohawk, flips Kane off. Kane frowns. XERXES, the Hispanic vampire, crosses his arms and glares.

> KANE
> Lucille, Felicia...

LUCILLE, a blond sexy female vampire, bares her teeth. FELICIA, a red-headed busty female vampire, licks her lips and pointed fangs.
Kane stands back. He points out to the cemetery.

> KANE
> Bring those humans to me.

Emilio and Elias move forward belligerently.

> ELIAS
> Have we not done enough for
> you? How many more people
> do we have to kill to make
> you happy?
> KANE
> Kill them and get the medal-
> lion. Bring back what they
> have taken from me. Now.

EMILIO

I've had enough of this shit.
Fuck you, Kane -- I'm not
breaking my ass for you
anymore!

KANE

Oh really?

Kane violently grabs Emilio by the neck, strangling him. He rips out Emilio's heart with his right claws. Emilio's body falls down, twitches, falls still.

Kane holds the heart in his hand.

KANE

He had such a heart...

He tosses it aside.

KANE

...anyone else got questions?

The vampires shake their heads, fearful -- except Elias, who affects nonchalance, and Nicholas, who grins and raises an eyebrow.

KANE

Good. Now, Obey.

FELICIA

Kane, those humans are
nothing...

KANE

Their bloodlines are inter-
mingled with those who

murdered me. I want them
dead. Now! Kill them all.

Kane summons magical energy, and SHOOTS electricity into all the vampires.

Shocked and crackling with energy, the vampires fall to the ground and writhe there.

Kane's attack ceases. The stunned monsters slowly crawl to their feet.

Now, each individual vampires eyes glow in colors of red, bright blue, or yellow. They are possessed by Kane's evil.

KANE

Now get to work.

The vampires run off into the foggy cemetery.

EXT. OLD CEMETERY - LATER

Misty and foggy. THUNDER and lightning play across the cloudy sky.

Lisa stands alone, with her camera, flashlight and her cell phone.

She attempts to call 911 on her cell phone. The display reads "NO SIGNAL".

Lisa looks up at the spiked metal gates towering over her head. She starts to climb. Despite dubious handholds on the wet iron, she gets to the top.

Lightning strikes, and THUNDER crashes -- startled, Lisa loses her grip and falls to the ground.

Roxy appears, sees what's up. She helps Lisa to her feet.

ROXY

You okay?

LISA

Nothing broken.

ROXY

Let's keep checking the fence.

The two move off together.

> ROXY
> You try calling again?
> LISA
> Yeah. No luck. You?
> ROXY
> Nothing. We're in a dead zone.
> LISA
> You're tellin' me.

Lisa and Roxy walk around the cemetery gates. Lisa stops suddenly and turns to Roxy.

> LISA
> Hey, Roxy... you know... thanks
> for always being there for me.
> ROXY
> What are sisters are for.
>   (smiles)
> Don't worry. We'll get out of
> this, I promise you.
> LISA
> Will we?
> ROXY
> Yeah. And when we do --
> promise me you'll find a less
> freaky way to get us extra
> credit on a assignment.
> LISA
> I promise.

Suddenly, Elias and Xerxes leap from the bushes out in front of them. Lisa and Roxy scream.

The vampires transform from their human form into gruesome-looking creatures. They roar at the girls and slowly move toward them.

> LISA
>
> Run!

Lisa and Roxy haul ass in the other direction.

Elias and Xerxes lope, on all four limbs like animals, after the girls.

Lisa pulls out her gun and, still at a dead run, fires four shots behind her.

The vampire creatures dodge Lisa's shots from side to side and fall back slightly.

EXT. BUSHES - MOMENTS LATER

Lisa and Roxy round some bushes and hide, panting.

> LISA
>
> I don't think they saw us turn
> in here.
>
> ROXY
>
> What in hell were those
> things?

Through the bushes, the girls see Elias and Xerxes pull up, some distance away. They've lost the girls.

Xerxes, like a dog, sniffs the ground to pick up the scent. He growls in frustration, then wanders off, leaving Elias there.

> ELIAS
>
> (sing-song)
>
> Come out, come out, wher-
> ever you arrrre...

Roxy and Lisa tremble.

>   ROXY
>   (whispers)
>   You see those fangs? There
>   vampires!
>   LISA
>   So what the hell do we do?
>   ROXY
>   (whispers)
>   Shhh, they'll hear us.

Elias leaves the scene as Lisa and Roxy watch.

Suddenly Xerxes leaps up behind them, and launches himself at Lisa.

Lisa wrestles with Xerxes, who snaps at her throat. Roxy tries to pull him off, but he hurls her back.

Xerxes' saliva drips on Lisa's face, as he pushes in, closer and closer. Suddenly -- BLAM!

Xerxes flies back.

Lisa holds the smoking gun. She grins.

Xerxes grins back. His chest gushes a trickle of gore, but otherwise he's fine.

>   XERXES
>   You can't kill a vampire with
>   bullets, bitch!

Suddenly, a wooden stake thrusts out of his chest, dead center! A fountain of gore shoots out!

Roxy rises up behind him.

>   ROXY
> That's right. It takes a wood-
> en stake through the heart.
> Bitch.

Xerxes goes down. Roxy and Lisa stare down at him.

The sound of RUNNING FEET -- Elias, still in creature form, appears! He looks down at his fallen comrade, and up at the girls. With a growl, he lunges--

Lisa fires! BLAM BLAM BLAM! Elias' head explodes!

Blood splatters on Lisa. She quickly wipes the blood off her with her dress. Elias' decapitated body falls down dead.

>   LISA
> Is that it? Are they dead?

Roxy kicks one of the vampire corpses.

>   ROXY
> Looks like.

Lisa finds a small shallow grave and small shovel.

>   LISA
> We better make sure.

>   ROXY
> How?

>   LISA
> Slice' em up. Then we'll bury
> the bodies.

> ROXY
>
> With pleasure. We'll hack'em
> into bat shit.

She starts hacking.

Nicholas watches this activity from a nearby bush. He shakes his head. Then, with a burst of speed, he's gone.

EXT. OLD CEMETERY - NIGHT

The wind dies down. The fog lies thick. Switch and Ricky come from opposite directions, and back into each other. They jump back, brandishing their weapons!

> SWITCH
>
> Whoa, you scared the shit out
> of me!
>
> RICKY
>
> Sorry man! You find a way
> out?
>
> SWITCH
>
> Think we'd still be here if I
> had?

With a scream, vampires Anton and Jacob descend upon them from above!

Anton strangles Switch, who drops his axe. He struggles to break Anton's iron grip.

The two fall to their knees, which makes it easier for Switch to get his axe. He flails for it -- grabs it --

-- then slings it right into Anton's skull!

Red blood squirts on Switch's face and the dead vampire releases his grip from Switch's throat.

Meanwhile, Jacob pins down Ricky and bites him on the shoulder! Ricky screams in pain.

Jacob tastes Ricky's blood. He laughs his clownish laugh, and prepares to make his kill...

AN AXE strikes Jacob's back! Blood squirts! He howls in frustration and rage!

Ricky jumps up off the ground, grabs his shovel.

RICKY

Batter up!

Ricky swings his shovel and knocks Jacob's head right off! It flies off into the bushes. A red gusher fountains out of the neck hole.

Switch and Ricky stand, panting, pissed off.

In frenzy, they hack the living hell out of the corpses with their weapons until the former vampires are more like two stains on the ground.

With nothing left to chop, the two boys stand back, chests heaving. They wipe the blood off their faces.

Ricky clutches his shoulder wound.

SWITCH

You okay, buddy?

RICKY

(wincing in pain)

What's it look like? That thing fuckin' bit me!

Switch inspects Ricky's shoulder wound.

SWITCH

Holy shit that's deep. Here, keep pressure on it.

Switch hands Ricky his torn sleeveless jacket. Ricky applies pressure on the wound to stop the bleeding.

The two friends limp off in the darkness.

EXT. CEMETERY BACK GATE - NIGHT

Switch finds another gate. Like the front gate, it's sealed shut and locked.

SWITCH

Ricky, over here!

Switch pulls his switchblade, and tries picking the lock. The blade breaks off.

SWITCH

Damn it!

He swings at it with his axe, but nothing doing.

Ricky shows up with his shovel.

RICKY

Oh, excellent!

Ricky looks at the lock and finds the door jammed.

RICKY

(aggravated)

You idiot! You jammed the fucking lock!

SWITCH

(defensively)

Eat me!

Ricky tries to break the gate with his shovel, but Switch stops him.

> SWITCH
> Forget it, that thing is sealed
> shut. There's no way in hell
> we can open that up.

Ricky and Switch sits next to a large tree and bushes. An eerie wind rustles the bushes and WAILS in the night air.

Switch fumbles through his pockets for something. He comes up with a cigarette pack -- empty! He crumples it up and hurls it away disgusted.

> SWITCH
> Man this place... I can't han-
> dle all this... damn vampires,
> freaking zombies, what's
> next? Aliens and fucking
> werewolves?

Switch is panting and shivering. He's in the midst of a freak out.

> RICKY
> Damn, I never seen you this
> scared before.
> SWITCH
> Well fuck, don't get used to
> it. I'm human too, you know.
> Shit.

Ricky tries to rally his friend.

> RICKY
> Hey, that was cool back there,
> the way we nailed those freaks.

SWITCH
(not in the mood)
But that guy bit you... you
don't think you're going to
turn into one of those... one
of those...

He can't come up with a word to describe them. Concerned, Ricky lets off
the pressure to check his seeping wound.

RICKY
I don't know, man.

He turns and looks Switch in the eye. Man to man. Serious.

RICKY
If I do, promise you'll kill me.
I don't want to hurt anyone.

SWITCHO
No way, you're my best friend!
RICKY
(commandingly)
Promise me!

Switch shakes his head, looks wretched. Ricky's dead serious.

SWITCH
Alright. I promise.
RICKY
Okay. If the same thing hap-
pens to you, I'll do the same.

Switch looks up.

> SWITCH
> Dude, I'm fine, nothing bit me.

> RICKY
> (lightly joking)
> Well man we can't take chances! Can't we? The moment something bites you -- vampire, werewolf, zombie, whatever -- I'm cutting your puss ass head off!

Switch stares -- then Ricky smiles. They burst out laughing. They laugh and laugh. Finally, it subsides.

> SWITCH
> Crazy fucker. Thanks man, that was a good one.

> RICKY
> But seriously... if I turn, kill me. Just do it quick.

> SWITCH
> You ain't gonna turn, man. These are just like... there's a rational explanation for all this shit. You're gonna be fine. You just got bit.

> RICKY
> Think so?

> SWITCH
> Gotta be. Look, let's just get
> the girls and find a way over
> this fence.

The two chuckle. Suddenly, there are two more voices laughing. Ricky and Switch look up.

The female vampires -- Lucille and Felicia -- stand there. Hot. Evil, but hot. They are laughing ironically.

> LUCILLE
> What's up boys?

Switch and Ricky stare. They stand up and face the girls.

> SWITCH
> Hiya. Come here often?
> FELICIA
> Not really. It's kind of a meat
> market.

The boys tighten their grip on their weapons. Even in the dim light, they can see these girls are monsters.

> LUCILLE
> Yeah. Dead meat.
> (sweetly)

Faster than the eye can see, they attack!

Switch swings his axe, but Lucille ducks under and kicks him in the balls. Felicia disarms him and the two knock him down and start feeding.

It took two seconds. Ricky stares, stunned. He tries to raise his shovel -- but then drops it and runs away.

The girls hardly notice. They take healthy bites of Switch's succulent flesh, blood covering their faces like sauce from barbecued ribs.

Sated, they loll back with a languorous sight.

> LUCILLE
> The sweet flesh of youth.
> Time to die lover.
> FELICIA
> I'm ready for seconds.
> LUCILLE
> Felicia... your diet.
> FELICIA
> Screw my diet!

They turn to look for Ricky, but he's long gone.

> FELICIA
> Little creep got away.
> LUCILLE
> (sniffs)
> Don't worry. They won't be
> hard to track.
> (sniffs)
> Body spray... and weed.

Felicia licks Ricky's blood trail from the ground.

> FELICIA
> His blood is sweet. I want
> some more.

> LUCILLE
> Remember what Kane said,
> Felicia -- get the medallion.
> If we don't, we're dead.

> FELICIA
> Oh fuck Kane, I don't care
> about the medallion, I want
> blood! Now. It's been a while
> since I had some this good.
> LUCILLE
> Control your thirst! They'll
> be time for that later.

Lucille sniffs, senses Ricky.

> LUCILLE
> Let's go.

The female vampires follow Ricky's trail.

Nicholas steps out from behind a tree. He was watching the whole thing. He moves off.

INT. MAUSOLEUM - NIGHT

Kane sits inside the mausoleum, breathing slow and smooth. He seems to be meditating. The Loa idol glows.

Nicholas enters.

> NICHOLAS
> They've killed four of ours.
> Emilio, Xerxes, Anton and
> Jacob. The girls are still
> searching.

KANE

Did you get the medallion?

NICHOLAS

No.

Kane gets angry.

KANE

That medallion is all I have
left of my wife and daughter.
Those families took everything from me. Get it now!

NICHOLAS

Show me where they are,
then I'll bring you the medallion. But afterward let me go.
You owe me.

KANE

I don't owe you anything --
you owe _me_. I was the one
who saved you.

(A beat)

KANE

You should thank me for
making you what you are.

NICHOLAS

I thought you'd bring me
back to life as a human, not a
goddamned monster!

Kane shrugs. Not his problem.

> KANE
>
> That's not my concern. You made the deal. Whatever you are, you're here now. You don't like it, too bad. Live with it. I was not the one who called out for help. You did. Keep your word and obey me.

(A beat)

> KANE
>
> Just like the good little bitch that you are. You're my dog, until I say it's over, boy.
>
> NICHOLAS
>
> You're a bastard. This isn't about revenge for you and you know it. You kill because of the thrill. Because you love it.
>
> KANE
>
> Well, sure! Who wouldn't? Who wouldn't love the god-like feeling of power one gets from killing innocents? It feels good. Doesn't it. You should know from experience Nicholas after all you've murdered many lost souls

lately. I can smell the death all over you. So now... one good kill deserves another.

NICHOLAS

I killed them because of what I am. Do you think I am proud of that. No. My cursed nature is the cause. The guilt I feel is beyond anything you could ever know. I regret killing innocents. You don't. That's what makes us different.

KANE

Spare me the sermon, boy. One day you will come to accept what you are. A killer. Be proud of that. For what I gave you is better than being human. I gave you the power of a god. Eternal life. That is better than living the life of being human. You never had your family taken away from you, like I did. My wife and son were murdered alive as I had to watch them die before my very eyes and I couldn't save them. So don't you dare speak to me on regret!!! The people I killed in return for their crimes against my

family deserved to die. What
I did, I had to do. That is
true justice. Revenge.

Nicholas snaps.

NICHOLAS

I hate you! I would rather rot
back in the ground than be
this thing you made.

KANE

Yes, well... you may soon get
your wish. Until that time,
you'll do what I tell you to do.
Or suffer.

NICHOLAS

I won't do it.

KANE

You will! Go now or I'll kill
you in such a torturous way,
you'll scream for death! Do it.

Kane laughs. He pats Nicholas in a fatherly way and turns away. Nicholas
turns and rushes out.

EXT. OLD CEMETERY - NIGHT

Lisa and Roxy stumble along, searching for a way out.

They notice a bloody trail next to them.

Roxy points it out. The two follow it.

Ricky, out of breath, appears from the bushes before them.

ROXY

Ricky!

Ricky collapses, while Lisa and Roxy come to his aid. They stare wide-eyed at the huge wound on Ricky's shoulder.

> LISA
> Oh my God, what did they
> do to you?!

Lisa hangs back, squeamish of the blood. Roxy clamps the wound with Lisa's handkerchief.

> LISA
> Hey I wiped my puke on
> that...
> ROXY
> I need to stop the bleeding,
> don't I?

Roxy ties Ricky's wound firmly with Lisa's handkerchief.

> ROXY
> There. That'll do for now.
> LISA
> (to Roxy)
> Will he turn into one of
> them?

Roxy shrugs. Ricky, pale and weak, pants in pain and fatigue..

> RICKY
> Guys, they got Switch.
> ROXY
> What?!

> RICKY
>
> I watched those freaks... they
> tore him apart. He's dead.

Ricky hands Roxy Switch's broken knife and car keys.
Roxy breaks down in tears.

> RICKY
>
> I went back to where his
> body was laying and picked
> these up.
>   (sighs)
> I feel like it's my fault... I
> should have...
>
> LISA
>
> There was nothing you could
> have done.
>
> RICKY
>
> Listen, you guys. If I start
> to turn into one of those
> things... you have to kill me.
>
> LUCILLE (O.S.)
>
> Why wait?

Lucille and Felicia appear behind the girls and backhand them to the ground.

Lucille searches Roxy and finds the medallion. She holds it up to show Felicia.

Ricky grabs his shovel and hauls back for a weak swing -- Lucille nonchalantly knocks it out of his hand.

She gets close to Ricky, hypnotized by him. She sees some blood trickling from the corner of his mouth. She kisses him, long and deep. Felicia watches, turned on.

Lisa works her gun free and points it at the vampires.

Lucille breaks the kiss. Ricky's blood is on her lip. She licks it off with a long tongue.

> LUCILLE
>
> So sweet.

Lisa shoots. CLICK! Tries again. CLICK! CLICK! Empty. And the box of bullets? Also empty.

> LUCILLE
>
> No ammo, ain't that a bitch.

Lucille knocks Lisa's gun out of her hand. Lisa reaches for Roxy's sword -- Felicia steps on it. She pins Lisa down.

Suddenly, Nicholas arrives.

> LUCILLE
>
> Nicholas! So glad you could join us.
>
> NICHOLAS
>
> Do you have the medallion?

Lucille reveals the medallion to Nicholas.

> NICHOLAS
>
> Good. Give it to me.

He reaches out, but she snatches it back.

> LUCILLE
>
> No! It's ours. We found it first.

NICHOLAS
Fine! But let me kill them.

Roxy, Ricky and Lisa stare up at the group, watching for any chance to break free.

Nicholas picks up Roxy's sword.

ROXY
You bastards! You killed
Switch!

Felicia slaps Roxy to shut her up.

FELICIA
It was us, bimbo. He tasted
so sweeeeeeet. I would not
have mind fucking him, if he
wasn't so pathetic. You bunch
of losers.

Roxy doesn't seem to hear. She stares, fixated on Nicholas. Felicia licks her monstrous teeth.

Nicholas raises the sword over Roxy. She quails, and closes her eyes at her imminent death...

Nicholas swings the sword --

-- then slashes Lucille and Felicia!

NICHOLAS
(to the humans)
Run!

Lisa, Roxy and Ricky scramble to their feet and flee.

Lucille and Felicia recover quickly, and transform into their vampire forms.

LUCILLE

You traitor!

NICHOLAS

Go to hell!

Nicholas turns into his vampire form. He squares off, brandishing the sword with a practiced hand.

Lucille's too fast -- she knocks the sword right out of his hand and out of reach.

Nicholas sets, shaking out his hands, light on his feet. He's confident fighting hand to hand as well.

The two charge at him. Anticipating this, he sidesteps, then sweeps a kick at their backs, sending them face first into the ground.

The girls snarl and get back up. They circle him, one on either side.

Lucille lunges, Nicholas counters. Felicia lunges, Nicholas jumps back. Lucille slaps him on his blind side, and he spins around.

The two charge again. This time, he flips back over their heads, and they slam into each other and carom off into the bushes.

NICHOLAS

You fight like girls.

LUCILLE

That's 'cause we are.

FELICIA

And... we bite!

Supernaturally fast, they fly at him. Each chomps an arm.

Nicholas screams! He flails, but they're locked tight.

He kicks Lucille in the crotch. She laughs, says something garbled by her bite.

NICHOLAS

What?

Lucille lets go for a second.

> LUCILLE
> I said, I'm a girl, dummy, I
> don't have--

Nicholas punches her hard in the face and she reels back.

> FELICIA
> Hey, you big bully!

She's let go to speak too. He kicks her in the chest and sends her flying.

Lucille, dazed, tries to shake it off. Felicia does shake it off, and charges at Nicholas again--

Only to be SLASHED in two! From crown to crotch, Nicholas bisects the poor vampire. The sword drips with blood and gore.

> LUCILLE
> (anguished)
> Felicia!

She climbs to her feet and attacks. He slashes at her -- she takes it on the arm, to tie up the sword, and with her other arm, knocks him down. She lands atop him.

> LUCILLE
> Why would you do this to us?
> We loved you!

Lucille opens her cavernous mouth with its monstrous teeth, and leans forward to take a bite--

Claws extend from Nicholas' fingernails. He slashes Lucille's throat!

Blood fountains down from the cut. Lucille frowns, sadly, pathetically. She clamps her hands to her throat, but the blood just jets through.

She falls back, choking and gargling. Then lies still.

Nicholas crosses to her. He grabs her hair, and rips off her head. The eyes still blink, the lips quiver. The spine swings crazily, dripping.

> NICHOLAS
>
> You two never loved anyone
> but yourselves!

He hurls the head contemptuously into the gore that once was Felicia.

He picks up the medallion and storms off.

EXT. CEMETERY BACK GATE - NIGHT

Lisa and Roxy help Ricky limp to the back gate of the cemetery.

There, they come upon the remains of Switch. Nothing more than a shredded carcass.

Roxy falls to her knees, in shock. She weeps. Lisa comforts her.

Lisa then goes to the back gate and tries to open it. Just like before, it's sealed shut.

> RICKY
>
> It's no use.
>
> LISA
>
> Then we're dead. There's
> no way out of here. We'll be
> dead by dawn. If we last that
> long.
>
> NICHOLAS (O.S.)
>
> I can help you get out of here.

They turn. There's Nicholas. With the bloody sword. He's in his human form.

Lisa and Ricky stare up at him in mingled terror and hope.

But Roxy's only got anger. She rises from Switch's side and rushes at Nicholas.

> ROXY
>
> You killed my boyfriend!

Nicholas holds her at bay with a long arm.

> NICHOLAS
>
> It wasn't me.

Lisa points her empty gun at him.

> LISA
>
> Don't move or I'll shoot!
>
> NICHOLAS
>
> Hey I just saved your lives! So this is how you want to repay me?
>
> RICKY
>
> What the hell you waiting for? Fucking shoot him already!
>
> NICHOLAS
>
> If you shoot me, you won't live through the rest of the night. You have to trust me.

Roxy stands there, staring at him, chest heaving.

> LISA
>
> Why should we?

> NICHOLAS
> You've got no choice. Do you
> want to live. If not, you're
> dead, otherwise.

The fog clears up some. Nicholas points.
The kids see a small church standing right next to the cemetery.

> NICHOLAS
> We'll be safe enough in there.
> Come on.

Nicholas goes to the gate which leads to the church. It's locked tight.

> LISA
> Who are you?

Nicholas summons his claws, and breaks open the back gate.

> NICHOLAS
> I'll explain everything once
> we get inside. Let's hurry in-
> side before someone sees us.

Nicholas leads the human group out of the cemetery and into the church.
Watching from the shadows... KANE. His eyes narrow in rage.
He disappears.
INT. MAUSOLEUM - NIGHT
Kane appears in a burst of light, already screaming!

> KANE
> God damn you Nicholas!
> You traitor! You'll regret this

night when I get my hands on
you. I'll skin you alive.

He smashes some statuary in an explosion of stone and dust.

KANE

You want something done
right, you gotta do it yourself!

He moves directly to his altar, and begins muttering spells and incantations,
rapid fire. His Loa idol sputters and glows... brighter... brighter...

INT. SMALL CHURCH - NIGHT

Nicholas leads the surviving humans inside the church, and shots the doors
tight.

He glances at the candles -- his eyes flash fire red -- the candles are lit.

The church is a large wooden structure with a huge cross hanging high on
the wall, stained glass windows, an altar and rows of large wooden pews.

Lisa, Ricky and Roxy catch their breath. Suddenly, Roxy lunges at Nicholas,
enraged.

ROXY

You killed Switch!

She punches and kicks at him. He blocks her attacks, then thrusts her gently
to the ground. Lisa rushes to help her, but Roxy pushes her back.

She gets up to rush at Nicholas again, but Lisa restrains her.

LISA

Cool it! He saved us!

ROXY

But he killed Switch!

RICKY
No he didn't! Those two
bitch freaks did!
(snarls)
But he's still one of them!
LISA
Will you two just shut up a
minute. Let me handle this.

Roxy calms down. Tears run down her face, smearing the black makeup on
her cheeks.

Lisa points her gun at Nicholas.

LISA
I want to know what the hell
is going on here! Who are
you? Why'd you save us? I
want some answers, now!

Nicholas, with superhuman speed, grabs the gun.

NICHOLAS
If you want answers, calm
down and shut up. I'm sorry
about your friend's death. And
by the way. That gun is empty.

Lisa looks embarrassed. The others smile. Nicholas tosses it back to her. He
paces a few feet away, then turns around to face them.

NICHOLAS

How could you all be so monumentally stupid as to awake that bastard Kane?

LISA

We didn't know. We're here for a school project. We were just trying to get extra credit for a project!

NICHOLAS

Extra credit? You'll need more than that if you want to survive! How about a brain for starters. Not only did you awaken Kane -- you also awakened the spirits he commands. Like it or not, right now we are fucked.

LISA

What are you talking about? Who the hell is this Kane? Really?

RICKY

That stuff that the old man was saying was true. Wasn't it?

NICHOLAS

You heard the story, then?

LISA

Only some of it.

NICHOLAS

Okay, well... listen up.

Nicholas sits on the edge of the stage. The kids take sets in the front pew.

<u>FLASHBACK</u> - EXT. COTTON FIELDS - DAY

A young Kane, 20s, works his cotton field. A simple farmer, dressed in drab clothing, he's the picture of health and upstanding industry.

> NICHOLAS (V.O.)
> Kane Louis Williams was a
> cotton grower in the 1960s.
> He had a wife and a child. He
> loved them very much.

EXT. KANE'S HOUSE - DAY

His wife, YOLANDA, 20, a beautiful African-American woman, stands outside their ramshackle house, holding an infant child.

She waves at Kane out in the fields. He waves back with his hat.

She smiles and goes inside the house.

A roostertail of dust approaches the house.

EXT. COTTON FIELDS - DAY

Kane sees the dust. His eyes lose their twinkle and become alarmed.

A beat-up old 1950s roadster convertible appears, bearing a group of hooded KKK members.

Kane throws down his farming implements and begins to run.

It's very far.

EXT. KANE'S HOUSE - DAY

The Klansmen jump from the car. One wedges the house's front door shut as two others light Molotov cocktails.

They hurl the flaming bottles through each of the two front windows.

The house goes up like a torch!

> KANE (O.S.)
> Yolanda!

The Klansmen see him running. They jump back in their roadster and speed off.

By the time Kane reaches the house, it's fully engulfed. He tries to get in, once... twice... but the heat is too intense.

The roof collapses in a fountain of flame and sparks. Nothing could've survived this.

> KANE
>
> Yolanda!

INT. SMALL CHURCH - NIGHT (BACK TO PRESENT)
Nicholas sighs, looks off into the distance.

> LISA
>
> Why did they do it?
>
> NICHOLAS
>
> The town was afraid of him due to him being a local shaman besides a farmer. Surprisingly, he helped a lot of people, but I guess fear turns humans into monsters.
>
> (beat)
>
> After his family was killed, he became a broken man. He kept a medallion to remember his family.
>
> LISA
>
> So that's why he killed those children. It was revenge.

Roxy slowly picks up the sword, and eyes Nicholas. Nicholas, paying no attention, launches into more of the story.

FLASHBACK - EXT. HELL - NIGHT

Or is it day? Who can tell -- all we can see are the crags of a burning red wasteland, swarming with imps and demons. Lava flows, and lightning crackles.

> NICHOLAS (V.O.)
> Kane made a deal with Baron
> Samedi, the god of Hell.

On blackened hilltops, littered with skulls and skeleton parts, lies a city of twisted and freakish architecture. In the background, a giant fortress reaches high in the air.

Closer to the pits below, commanding a wide prospect, stands a giant three-story colonial mansion.

INT. BLOOD POOL CHAMBER - NIGHT

In this ancient torchlit room, a large pool filled with dark read and black blood bubbles like tar.

Baron Samedi "baptizes" a screaming, naked Kane Williams in the pool. Kane struggles, to no avail, and is fully submerged in the burning liquid.

An image in steam of a demonic skull-like face in living fire roils up from the pool as Kane sizzles.

Kane resurfaces. A remarkable transformation has occurred. His green eyes burn brightly with malevolent purpose. He's a living demon in human form.

Kane's chest has runes tattooed on it -- they dissolve into his flesh.

Baron Samedi's new creation has been born.

INT. LABOU CHURCH - NIGHT

Inside this dark candlelit church, Kane bustles about in front of the altar.

> NICHOLAS (V.O.)
> He slaughtered babies and
> children to make the towns-
> people suffer.

Kane lights two black candles. He arranges ceremonial knives and other implements.

> NICHOLAS (V.O.)
> No one could stop him -- not until 1984, when he made the mistake of kidnapping the infant daughter of the town's first black mayor.

Kane places a black infant wrapped in a baby blanket in the center of the altar.

Kane raises the knife.

A team of police officers and the sheriff burst through the doors and shoot Kane down in a hail of bullets.

Kane falls, shot non-fatally in his extremities.

> NICHOLAS (V.O.)
> Lucky they got him in time.

The baby squeals. A policewoman gathers her up and comforts her.

INT. SMALL CHURCH - NIGHT (BACK TO PRESENT)

Roxy points her sword right next to Nicholas's neck.

> LISA
> Roxy! What are you doing?!
> ROXY
> Let me kill him! He has to pay for what he did!
> NICHOLAS
> You boyfriend's death was not my doing. It was Lucille

and Felicia's. There dead so
consider it even.
ROXY
Killing your own won't bring
him back!
NICHOLAS
No, but I kept you from suf-
fering the same fate.

Ricky, weakened by loss of blood, slumps suddenly to the floor.

LISA

Ricky!

Lisa kneels down beside Ricky. Nicholas, ignoring Roxy and the sword, joins
her. He inspects Ricky's vampire wound.

LISA
Is he going to turn into a
vampire like you?
NICHOLAS
No. In order for your friend
to become like one of us,
he would have to drink the
blood of the vampire that bit
him. That's how it works.

Nicholas reaches for Ricky's wound -- and Lisa snatches his hand away. She
shields Ricky with her body.

LISA
(defensive)

You're not going make him
into one of you!
NICHOLAS
I wouldn't presume that. But
he'll die from the infection
if this wound is not treated.
The bite is deep and he's lost
a lot of blood.

Roxy points her sword at Nicholas.

ROXY
And you expect us to trust
you?

Nicholas barely glances at Ricky.

NICHOLAS
Yes. Besides, I know you
want to get out of here just as
much as I do!
ROXY
You're lying!

Roxy jabs with the sword. It cuts Nicholas slightly. The pain does not even
bother him, he almost wants her to kill him, but he is calm about it.

NICHOLAS
(gently)
Believe me, I know what
it's like to lose a friend. Just
know this -- if you kill me,

you'll be no match for Kane.
He's too powerful.
                    LISA
Meaning?
                    NICHOLAS
He'll butcher you all like pigs.
You'll be dead.

Roxy wants desperately to kill Nicholas. Her forehead sweats... her face shows her conflict...

Finally, she drops the sword with a CLATTER. She bursts into tears and rushes out.

                    LISA

          Roxy!

Nicholas roots in a cupboard, and comes up with a bottle of wine. He hands Lisa the wine, along with a piece of cloth.

                    NICHOLAS
          Pour this wine on his wound.
          It'll kill the infection.

Lisa does so. Nicholas composes himself. Lisa glances back at him.

                    LISA
          What are you doing?
                    NICHOLAS
          I'm going to heal him. Back
          off.
                    LISA
          What?

NICHOLAS
Just watch.

Nicholas put his right hand on Ricky's wound. He concentrates. Lisa stands back, uncertain.

A greenish light flashes between Nicholas' fingers. Nicholas lifts his hand.

RICKY
Whoa...

Ricky, completely restored, removes the bloody handkerchief.

RICKY
Thanks man! Neat little trick!
NICHOLAS
(smiles)
Maybe I'll show you how to
do it sometime. My name is
Nicholas, by the way.
LISA
Lisa.
RICKY
And I'm Ricky.
LISA
How did you get involved in
this?

Nicholas smiles.

NICHOLAS
You wouldn't believe me if I
told you.

                    LISA
        After what we've seen, I'd
        think we'd believe anything.
                 NICHOLAS
        I was once part of a metal
        band called "Black Voodoo".
        Back in 1989, we were travel-
        ing from city to city, playing
        gigs across Louisiana...

FLASHBACK - EXT. OLD CEMETERY - NIGHT

In the cemetery a younger Nicholas hangs out with three band mates.
They're all decked out in 80's rocker gear.

They pass around a bottle and a joint. Drunk, laughing, everyone's having a
weird old good time.

                 NICHOLAS (V.O.)
        We dropped out of school
        to become rock stars. It was
        going well -- we were paying
        our dues and making connec-
        tions, but we didn't mind...

Behind the tombstones, some seedy street punks spy on the band mates.

                 NICHOLAS (V.O.)
        We heard about this place one
        day, and came down here to
        party. For us music was life. It
        was all good times. Until some
        locals decided to join us...
        that's when things got ugly.

One punk steps forth, swinging a chain.

Nicholas looks up.

The punks descend on the rockers and beat them savagely.

                    NICHOLAS (V.O.)
                    We were just a bunch of
                    young kids. No match for
                    them. I remember seeing
                    those bastards as they beat
                    my buddies to death. All
                    over, a few wallets to pick for
                    just three hundred bucks.

The punks beat and stab the four band members to death.

                    NICHOLAS (V.O.)
                    They killed us all.

One punk wipes his knife on Nicholas's shirt and pick pockets Nicholas of his money. Nicholas reaches out -- his hand closes on nothing as the punk walks off.

Nicholas falls to the ground. Dead.

EXT. HELL - NIGHT

A naked, bruised Nicholas lands sprawling on the rocky ground of Hell.

                    NICHOLAS (V.O.)
                    I'd lived my life on my own
                    terms most of the time. No
                    restraint, no morality, no re-
                    grets. Total freedom. And
                    for that it cost me my immor-
                    tal soul. Then I saw his face.
                    And heard those haunting
                    words...

A hand extends. Nicholas looks up to behold: Kane Louis Williams.

> KANE
>
> I've been waiting for you my
> friend. I can send you back.
> Serve me if you will and live
> forever!
>
> NICHOLAS (V.O.)
>
> When Kane found me, he
> offered me a chance to have
> my revenge. So I made a deal
> with the devil, anything to
> get revenge.

Nicholas reaches out and takes Kane's hand.

INT. BLOOD POOL CHAMBER - NIGHT

Just like before, only the players are different -- Kane now "baptizes" Nicholas in the tarry pool of blood. The same skull-like face of fire congeals above the pool.

A beautiful woman peeks into the Chamber, witnessing Nicholas' transformation.

Nicholas resurfaces. Fully restored, eyes glowing with dark powers.

Kane magically wraps energy around Nicholas' body -- and Nicholas is again clothed in his old rocker clothing.

Kane opens a portal.

> KANE
>
> Find the ones who sent me
> here and kill them all. When
> the proper time comes, I'll
> shall release you. Now go
> and kill for me. Avenge
> yourself.

Nicholas steps through the portal.
INT. SMALL CHURCH - NIGHT (BACK TO PRESENT)
Nicholas gestures to himself.

> NICHOLAS
> He made me this way, the same way the Baron made him into the demon that he now is. The deal was, I would be granted my revenge if I served him.

FLASHBACK - EXT. KANE'S MAUSOLEUM - NIGHT
Kane's spirit in ghostly transparent form walks through the cemetery haunting the place.

> NICHOLAS (V.O.)
> Kane's spirit would haunt the cemetery but he could not come back. That is, not until you all resurrected him, you see you guys are the descendants of the townspeople that killed him.

INT. SMALL CHURCH - NIGHT (BACK TO PRESENT)
Lisa and Ricky sigh and bow their heads in despair and understanding.

> RICKY
> It all makes perfect sense now.
> LISA
> Yes, it does.

FLASHBACK - EXT. OLD CEMETERY - NIGHT

The punks from before laugh and drink among the tombstones. Nicholas, restored, now watches from the shadows.

> NICHOLAS (V.O.)
> I killed those punks without
> any mercy. I got revenge.

Nicholas whirls through the punks, slashing death. The punks drop like flies.

> NICHOLAS (V.O.)
> It was sweet.

Nicholas is covered in blood. He tastes it. A heavenly look crosses his face.

> NICHOLAS (V.O.)
> As soon as I got my first taste
> of human blood the thirst
> took over...

He bends down and starts to suck the blood of one of the street punks.

> NICHOLAS (V.O.)
> The hunger was unbeliev-
> ably addicting. It felt great;
> the taste was better anything
> I had ever tasted before. Just
> like a drug, I wanted more
> and more, the blood was nev-
> er enough.

One-by-one, Nicholas drinks dry all the punks.
Covered in blood, he screams in rage and exaltation.
INT. SMALL CHURCH - NIGHT (BACK TO PRESENT)
The Nicholas we now see looks rather different -- sad and pensive.

NICHOLAS

As time goes on, you begin to feel truly dead inside. Your soul rots. But somehow over the years, my feelings began to change about hunting humans. After all, I was -- had been -- one of them. I missed it. I hated what I was doing. That's loneliness and inner turmoil of being a vampire... that's the price you pay for eternal life. It's not all red wine and roses like the movies and novels that portray it to be.

The two gaze up at him. They seem compassionate.

NICHOLAS

Just imagine -- every night you wake up, and there's no family to see or to love, no true friends to keep you company, no purpose to your existence. You're trapped, in a kind of half-life, a prisoner in an immortal, undead body, with only a terrible, insatiable hunger inside you. Killing and feeding. Killing and feeding. That's all you have left in the end.

Lisa gives Ricky the wine bottle. He takes a drink, makes a face.

LISA

That's so sad.

Nicholas looks down at himself. The sadness in him is palpable.

LISA

The vampires that attacked us. They were once human?

NICHOLAS

Yeah.

LISA

I feel sorry for you.

NICHOLAS

Don't be. I chose this type of life. Good or Evil, it's the choices, we all make them. I just made the wrong ones. I know that now.

Lisa looks into Nicholas' sad eyes. She moves up next to him and gives him a tender kiss on his lips. Much to his surprise.

RICKY

Hey!

The two stare down at him.

> LISA
>
> Oh, relax. I'm just trying to be nice.

Ricky can't believe it. He gets up.

> RICKY
>
> Hell with this.

He stalks out.

> LISA
>
> Ricky!
>
> NICHOLAS
>
> Why did you just kiss me?
>
> LISA
>
> You're not like all the other vampires ...you've have a good heart.

She smiles. He leans down and kisses her back.

Lisa's into it. She becomes extremely turned on. The two kiss deeply and embrace feverishly.

Lisa kisses his neck. Nicholas's eyes glow red. Lisa's tender white neck extends before him. He fights temptation -- his eyelids flutter...

Nicholas leans down, about to bite -- then spots the crucifix on the wall.

He pushes her gently, but inexorably, off him.

> LISA
>
> Why did you stop?

> NICHOLAS
> I don't want to hurt you. I
> have never been treated so
> kindly like this by anyone.
> Ever.
>
> LISA
> I know you're in pain. Let me
> in. Let me help you.
>
> NICHOLAS
> What are trying to say?

Lisa stares lovingly up at him. She's completely smitten.

> LISA
> I don't know, I really like you,
> I guess. I feel for you.
>
> NICHOLAS
> But I'm not human.
>
> LISA
> Yes, you are... you just don't
> know it.
>
> NICHOLAS
> Trust me, you don't want to
> be like me.
>
> LISA
> (compassionately)
> Maybe you're right. But you
> helped us out -- let me help
> you. I mean... let us help you.
>
> NICHOLAS
> (smiles)
> Okay. Deal. I guess that's
> what friends are for.

EXT. SMALL CHURCH - NIGHT

Roxy stands alone outside the church.

She stares down at Switch's broken switchblade, in her hand.

A dark spiritual force travels around the church, like a rush of smoke. It zeroes in on Roxy.

She looks up and sees it! She screams!

INT. SMALL CHURCH - NIGHT

Lisa and Nicholas hear the scream.

Startled, they rush outside.

EXT. SMALL CHURCH - NIGHT

Lisa and Nicholas see nobody.

> LISA
>
> Roxy!

Nicholas and Lisa search the immediate area.

> LISA
>
> Roxy!!

Lisa moves to the fence to the cemetery. Her foot kicks something. She looks down.

Switch's broken switchblade lies there.

> LISA
>
> Roxy! Where are you?

Suddenly, Kane appears out of nowhere in his demonic form -- devilish red eyes, his monstrous razor sharp teeth and menacing claws. He roars!

Lisa trips and falls to the ground in horror. She tries desperately to crawl back to the church. Kane easily closes the distance.

LISA

Ricky! Ricky!

BEHIND THE CHURCH
Ricky sits, brooding, in a corner behind a gravestone.

LISA (O.S.)

Ricky!

He glowers, shakes his head, puts his hands on his ears.
BACK TO SCENE
Kane grabs Lisa's shoulders and her neck.

KANE
(demonic voice)
Soon child... you and your
friends will make perfect
slaves.
(leers)
Such a pretty girl. You're too
beautiful to kill... yet.

He laughs maniacally and kneels over her, groping her in a sexual manner.
Lisa screams out loud and bursts into tears.

Suddenly, a sword stabs out through Kane's chest!

He screams in pain and rage!

Wielding the sword -- Nicholas. He savagely twists it!

Kane releases Lisa, and she scrambles away.

He strikes Nicholas with his right elbow, sending Nicholas reeling back.

Kane turns around, pulls out the sword and tosses it. His wounds disappear
as his flesh regenerates.

Nicholas rushes in for the attack, but Kane steps aside and clotheslines him
with a stiff arm.

Nicholas falls back, stunned -- and Kane lunges forward and grabs his neck.

> KANE
> (demonic voice)
> You're mine.
>
> NICHOLAS
> (gagging)
> I won't let you kill any more
> people!
>
> KANE
> Really? So, rather than me
> killing your new friends -- I
> think I'll kill you instead.

> NICHOLAS
> Try me...

Kane looks at Nicholas in disappointment.

> KANE
> Fuck it, just die!

Kane raises his claws, ready to kill Nicholas.

Lisa stares. She can't let this happen. She quickly grabs the sword, closes the distance and SWINGS!

Kane's right claw falls away in a fountain of blood.

Lisa turns and slashes his leg.

Kane screams in pain and falls to his knees.

Lisa holds the sharp edge of the sword up to Kane's neck.

> LISA
> Where is Roxy? What have
> you done with her?!

Kane laughs maniacally. His severed claw regenerates itself in a flash.

                    KANE
            It's too late. She's mine.

He grabs the sword and breaks it in half!
He then suddenly vanishes from sight.

                    LISA
            Noooooooo!!!!

Lisa rushes toward the cemetery -- Nicholas restrains her.
Together, they watch evil spirits roam and moan in and out through the tombstones of the cemetery.
INT. MAUSOLEUM - NIGHT
Kane reappears. In his human form. He stretches, cracks his neck.
Roxy struggles, chained to the altar. She screams. Tears run freely down her face.
Kane pulls out his ceremonial dagger, with a dark black handle and a rusty blade.
He slowly cuts Roxy's right leg. She wails and gnashes her teeth.
He licks the blood as it seeps down her leg. It gives him energy. Restores his vitality.
Kane stands, caresses her face gently.

                    KANE
            Thank you for bringing me
            back, child. I'm going to let
            you live a little while longer.
            Just enough time to feel the
            pleasure of pain before you
            die.

Kane slices Roxy's stomach. Roxy screams in agony.

Kane licks the blood off his dagger. He smiles cruelly at her.

He then bites her shoulder with his sharp, jagged teeth -- and sucks the blood from the wound.

                    ROXY
          God help me! AAAAH!!!!
                    KANE
          God? I'm God! Your soul is
          so pure, so fresh. Worship
          me and live.
                    ROXY
          Never!
                    KANE
               (chuckles)
          Let's take it from the top
          then, shall we?

Kane cuts her forearm slowly. Blood seeps from the cut.

                    ROXY
          What do you want!
                    KANE
               (roars; demonic)
          You!

INT. SMALL CHURCH - NIGHT

Nicholas and Lisa sit in the candlelit church. Ricky enters.

                    RICKY
          Where's Roxy?

LISA

Where the hell were you?
Didn't you see that bastard
attack me?

RICKY

Out back... I... where is she?

LISA

She's gone. They got her.

RICKY

Is she dead?

LISA

I don't know. It doesn't matter anymore.

Ricky grabs Lisa's shoulders. He shakes her.

RICKY

Lisa, what the hell! Is she
dead or not?

Lisa doesn't answer. She just closes her eyes and looks down.
Ricky turns to Nicholas.

RICKY

Well?

Nicholas didn't say a word either.

RICKY

(freaking out)
Oh, fuck! We're fucked man!
We're so fucked!

He stumbles off, collapses in a heap against the back wall.

                    NICHOLAS
             Keep cool man. We'll get her
             back.

Ricky thinks of something. He turns and scrutinizes Nicholas.

                    RICKY
             Hey... wait a minute. I <u>know</u>
             you... don't I?

Nicholas stares back at Ricky.

                    RICKY
             You're Nick Napalm! The
             drummer and second lead
             vocalist of Black Voodoo!
             You were the best!

Nicholas is surprised and pleased to have met a fan in such a place as this.

                    RICKY
             My mom told me about you.
             She was your biggest fan,
             back in the day. She got
             me into all your music -- it's
             why I joined a heavy metal
             band! To rock like you guys
             did!

Ricky paces and laughs.

RICKY

Damn I mean... I still don't
like you kissing the girl I love,
but... well hell, man, you're
freakin' Nick Napalm!

Lisa, taken aback, rounds on Ricky.

LISA

What? You love me? Really?

RICKY

Yeah, I do ever since back in
the day. Not that it matters
now, now that it's too late.
You got a new boyfriend now.
That's fine. I really don't care.
I just want us all to get out of
here now and go home in one
piece.

Nicholas stares at his claws and face in a old mirror hanging on the wall.
He suddenly, violently, smashes the mirror. Pieces of glass falls to the ground.
The other two watch this outburst warily.

NICHOLAS

I used to be Nick Napalm. Now
I'm this...a damn monster.

RICKY

Dude, don't you see... you're
still alive. Still kicking. You
can still be human...

NICHOLAS

I gave that up a long time ago.

                    RICKY

I don't believe that. Being human is a choice. You helped
us back there. You stood up,
did the right thing. If that's
not being human, then what
is?

Ricky takes a deep breath, shakes out his arms.

                    RICKY

And now we got a job to do.
Let's go get Roxy.

                    LISA

Ricky... surely that monster's
killed her by now.

                    NICHOLAS

No. She's alive, you can bet
on that. Whoever awakens
Kane will have his or her life
spared for a short period of
time.

                    RICKY

Then what?

                    NICHOLAS

Then...

        (reluctantly)

...the summoner will be ritu-
ally sacrificed, and their soul
will be taken. Just like all the
others.

                    RICKY
          Well, shit -- there's no time to
          lose, let's go!

Ricky moves toward the door, but Nicholas grabs his arm.

                    NICHOLAS
          I wouldn't go outside if I
          were you.
                    RICKY
          That psycho's gonna kill her!
                    NICHOLAS
          If you two go in there alone,
          you won't come out. But... if
          all three of us strike at the ex-
          act same time, we might have
          a good chance to take him
          down. It's the only shot we
          got, trust me.

Ricky and Lisa exchange a glance. They nod in unison.
Ricky grabs a broken length of jagged wood.

                    RICKY
          Fine, we will. But listen up...
          you try anything, you even
          look for one second like
          you're gonna turn on us...
          then the hell with how much
          I like your music. I won't hes-
          itate to stake your sorry ass.

NICHOLAS
Fair enough. Let's get moving.

Just within the open front door, they hear THUNDER and see multiple bolts of green lightning strike the nearby ground.

LISA
What's happening?
NICHOLAS
It's Kane. He's doing something.

Suddenly they hear the WAILING of people -- or something -- close by.

RICKY
What the hell? You hear that?
LISA
What is that?

Nicholas goes next to the front entrance and looks through the port hole.

NICHOLAS
It's Zombies. Damn it.
RICKY
Great. More fuckin' zombies. Where's Bruce Campbell when you need him.
NICHOLAS
Take it easy. We can handle this. Come on.

Nicholas leads them away from the front entrance.
EXT. CHURCH REAR DOORS - NIGHT

Nicholas, Lisa and Ricky quickly leave the church through the back entrance.

Nicholas takes the humans over to a ramshackle garage. Within is a form draped in dirty white sheet. Nicholas whips the sheet off, revealing --

A black 1960 fully customized four door Cadillac Eureka Landau 3-Way Hearse.

> NICHOLAS
> Meet Betty.

The thing is a gleaming, tricked out, cherry. "RIDE LIKE HELL" is painted in ornate scrollwork on the side. Bats erupt from an inferno of painted flames. The hood ornament: a gleaming chrome gargoyle, leering menacingly.

With his finger, Ricky traces a hatch above the driver's compartment. He grins up at Nicholas.

> RICKY
> A sunroof? On a hearse?

Nicholas grins crooked.

> NICHOLAS
> Hey... you don't stop bein'
> cool, just because you've been
> to Hell.

Nicholas pulls out his car keys from his inner jacket pocket. He unlocks the driver's side door and reaches inside. He tosses Ricky a Colt Anaconda .44 Magnum.

> RICKY
> Wicked!

He pops it, spins the barrel, jerks it closed. Nicholas, meanwhile, is packing a Mossberg sawed-off combat shotgun.

Lisa sneers.

LISA

Boys and their guns.

Nicholas tosses something which she juggles and catches. Keys. He cocks the shotgun.

NICHOLAS

Its boom stick time!

EXT. CHURCH - MOMENTS LATER

Zombies shamble toward the church doors. The ROAR of a souped-up engine screams out into the night.

From around the church, high beams burning, bursts the Hearse. Lisa's driving. Nicholas pops out of the sunroof. He aims at the two nearest zombies.

LISA

Lets rock!

Nicholas lays off. Lisa mows down the zombies in a cloud of green-black spray.

LISA

Hell yeah!

EXT. LABOU BAYOU - NIGHT

The hearse prowls through the grassy bayou. Nicholas and Ricky blast zombies at will.

A whole crowd of the undead infests the bayou and cemetery.

INT. HEARSE - NIGHT

Ricky snaps on the radio. He fiddles with the stations. Comes up with a HEAVY METAL song.

>   RICKY
>   Holy crap! Hey, Nick! It's
>   your song!

Ricky rocks out. He sights in and BLASTS -- another zombie head ventilated!

EXT. HEARSE - NIGHT

Nicholas smiles in recognition.

>   NICHOLAS
>   I don't believe it. Let's shock
>   it.

He draws a bed and fires! A zombie head blows apart!

MUSIC POUNDS as the hearse crashes through the back gate of the cemetery and heads inside.

EXT. OLD CEMETERY - CONTINUOUS

Zombies crunch under the wheels.

Nicholas and Ricky point, fire and shoot. Methodically, quickly.

INT. HEARSE - NIGHT

Ricky reloads. Lisa thumps over another zombie. Ricky drops a few bullets.

>   RICKY
>   Watch it!

>   LISA
>   Hang on guys.

Ricky finishes reloading, squeezes off several more shots. The shotgun ROARS repeatedly above their heads. Zombies disintegrate right and left.

The mausoleum comes into view. Nicholas drops down into the front seat.

EXT. MAUSOLEUM - NIGHT

Kane comes out of the mausoleum. He shoots lightning from his hands into the sky, causing a lightning vortex.

> KANE
> Come on, you little bastards!
> Come and get me!

He laughs maniacally.

INT. HEARSE - NIGHT

Lisa floors the accelerator, aiming directly for Kane.

> NICHOLAS
> Run him down!

EXT. MAUSOLEUM - NIGHT

Kane shoots a lightening blast from his hands directly at the car -- a fireball slams into the hearse's hood!

INT. HEARSE - NIGHT

Lisa loses control of the hearse. The car swerves wildly.

EXT. OLD CEMETERY - NIGHT

The hearse swerves away from the mausoleum, flips over, and crashes into a tree.

EXT. MAUSOLEUM - NIGHT

Kane smiles.

> KANE
> Good riddance.

He goes back inside the mausoleum.

EXT. CEMETERY - NIGHT

Nicholas, Ricky and Lisa crawl, battered and bloodied, out of the car.

> NICHOLAS
>
> C'mon -- Get out she's going
> to blow!

He rushes them away from the car as the hearse EXPLODES in a blazing fireball!

INT. MAUSOLEUM - NIGHT

The THUNDER of the explosion sounds, as Kane crosses the room with a small wooden box. Roxy moans, bloodied and semi-conscious.

Kane opens the box and pulls out a set of different types of blades, knives, and scalpels with little hooks.

He lays each instrument out on a stone tablet, humming merrily all the while.

Roxy sees the implements laid out. She struggles against her bonds.

> ROXY
>
> You're not gonna get away
> with this!
>
> KANE
> (chuckling)
> I already have.

Kane bars the door with a wooden beam. He grabs a roll of duct tape from his knife bag.

> ROXY
> (enraged)

When my friends get here,
they're gonna massacre your
ass and cut your balls off! If
you even still got any balls.

Kane duct tapes Roxy's mouth.

KANE

You let me worry about my
balls, my dear. Relax. It'll all
be over in a moment.

EXT. MAUSOLEUM - NIGHT
Nicholas, Ricky and Lisa stand outside the Mausoleum, staring at the closed door.

Ricky hauls back and kicks it. Solid. He dances back, moaning in pain, hopping on one foot.

INT. MAUSOLEUM - NIGHT
Kane takes out his sacrificial dagger. He stands before the Loa idol and altar, and composes himself in reverence.

KANE

Sataiya   Usekala   Shanda
ISKAH – great Samedi grant
me her soul, that I may sacrifice this token of flesh and
blood to you!

BAM! BAM! The door pounds, but holds.
Kane glances slightly toward the noise, but returns to his incantation.
EXT. MAUSOLEUM - NIGHT

Lisa and Ricky bang on the door with arms, shoulders. Just doesn't give at all. They fall back, winded.

> NICHOLAS
> Care to let the undead guy
> have a crack at it?

The two wave their hands: be our guest.

> NICHOLAS
> Stand back.

Nicholas rams the door with all of his might.
INT. MAUSOLEUM - NIGHT
CRASH! The doors burst inward, and Nicholas comes tumbling after.

> KANE
> Shit!

Lisa and Ricky enter -- the three rush toward Kane.
Kane brandishes his dagger.
He swipes at Nicholas. Nicholas dodges, then sidekicks Kane into the wall.
Kane leaps back into the fray, snarls, and DISAPPEARS.
Lisa and Ricky stand frozen.

> NICHOLAS
> Get Roxy!

Nicholas runs outside.
The two rush to Roxy and work on releasing her from her bonds.

ROXY

You guys oh I love you. Thank
God...
    (suddenly pissed)
Get these fucking chains off
me.

Lisa reaches out, yanks her hand back. There's blood on the chains.

ROXY

Dammit, Lisa, it's just blood!
You got plenty on you already!

Lisa overcomes her fear, and renews her efforts.
EXT. MAUSOLEUM - NIGHT
Nicholas and Kane, in his monster form, come face to face.

KANE

You've interfered with me for
the last time boy!

NICHOLAS

Too bad -- live with it!

Nicholas transforms into his beastly vampire form. He rears up, and charges.
Kane dodges his attack and slashes Nicholas across the chest.
Nicholas falls to the ground, wounded.
INT. MAUSOLEUM - NIGHT
Ricky and Lisa see Nicholas fall, and move to the door to assist. Roxy is still chained.

> ROXY
>
> Hey! Come back here, dam-
> mit!

Ricky goes back to Roxy.

> RICKY
>
> Listen -- just sit tight for one
> sec...

Her screams of protest are muffled as he replaces the duct tape on her mouth.

EXT. MAUSOLEUM - NIGHT

Kane stands over the wounded Nicholas, chuckling with satisfaction.

Lisa and Ricky slip out of the mausoleum, unseen by Kane.

> KANE
>
> You arrogant pup. Don't you
> realize who I am? Don't you
> realize my power? Did you
> really think you could--

Kane chokes off his words in pain. He drops his dagger.

With a roar, he turns to face Ricky. A stake sticks out of Kane's back.

Kane reaches back, as if gingerly probing for damage. Ricky isn't prepared for the speed at which Kane whips out the stake and SLAMS Ricky across the face. Ricky goes flying.

Lisa grabs Kane's dagger, spins, and PLUNGES the blade into his heart!

Kane coughs up blood on Lisa's face. Lisa spits it back at him.

> KANE
>
> You cannot kill me. I am a
> living god! I am the demon of
> shadows. I AM KANE!!

Kane pulls the dagger out, backhands the girl, and runs back inside the mausoleum.

INT. MAUSOLEUM - NIGHT

Kane goes next to the crystal Loa idol and kneels.

> KANE
>
> Baron Samedi -- send your
> legions of the Loa to me --
> protect your servant on the
> Earth, I evoke you. Give me
> all your power I beg of you!!!

EXT. MAUSOLEUM - NIGHT

Nicholas and the humans slowly collect themselves, and try to rise.

Only Lisa stumbles shakily to her feet.

INT. MAUSOLEUM - NIGHT

Kane levitates into the air.

The Loa idol glows and trembles with contained power.

Spirits begin to issue from within the idol.

Roxy, eyes wide, screams her muffled screams, and whips her head from side to side.

EXT. MAUSOLEUM - NIGHT

Lisa still has her gun. She digs in her pockets.

She comes up with two bullets. Just two.

With exhausted fingers, she shoves the bullets in her gun and snaps it closed.

She stumbles toward the mausoleum. The NOISE and light from inside is fearsome. Undaunted, she enters.

Outside, zombies shamble into view and move slowly toward the dazed Nicholas and Ricky.

INT. MAUSOLEUM - NIGHT

Lisa falls against the lintel. She's totally drained. She raises her gun and aims at Kane's head.

BANG! She misses Kane -- but hits the idol!

A piece of crystal flies off of it.

Kane immediately screams in pain -- lightning charges out of the idol and sizzles his body!

Kane turns to see who his assailant is. With a growl, he staggers toward her, dagger outstretched.

Lisa realizes the truth of his power. She focuses in on the idol... aims her gun directly at it...

Kane raises his hand -- a yard away --

BANG! Lisa fires her last shot!

The crystal Loa idol explodes in a thousand pieces!

Kane emits a bloodcurdling scream!

He spins in the air, bolts of white light cutting through his body -- cracking him apart --

-- and EXPLODES in a burst of ash, flame and wind.

Lisa collapses to the ground. She smiles weakly.

EXT. MAUSOLEUM - NIGHT

The ten zombies dissolve, back into the dust from whence they came.

Nicholas and Ricky stand together, staring uncomprehendingly.

Hundreds of souls, freed from Kane's evil, fountain up into the sky. Lighting flashes to greet them, and THUNDER rolls a final gravestone over them as the bayou falls silent.

The battle is over.

INT. MAUSOLEUM - NIGHT

Nicholas enters the mausoleum. He sees Lisa lying there, seemingly asleep. He kneels down next to her.

NICHOLAS

Hey.

Lisa's eyes flutter open.

LISA

Oh, hey you.

Nicholas lifts her to her feet.

LISA

Is it over?

NICHOLAS

It's over.

Nicholas's skin color changes from pale and deathly -- to pink and living. He looks down at himself, noticing the change.

NICHOLAS

It's over. I'm back. I'm human again.

Ricky runs back in. He and Lisa hug tightly.

A MOANING VOICE sounds O.S. -- the three turn, alarmed -- it's just Roxy!

Ricky rushes to her and rips off the duct tape.

ROXY

Ow! Damn that hurts!
(to Lisa)
Hey, sis... nice shot.

Lisa nods, smiles.

                    ROXY
          Now will you guys <u>please</u> get
          this shit off me?

Nicholas crosses and yanks on the chains. Surprised that he didn't rip them
to shreds like paper.

                    ROXY
          Just when we could've really
          used your vamp powers --
          you go and turn human on
          us.

The three gather and free Roxy.

                    RICKY
          You're bleeding.
                    ROXY
          I'll be fine, lets just get out of
          here.

Roxy looks at Nicholas. She grins lopsidedly and gives him a big hug. She
breaks it off, holds him at arm's length.

                    ROXY
          Thank you.

Nicholas nods his head.

                    NICHOLAS
          Let's go back to town and get
          shitfaced. We need it.

> RICKY
> Amen to that.

The foursome head to the mausoleum door.

> ROXY
> Hey, wait... where's that me-
> dallion thing? We don't want
> this crap to happen all over
> again...

Nicholas pulls the medallion from his pocket. He dangles it before the re-lived humans.

> NICHOLAS
> You didn't think I'd be so stu-
> pid as to give it to Kane, did
> you?
> ROXY
> Hell no.

Nicholas puts the medallion back to his pocket.
They exit the mausoleum with their equipment. The doors close.
Blackness.
EXT. OLD CEMETERY - MORNING
The four stand around a fresh grave. A hump of rich brown soil, headed with a crudely-made cross.

> RICKY
> (to Switch's grave)
> Buddy, I'm really going to
> miss you. See you on the oth-
> er side. Rest in peace buddy.

>   ROXY
>   (to Switch's grave)
>   Baby, you were the best.
>   Sleep well.
>   LISA
>   (to the sky)
>   Good God -- take him home.
>   NICHOLAS
>   At least he's rocking in a bet-
>   ter place now.

A moment of silence.

>   LISA
>   Come on guys, let's go.

The four leave. Switch sleeps peacefully in the morning sun.
EXT. CEMETERY GATE - MOMENTS LATER
The four watch the sun clearing the distant horizon.

>   NICHOLAS
>   I haven't seen the sun in so
>   long. It feels kind of good.

The gate is closed.

>   ROXY
>   Oh, hell. It's still locked.

Lisa goes to the gate and pushes. It swings open easily. They laugh at the irony.

LISA

After you.

The four chuckle and exit the cemetery.

EXT. LOUISIANA ROADWAY - MORNING

The four walk together as group. Lisa comes up to Nicholas.

LISA

Thanks for saving our ass, Nicholas. I mean Mr. Napalm.

Roxy looks up sharply.

ROXY

Say what?

She looks closely at Nick.

ROXY

Holy crap, it is! You guys rocked! Man, I can't believe I didn't notice.
(to Lisa)
Hey, how'd you figure out the idol was the source of his power?

LISA

Dumb luck.
(to Nicholas)
I thought it was his medallion.

NICHOLAS
Nope. The medallion was
just a keepsake.
ROXY
But the inscription...
NICHOLAS
It was written by Marie
Laveau, the voodoo priestess.
She was Kane's ancestor.

The bright sun splashes the bayou with gentle golden light.

RICKY
Hey check out the horizon.
Dawn never looked so good.
LISA
(to Nicholas)
So what happens to you now?
NICHOLAS
I'm free. I saved you... and
you saved me. We're even
then.
ROXY
No, Nicholas -- we're any-
thing but even.

Nicholas looks curiously at her. She pats him on the back.

ROXY
What I mean is -- we're
friends. Friends. For life.
LISA
That's right.

NICHOLAS
Well, okay -- how about this.
I understand your band needs
a   new   drummer...besides
three's a crowd if you know
what a mean.

Roxy is stung by the remembrance. There's a moment of silence.

ROXY
Yeah, you know... we could
maybe audition you.
NICHOLAS
What?
LISA
It's been awhile. You're prob-
ably pretty rusty though.
NICHOLAS
Hey, I freakin' rock!
RICKY
Maybe back in the eighties.
You've been undead a long
time. That can really fuck
with your rhythm.
NICHOLAS
Bullshit! I'm still solid as a
rock.
RICKY
Oh, did you get a lot of prac-
tice in, while you were...
    (scary fingers)
...haunting people?

LISA

Sucking blood?

NICHOLAS

Okay, okay. So that's the way it's gonna be, eh? Jesus, you suck a few people dry and look at all the shit you gotta put up with. I can still play well you guys, trust me.

ROXY

(smiling)

Hey Nicky, we're just kidding. What I mean to say is. Well Lisa, you tell him.

LISA

We want you to be in the band with us.

NICHOLAS

Cool.

The group walks off into the distance, razzing and shoving each other.

EXT. LOUISIANA ROADWAY - LATER

The stolen van sits by the side of the road.

Charlie sleeps off a drunk in the grass beside the van. An empty bottle of booze lies nearby.

The four arrive, and stare down at the pathetic display.

Ricky peeks in the driver's window.

A spaghetti of wires sticks out from under the dash.

RICKY

Well look who we got here, it's the dickless hick who hot-wired our ride. Son of a bitch.

Lisa looks into the back.

> LISA
>
> The gear's still here, thank God. Looks like the bastard didn't have time to fence it.
>
> ROXY
>
> This guy deserves an ass kicking.
>
> NICHOLAS
>
> Let's have some fun with him instead. I got a cool idea. Wake him up.

Roxy kicks Charlie awake.

> ROXY
>
> Hey. Dickhead. Get up.

Charlie's eyes open. He takes a moment to register where he is, and who's looking down at him.

> CHARLIE
>
> Oh, hey kids! You made it! Praise the Lord! Oh, I'm so relieved! Boy, I didn't--

Ricky appears with some rope. He looks at the others. They smile.

> CHARLIE
>
> Hey, now, wait a minute... no harm no foul, right? Hey, come on, you guys...

NICHOLAS

Get him!

Charlie screams and struggles as the four descend upon him.

EXT. LOUISIANA ROADWAY - LATER

Ricky drives the van, looking relaxed, even though he's dirty and bloody.

Nicholas sits shotgun.

Behind the van, the doors are open.

Lisa and Roxy stare out at a rope.

The rope undulates out behind the van.

CHARLIE (O.S.)

(panting hard)

Please... kids... I can't...

Charlie, naked, hands tied in front of him, jogs desperately behind the moving van.

CHARLIE

I got a... a heart condition...

I'm tellin' ya...

ROXY

Oh really?

(to Ricky)

Hey, Ricky -- he's got a heart

condition he says!

Ricky responds by pressing the gas pedal.

RICKY

(pretending to hear wrong)

Faster? Sure, I can go faster.

(to Nicholas)

Man, that Charlie. He's an
animal, isn't he?
NICHOLAS
Yeah, a true iron man. Ozzy
Osbourne, would be proud.

The gang laughs all except Charlie.

The van moves on, Charlie bleating, yelling, struggling along. In the distance, the old cemetery gates stand open. The band is busting up laughing their
asses off.

INT. CLUB - NIGHT

A small grimy rock club. The stage is set up for a show, instruments waiting.

Off to the side, the four Midnight Freaks, in coordinated black leather rocker outfits, sip beers and wait to be introduced.

LISA
Oh, hey...

She digs in her bag and passes out necklaces to each.

LISA
I made these for us as a sou-
venir of our little adventure.
Come on, Put 'em on!

Ricky takes a good look at his: it's a silver skull, with a leering grin.

LISA
It's kind of a symbol of what
we went through. You know
a memorial. For Switch. We
should dedicate this show
to him. Besides maybe its a

sign of good things to come.
Who knows.

Nicholas drains his beer and takes a closer look at the skull.
The eyes glint. Some sort of black crystal.

                    NICHOLAS
          (concerned)
     Lisa... what are these jewels in
     the eyes here?
                    LISA
     Oh!
          (laughs)
     Shards of that crystal idol
     Kane had. I picked 'em up on
     our way out.
          (snickers)
     Maybe they'll give us <u>powers</u>
     or something. I thought it be
     good for a joke.

Nicholas looks wary, but he puts his on anyway. They all have them on.

                    NICHOLAS
     Ahh. Why not?

The lights go down.

                    LOUDSPEAKER (V.O.)
     And now, ladies and gentle-
     men, bitches and bastards --
     the most badass hardcore
     thrash band you ever heard --

direct from Hell -- The
Midnight Freaks!

The crowd roars. The band takes the stage.

A quick drumstick four-count from Nicholas -- and the band slams into one of their songs.

The band rocks! The kids are totally into it. The crowd is totally into it!

Roxy's eyes glow RED.

Ricky's eyes glow RED.

Lisa's eyes glow RED.

Nicholas's eyes glow RED.

The band begins to change. Muscles ripple under their skins, veins protrude, claws extend... teeth elongate...

The crowd notices. It's weird. They shrink back in a hubbub.

The Freaks continue to rock. Lisa, transformed into an uber-hot bitch goddess, hits the mike--

LISA (V.O.)
Alright! Let's get this party
started!

The crowd CHEERS! Whatever's going on up there, they love it!

Roxy, Ricky, Lisa, all gaze at each other. They're aware of the change, but they dig it!

Nicholas looks out at them all. He feels the power. His eyes glow.

He grins, and hits the CYMBALS --

FADE OUT.

TO BE CONTINUED

NIGHT OF THE FREAKS 2

Night Terrors
[Book 2]

DOMINIC R. DANIELS

WGA Registered.
Dominic Rocky Daniels
Email: dominicdaniels777@gmail.com

F ADE IN:

INT. NEW ORLEANS - COBRA CLUB - NIGHT

The stage is pitch black.

It is Halloween Night at 10:00 PM in the world-famous Cobra Bar and Nightclub.

Strobe lights with thunder sound effects quickly flash on the dark stage with smoke machines going on the floor.

Four silhouettes enter the dark stage.

Eerie instrumental introduction music plays.

Black lights with cool dark blue and purple colors light up behind the silhouettes on the stage.

The female lead singer's eyes lights up glowing red. Slightly revealing her vampiric face.

Quick transition of the rest of the band's eyes lights up glowing red. Slightly revealing their vampiric faces.

The stage lights blast into red and orange, revealing the full stage with the band in view, with the smoke and light resembling fire in the presence in front of the crowd.

A banner above the stage lights up, reading, "THE MIDNIGHT FREAKS".

The MIDNIGHT FREAKS rock out on stage:

LISA, 22, a blond bombshell with a tough-as-nails attitude, sings lead.

NICHOLAS, 47 (but looks 28), plays drums. He's an 80s metal style rocker, collected, smart, and full of cunning.

ROXY, 25, the mistress of the night, Goth queen and free-spirited beauty, plays keyboards.

RICKY, 23, the clown prince of rock and roll, funny, charming and goofy, plays lead guitar.

The Midnight Freaks are a vampire horror themed heavy metal band with the similar singing and guitar playing styles of the real life band Doro and Warlock, but with more emphasis on horror and theatrics. Their vampire appearances are demonic, frightening but mysterious.

The Midnight Freaks play a cover of "Fight for Rock" from the band Warlock.

Lisa rocks it out on stage, singing. The other band members join in.

Ricky strums the guitar with a strap around his shoulder. Holding it in a position similar to real life guitarist Zakk Wylde. He raises his guitar above his head, then brings it back down. Ricky's right claws strum with a pick and left hand fretting.

Roxy plays the keyboards with elegance and wicked passion.

Nicholas drums with power while singing background vocals for Lisa.

The band plays as Lisa sings with the elegance of fallen angels.

The Cobra Club venue is the size of the real life rock night club "The Whiskey a Go-Go" in Hollywood, CA. It has a bar on the back side like the real life club "Busby's" in West Los Angeles, CA.

The club is dimly lit, decked out for Halloween with hanging skeletons on the walls, and freshly carved glowing jack-o-lanterns on a few side tables and on the bar. Multiple electric candelabras give the room a dim-lit, spooky atmosphere. The club is decked out with large cobweb curtains draped everywhere and a large skull chandelier hanging from the ceiling over the middle of the club.

The sold out crowd are all standing -- no seats. They're into the band and really rocking out. The crowd is a mix of head bangers, punk rockers, goths, skaters, video gamer geeks, BD&SM people... even regular types. There is marijuana and alcohol circulating -- people drink and smoke out in the crowd, having a wicked good time.

The band plays on the stage and the crowd rocks out cheering.

After the song, the crowd goes wild and cheers for the band.

The band members bow gracefully.

INT. COBRA CLUB - BACKSTAGE - NIGHT

It is midnight at the backstage of the club. There is a ton of packed and un-packed audio and lighting equipment in the backstage area. There are black tarps and the room is dimly lit.

The Midnight Freaks, in their human appearance, wait around. The band is tired from playing after their two hour set and want to go home. Ricky and Roxy are smoking cigarettes. Lisa and Nicholas are drinking bottled water.

> LISA
>
> Nicky, where is Stevie? He should have been here twenty minutes ago.
>
> NICHOLAS
>
> Relax.
>
> RICKY
>
> If we weren't so desperate for cash, we wouldn't be playing four nights a week for this guy.

STEVIE, 37, the club owner, a drugged-out prick dressed sharp as a tack, arrives. He snorts a shot of cocaine from a fake car cigarette lighter, then tucks it away in his upper chest suit pocket.

> LISA
>
> (to Stevie)
>
> Stevie? Where the hell were you? We've just finished

playing a two-hour set. We
want to get paid and go
home.

STEVIE

Sorry, I had business to take
care of.

LISA

Do you have our money?
You owe us three thousand
bucks!

STEVIE

Take it easy, I got your money
-- here.

Stevie hands Lisa a wad of cash.
Lisa flips through the money.

LISA

(confused)

What's this? This is only thir-
teen hundred. Where's the
rest?

STEVIE

Sorry sweet thing, but I had
to take care of other expenses
for the club. Booze, payroll,
rent, and also renew my business license. You know how
it goes.

LISA

(angry)

Oh, the business, huh...

ROXY
(to the band)
Would you look at this asshole?
For someone with so much
money, take a look at this.

Roxy takes a speck of coke dust off of Stevie's coat with her finger.

ROXY
What's this shit on your coat?

She knows that Stevie is high. She grabs the coke lighter from Stevie's top
coat pocket.

ROXY
Oh, coke! Nice! Looks like
coke business to me.

Stevie freaks out, tries to grab the lighter back from Roxy.

STEVIE
Give me that! This is real ex-
pensive shit, man!
ROXY
Oh fuck you! Look at this!
Look at this!
Roxy and points at Stevie's
pink-eyed face.
LISA
(angry)
So this is what you have been
spending our money on! You
selfish dick.

Stevie is being defensive of his situation.

> STEVIE
> Well I, uh --
> LISA
> (interrupts)
> Oh this is business expenses!
> (sarcastically)
> Right! So it cost five hundred dollars an ounce to snort blow up your nose.
> (extremely pissed)
> Where is our money you promised us?
> STEVIE
> (interrupts back)
> Babe! Relax! Look I got more problems than you can imagine right now. The mob has fucking loan sharks crawling down my ass. If I don't pay them off first, I'll lose my club.

Stevie tries to play it cool, being slick.

> RICKY
> This is ridiculous! You're a damn liar! We're the ones who should hire the mob to break your legs!

> STEVIE
>
> Whoa! Whoa! If business was better, I would have paid you the full amount.
>
> ROXY
>
> We just gave you a sold-out crowd. People were scream-ing for us out there and this is how you repay us?
>
> RICKY
>
> Man! Fuck this! Let's go!

Nicholas jumps on board the conversation and tries to resolve the situation.

> NICHOLAS
>
> (to the band)
>
> You know this guy doesn't want to pay us.
>
> (to Stevie)
>
> You can get yourself anoth-er band to rip off with your bullshit and cheap lies. We're done here.

The Midnight Freaks exit the scene as a group.

> STEVIE
>
> Guys! Guys! Wait wait wait! Come back!

The backdoor slams shut.
Stevie's disappointed.

STEVIE

Aw shit!

EXT. DESERTED HIGHWAY - NIGHT

A Route 66-like highway with double yellow line and broken, cracked concrete asphalt.

A jet black Chevy van, wickedly detailed with illustrations of demons and monsters on it, moves up the road. The side reads, "THE METAL MACHINE".

EXT. MIKE'S MOTEL - NIGHT

It is now 1:00AM. November 1st.

The sign reads "Mike's Motel" -- a roadside motel, dimly lit, with a neon sign reading "Vacancy". The Metal Machine van is parked into the parking lot. The Midnight Freaks get out of the van and enter their room.

INT. MIKE'S MOTEL - ROOM 106 - NIGHT

The motel room is a torn to shit dump.

Roxy and Ricky crash on top of their bed. Nicholas is having a cigarette.

LISA

You guys, what are we going to do now? We really needed that gig.

NICHOLAS

Look, the guy screwed us over and besides, we have bigger problems to deal with. You three are at least up to seventy thou in college debt -- each.

RICKY

We couldn't even get ten grand for that fancy medallion from the historical

society in Labou. What a
bunch of fuckers.
LISA
You said it.
Ricky and Roxy lay on their
queen-sized bed, relaxing.
RICKY
How are we going to pay it
all off? We can't even get any
solid work.

Roxy is annoyed and complains sarcastically.

ROXY
Yeah, we got collection agen-
cies hounding us and con-
stantly calling us at every
hour of the day. Face it, we're
in hell.
RICKY
What the fuck were we
thinking? Shit, if we knew it
was going to be this tough to
find a gig after graduation,
we should have just dropped
out and saved ourselves a lot
of money.

Nicholas controls the situation as he tries to ease up the band's spirits. He
opens the mini fridge and pulls out a couple of blood packs with medium size
drink straws.

NICHOLAS
(to Ricky)
Take it easy. Have a little
blood and calm down, we'll
find a way to get the cash.

Nicholas tosses a blood pack with a straw to Ricky.

Ricky catches the blood pack with his hands. He takes the straw and pokes
a hole into and drinks it like a Capri Sun juice drink pouch.

ROXY
Nicky, I thought you said this
lifestyle would be easy.
NICHOLAS
I never said it would be
easy. How'd you think I got
around the last twenty years
this way? What did you expect this to be? Anne Rice
and velvet corsets? Come
on.
RICKY
At least we don't sparkle like
it is, in those shitty vampire
romance books. Who the
fuck writes crap like that?

(A beat)

Yeah, we got the good looks,
we got the style, but we don't
have any money and we're
running low on blood.

Nicholas sits down on a chair next to a coffee table putting his boots on the table.

NICHOLAS
Relax, we'll get some more.
Be patient.

Lisa sits down on the end of her and Nicholas' queen size bed, thinking -- her left hand on her cheek and her left leg crossed over to her right, right foot on the floor.

LISA
So what's Plan B?

Nicholas thinks for a brief moment, but he is unable to come up with a solution.

RICKY
We've called everywhere from Hollywood to New York for clubs and bars, but they are fully booked.
ROXY
We could always go to Vegas.
NICHOLAS
Vegas? Get real. We're good but we're not that good, yet. You guys know anyone we can try to call?

Neither Roxy nor Ricky answer the question. Until, Lisa thinks of someone.

LISA

Wait a minute... I know someone, Sherry Roberts.

NICHOLAS

Who's Sherry Roberts?

LISA

Sherry Roberts and her
band. "Black Death Babies."
They are our rivals from
back in the day but they are
still good friends with us.
Sherry is an awesome bassist
and singer. She runs a small
lounge club out at this little
hick town in Texas called El
Cortez.

NICHOLAS

Do you want to give her a
call?

LISA

I'm going to call her. Hang
on.

Lisa grabs the band's only cell phone out of her pocket and calls Sherry.
The line picks up and a sweet female voice answers the call.

SHERRY (V.O.)

Pistol Whip Bar and Lounge,
Sherry speaking.

LISA

Hey Sherry, it's Lisa. I'm sorry to bother you this late in
the evening. Are you still up?

We don't see Sherry's physical appearance; just hear her voice on Lisa's cell phone.

> SHERRY (V.O.)
> Hey Lisa, Yeah I'm still up.
> How you doing? I've haven't
> heard from you and the guys
> in such a long time.

> LISA
> We've been trying to hang in
> there. But we're running cold
> on gigs. Do you have any
> new lineups for shows at your
> place?

> SHERRY (V.O.)
> Why? What's wrong?

> LISA
> I was wondering if you can
> book us for a show in the next
> two days? We got screwed
> on the last gig that we were
> playing. The club manager
> scammed us, he wanted us
> to work for free. Can you be-
> lieve that?

> SHERRY (V.O.)
> I've had the same problem
> in the past. Look anyway,
> I can use some fresh talent
> out here. I can hook you
> guys up.

LISA

How come your band isn't playing? Just wondering.

SHERRY (V.O.)

Let's just say we broke up.

LISA

Oh, that sucks.

SHERRY (V.O.)

But, I still have my manager.

LISA

Cool. Do you think he would be interested in hearing our stuff?

SHERRY (V.O.)

I'll give him a call. Come on out. It'll be just like old times.

LISA

Great, we'll be there in two days. Thanks. See you soon.

Lisa hangs up the phone and tells the others to pack.

LISA

Get packing, it's time to rock.

RICKY

Let's roll!

The band grabs their duffel bags.

EXT. DESERTED HIGHWAY - DAY

The Metal Machine van drives down on a deserted highway.

SUPERIMPOSED on the scene -- a map with a red line traveling from New Orleans, LA to El Cortez, TX.

Instrumental 80's rock and roll music plays.

EXT. DESERTED HIGHWAY - DAY

SUPER:"Two Days Later"

It is now November 2nd. Mexican Holiday: Day of the Dead.

The sun sets. The Metal Machine van drives down the road, passing a sign: "Welcome to El Cortez. Population 200." Two red spray painted letters deface the sign, renaming the town "Hell Cortez".

INT. CHEVY VAN - MOVING - NIGHT

It is 7:00PM.

Inside the van, red leather seats and red fabric on the walls. In the back of the van are a bunch of musical instruments, mics, and a drum kit. Instrumental heavy metal music plays in the CD player.

Lisa is driving the van, while Nicholas is on the front passenger seat. Ricky and Roxy are next to each other drinking cans of energy drinks.

Suddenly, police lights flash and the police horn goes off. Lisa looks into the driver's mirror. She sees a police squad car on their tail.

LISA

Aw, crap. Here comes bacon.

Lisa pulls over to the right side of the road and turns off the music. The police squad car stops behind her. The siren goes off, the lights remain flashing.

EXT. DESERTED HIGHWAY - NIGHT

It is pitch black out. The only lights -- the cop car's cherries, headlights, and the van's headlights.

SHERIFF MITCH BARTON, mid 40s, a muscular and gray-haired brute of a man in uniform, exits his car and strides domineering toward the van.

He walks up to the driver's window and taps on the glass with his flashlight.

Lisa rolls down her side window.

LISA

Is there a problem, officer?

Mitch speaks in a deep, tough, strong voice.

> MITCH
> Yeah. Your left tail light is
> out.

Mitch points the flashlight in the band's eyes.

> MITCH
> Let me see your driver's li-
> cense and registration.

Lisa pulls out her driver's license from her wallet and registration from the glove compartment.
Lisa shows her driver's license to Mitch.
Mitch takes it and goes back his squad car to look for information.
INT. CHEVY VAN - NIGHT
Each member of the band is nervous -- only Nicholas is calm.

> RICKY
> If he finds the blood packs,
> it's all over.
> NICHOLAS
> Keep cool.

Mitch returns to the driver's side of the van.

> MITCH
> (to Lisa)
> Step out of the van, Miss.

Nicholas interrupts.

NICHOLAS

What the hell are you doing?

MITCH

(to Nicholas)

Back off boy! Or I'll have
your ass in a cell quicker than
a bitch in heat!

Lisa calms Nicholas down.

LISA

It's okay, Nicky.

Lisa calmly gets out of the van.
EXT. DESERTED HIGHWAY - CONTINUOUS
Mitch and Lisa are on the driver's side of the van.

MITCH

Lean yourself against the vehicle. Spread your legs.

Lisa obeys.

LISA

Am I being arrested for
anything?

MITCH

Stop talking!

Mitch frisks her down, while he calls up for back up.

MITCH

(into walkie talkie)

Barton here -- we got us a couple of punk kids on Highway
13, I pulled them over. They
are obstructing my investiga-
tion with the suspect. I need
some assistance, over.

DIXON (V.O.)
Copy that, Barton.

A Deputy squad car pulls up next to the Sheriff's squad car.
The driver is DEPUTY ERIC DIXON, late 20s, a clean cut cop with a strict
attitude and serious demeanor. Dixon arrives on scene and gets out of his car.
Deputy Dixon walks to Sheriff Mitch and Lisa.

DIXON
What seems to be the problem?

MITCH
Dixon, these kids have marijuana in their van.

Lisa interrupts.

LISA
That's not true.
MITCH
(to Lisa)
Shut up!

Dixon pulls out his flashlight and opens the van's sliding side door.

> DIXON
> (to the band)
> All of you! Step out of the
> van! Put your hands behind
> your heads and come over
> where I am standing!

The Midnight Freaks know that they are in trouble as they slowly exit the van. Deputy Dixon searches the van for drugs with his flashlight.

Deputy Dixon points his flashlight slowly in all directions of inside of the van. He finds nothing.

Dixon holds the flashlight and turns his head slightly to the left talking to Sheriff Mitch off screen.

> DIXON
> (to Mitch)
> Sheriff! I don't see any drugs
> in here.
> MITCH (V.O.)
> That's because they ate it!

Ricky interrupts trying to plead the band's case.

> RICKY
> That's bullshit!
> DIXON
> (to Ricky)
> Don't raise your voice to me,
> sir.

Mitch arrives while holding Lisa's right arm firmly.

MITCH

Cuff em' and put them in the
back of my vehicle. I'll call
the tow truck company to
come in and impound their
van. Book them for driving
under the influence of an un-
lawful substance.

Dixon slaps three sets of cuffs on Ricky, Nicholas, and Roxy and puts them
in the back of Mitch's squad car, while Mitch slaps a set of cuffs on Lisa. Lisa
stays in front of Mitch. The squad car back door is locked.

DIXON

(to Mitch)

I think you got everything
under control here. See you
later.

Dixon returns to his own squad car and drives off.

Now that Mitch and Lisa are alone, Mitch drags Lisa to a nearby tree six feet
away. Mitch violently gropes her trying to rape her.

Mitch grabs Lisa's throat and plants a big kiss in her mouth, his right hand
on Lisa's right shoulder.

Lisa removes Mitch's slobbery face from her mouth with her left hand.

LISA

Get the fuck off me!

Lisa vamps out in front of Mitch. Scaring the living hell out of him.

Mitch steps back real quick and quickly draws his Magnum with both hands
and shoots her.

BANG! BANG!

We see Lisa getting shot several times in the heart. Lisa falls down dead.

INT. SHERIFF'S SQUAD CAR - NIGHT

Nicholas, Ricky and Roxy are handcuffed in the back of the cramped up squad car.

They hear the gunshots. They know that Lisa has been shot. They break out of their cuffs, vamp out and rips the doors open.

EXT. DESERTED HIGHWAY - NIGHT

The Midnight Freaks exit the sheriff's squad car to attack Mitch, but they are all shot by the power of Mitch's gun knocking them down to the ground.

Mitch is scared as hell as he quickly runs to his squad car and drives away, burning rubber. Nicholas watches Sheriff Mitch Barton get away.

EXT. DESERTED HIGHWAY - MOMENTS LATER

Nicholas, Ricky and Roxy transforms into their vampire forms. They are still on the ground and hurt from the gunshot wound. Each of them pull the bullets out of their chests, with their wounds starting to close and heal up.

Nicholas and Ricky moan.

Roxy runs to Lisa's lifeless body.

Roxy screams in horror.

ROXY

Lisa!

Roxy shakes Lisa's body.

Ricky and Nicholas get to the scene as they are concerned about Lisa.

Nicholas shakes Lisa's lifeless body and cradles her in his arms. He tries to revive her, shaking her to wake her up... but it is no use. Lisa's heart has been blown to pieces with her body drenched in her own blood. He cries in anger mixed with sorrow and hugs her in his arms.

NICHOLAS
(desperately trying to hold it together)
Lisa! Come on, damn it!
Don't die!

Roxy cries hysterically. Ricky get pissed off and curses out of anger.

> RICKY
> I'm going to kill that sick son
> of a bitch if it's the last thing
> I do.

Ricky punches the tree, knocking it down with his vampiric super human strength.

EXT. DESERTED HIGHWAY - MOMENTS LATER

The Midnight Freaks bury Lisa in a shallow grave. Roxy holds Lisa's necklace to keep her memory alive. Ricky is holding a shovel -- the same shovel that he buried his dead friend, Switch with.

Nicholas makes a speech as he takes over leadership of the band.

> NICHOLAS
> There is only one thing left
> for us to do. We're going to
> find us that bastard and we're
> gonna kill him.
> ROXY
> He took the only family I
> have left. Let's do it.

Ricky doesn't say anything but closes his eyes, breathing heavy with anger. He clinches his right fist next to his knees.

> NICHOLAS
> You're wrong, Roxy. We are
> all more than just friends.
> We are a family, and a family
> sticks together. Come on, it's
> time to raise some hell!

The Midnight Freaks are ready to rock and avenge.

The Metal Machine speeds off the road, burning rubber to El Cortez.

INT. CHEVY VAN - MOVING - NIGHT

The van is speeding to El Cortez. Ricky is in the driver's seat, Roxy is in the passenger seat and Nicholas is in the back seat.

Nicholas pulls out a small foot locker and opens it.

In the small foot locker -- the revolver, a broken switchblade knife, some shards of a voodoo diamond skull and Nicholas's "Black Voodoo" CD album. He puts Lisa's Heart necklace in there and pulls out a civil war revolver. The revolver has been modified to work perfectly and shoot modern bullets. He closes the foot locker.

Nicholas loads the gun then stuffs the gun inside his chest coat pocket.

Ricky speaks to Nicholas, while he is driving having second thoughts.

> RICKY
> Maybe we should go to the
> cops. Instead of doing this.

> NICHOLAS
> We don't have a choice. They'll
> think we did it. They won't
> believe us, and they'll find out
> what we are -- vampires.

> ROXY
> We're not going to get any jus-
> tice with those pigs. How can
> you go to the police to report
> a murder when they are the
> ones who did it? You can't.

> NICHOLAS
> When the police break the
> law, then there isn't any law,

period. It's anarchy. It's now either us or them.

ROXY

Right.

NICHOLAS

Lisa was a good friend to you both. She was my girl... I loved her dearly. But I'm not going to let that monster get away with this. That fat good 'ole boy, fucker deserves a bullet in the head.

ROXY

Neither am I. Lisa was more than my best friend, she was my sister. That piece of shit needs to die.

RICKY

(to Roxy)

Turn on the radio, I don't want to even think about what just happened.

NICHOLAS

You have to deal with it.

RICKY

This stuff is really screwing with me man! One minute she was alive talking with us and now just like that, snap! She's dead! Man! She's freaking dead!

ROXY

Stay tough Ricky. Both of you
guys. We have to stay tough.

NICHOLAS

Yeah that's right. Tough.

ROXY

If we let it hit us in our minds,
we're not going to be able to
think straight. No matter if
we are upset or not.

RICKY

Look, let's just listen to something, anything. Please.

ROXY

Yeah, the radio would be
good right now. Let's listen
to something to help us cool
down.

Roxy turns on the radio, but instead of rock and heavy metal tunes, they get
a news report.

NEWS ANNOUNCER (V.O.)

There has been a string of
rapes occurring the past few
months by a mysterious suspect who has not yet been
identified. Authorities have
been conducting multiple in-
vestigations at this time. All
of the victims have ranged
from late teens to early twen-
ties. One of the victims has

been identified as 25-year-
old, Sherry Roberts, owner
of the Pistol Whip Bar and
Lounge in the small town
of El Cortez in Bellinghem
county. We will be bring-
ing you more on this story
when new information has
been released. This is David
Richardson reporting for the
ZTQ's News Radio Station,
Channel 89.7AM...

The Midnight Freaks hear about Sherry's rape, and are stunned. Meanwhile the radio static cuts out any further audio -- the radio's sound begins to die down to where it can barely be heard.

                    RICKY
          I don't believe it.
                    ROXY
          I do.

                    NICHOLAS
          Add it up and who do you
          think is responsible?
                    RICKY
          Let's go pay The Pistol Whip,
          a little visit.

Ricky turns off the radio and speeds up. The Metal Machine van heads to the Pistol Whip Bar & Lounge in El Cortez.

EXT. EL CORTEZ - NIGHT

It is 8:00 PM at the small but rowdy town of El Cortez. Bikers, gang bangers, cowboys, gamblers and criminals regularly visit the town. There are a couple of bars and strip clubs, small poker houses, barbecue house restaurants, a cigar lounge, a motel, general store and a hardware store.

The Metal Machine van enters the neon-lit town and arrives at the Pistol Whip Bar and Lounge parking lot.

The trio exits the van and enters the bar.

INT. PISTOL WHIP BAR AND LOUNGE - NIGHT

Inside is a lively place. A jukebox is playing Southern Rock music. The wooden bar is modestly decorated for the "Day of the Dead" Holiday. The entire bar is lit up red and orange colors with glass candle holders. Little red chili lights are hanging above the bar. Little Mexican skeletons are hanging on the walls and ceilings.

A giant wall sculpture of a Mexican Day of the Dead skull decorated with lights and glowing red eyes is on the background wall of the main stage. There are posters of famous rock bands from the 1970s and 1980s all over the walls of the lounge. Red and white Christmas lights illuminate the place.

There are drunken people everywhere.

Smoking hot and busty bikini clad go-go girls in black bikinis wearing black high heels and skull necklaces and earrings, dance on top of various tables. The girls are a mix of white, black and Latino.

A group of bikers are drinking around a few of the tables with a go-go girl dancing on top of their table. College guys and girls are dancing on the dance floor. The rest are locals kicking back having a good time. The place is understaffed.

Nicholas, Roxy and Ricky enter and are relaxed.

RICKY

This place is chill.

NICHOLAS

Since we're here, we might
as well calm down and get a
couple of drinks. Let's see if
we can talk to Sherry.

The band walks through the semi-drunken crowd in unison.

Nicholas leads his band to sit at the bar, to drink whiskey and to talk to LUCAS, the bartender, 28, African American, bald head, buff, tattooed, goatee.

NICHOLAS
(to Lucas)
One shot of whiskey, a cold
brew and a Bloody Mary for
my friends here.

Lucas winks his left eye and smirk at Nicholas.

LUCAS
You got it.

Lucas gets the drinks to the Midnight Freaks. Nicholas gives thirty dollars to Lucas.

NICHOLAS
(to Lucas)
Thanks. Keep the change.

The three raise glasses for a toast.

NICHOLAS
To Lisa!
RICKY & ROXY
(in unison)
To Lisa!

They clink their glasses and drink their drinks.
Lucas is cleaning a couple of glasses with a wet rag.

LUCAS

Sorry to interrupt you guys,
but I couldn't help but over-
hear. You said the name Lisa.
Are you Sherry's friends by
the way?

Nicholas talks to Lucas.

NICHOLAS

Yeah, we're all friends of hers.
Is she here?

LUCAS

She's upstairs in her pad taking the night off. Some asshole attacked her last night.
Cops didn't do jack about it.

ROXY

Yeah, we heard on the radio.
That's why we wanted to see
her.

Lucas turns around to the phone on the wall.

LUCAS

Alright. Let me call her
upstairs.

Lucas goes to the land-line phone and calls Sherry.

LUCAS

(into phone)

Yo Sherry! I got some people
who want to see you. They
said they're friends of yours.
(listens)
I understand.
(to Nicholas)
She doesn't want to see
anyone.
NICHOLAS
Tell her, Lisa's band is here.

Lucas turns around to talk on the phone.

LUCAS
(into phone)
Sherry. They're Lisa's band
members.
(listens)
Yeah... okay, cool.

Lucas hangs up the phone and turns around to the band.

LUCAS
I'll open the stairway door
for you. Go upstairs, knock
on the green door, and she'll
let you in.

Nicholas, Roxy and Ricky finish their drinks. Lucas walks towards a low half
door connected to the bar. He unlocks and opens the door, revealing a stairway.

The Midnight Freaks go through the low half door and through the small
stairway door that Lucas just unlocked for them. Lucas closes the stairway door
behind them.

INT. STAIRWAY - NIGHT

The Midnight Freaks walk straight up the wooden creaky stairway.

Nicholas is about to knock on the door, but Roxy stops him.

Roxy knocks on the door, but no one answers. Feeling that their time is wasted, the Midnight Freaks are about to leave. Then, the green door opens. They turn around and see Sherry.

SHERRY ROBERTS, 25, a beautiful redhead woman, half-Latina/Irish knock out, a badly-beaten and bruised mess. A sad but sweet train wreck of a girl. She has a lit cigarette in her right hand.

Roxy gives Sherry a hug, to comfort her.

> ROXY
> (to Sherry)
> We came as soon as we heard.

Sherry's speaks with a sweet voice.

> SHERRY
> Thanks, guys.

Sherry turns to Ricky and gives him a hug.

> SHERRY
> Hey Ricky. Where's Lisa?
> RICKY
> She couldn't come.
> SHERRY
> Why? What's wrong? I talked
> to her two days ago.
> NICHOLAS
> You better close the door and
> lock it. We'll tell you.

> SHERRY
> Who's this?
> ROXY
> Just close the door and we'll
> talk.

The remaining members of the Midnight Freaks enter into Sherry's apartment.

Sherry closes the door and locks it.

INT. SHERRY'S APARTMENT - LIVING ROOM - NIGHT

Sherry's apartment is a modern day apartment, with a wooden floor, wooden walls, large wooden blinds on the windows, a mini bar with a kitchen sink, an electric stove, an old refrigerator, a plush brown leather couch, a television with a wooden cabinet stuffed with DVDs and CDs, ceiling lights with a fan, red lava lamp on the kitchen counter, a tall lamp next to the couch, complete with a microphone stand with a mic, electric bass guitar and an amp next to the TV cabinet. The room is dimly lit with black lights.

The ceiling fan turns clockwise to keep the cool air flowing in the living room.

Sherry sits down on the couch, while Roxy and Ricky sit down the floor Indian style and Nicholas stands on Sherry's right side.

Sherry smokes her cigarette.

> SHERRY
> Mind telling me what's going
> on?

Nicholas turns to her.

> NICHOLAS
> Names's Nicholas Copeland.

Sherry sees Nicholas in person -- and her poster of Nick Napalm of Black Voodoo on the wall.

Sherry looks from Nicholas to The Black Voodoo poster on her wall then back to Nicholas.

Sherry gets up from her couch.

                    SHERRY
                (surprised)
            Nick Napalm? Oh my god!
            It's really you! I thought you
            and your band were killed
            in Labou, Louisiana, twenty
            years ago.
                    NICHOLAS
            We were.
                    SHERRY
            But how can you... you...
            you're standing right here in
            front of me for Christ sakes!
                    ROXY
                (to Nicholas)
            Maybe we should show her?
                    SHERRY
            Show me what?
                    NICHOLAS
                (to Sherry)
            Listen, you can't tell anyone
            about what you are going to
            see.

Ricky stands up quickly.

> RICKY
> (to Nicholas)
> Dude! You show her, she go-
> ing to freak out on us and get
> us killed.

> SHERRY
> What the hell are you talking
> about?

Nicholas stands up and vamps out in front of Sherry.

Sherry is horrified and screams.

Ricky runs towards her, tackling her to the ground and covers her mouth, while he is vamped out.

Sherry continues to scream.

> RICKY
> (to Sherry)
> Calm down! Calm down! We
> came here to help you, not
> hurt you!

Ricky nervously tries to cover Sherry's mouth as she keeps on resisting and screaming.

Roxy walks to Sherry, already vamped out. She grabs Sherry by the shirt with her right hand. She puts her finger to her own lips, shushing her.

Sherry stops screaming but she is paralyzed with fear. Her eyes roll and she passes out.

FADE OUT.

FADE IN:

INT. SHERRY'S APARTMENT - BEDROOM - NIGHT

Sherry wakes up lying down on her bedroom. Her room contains, a brass framed bed, a nightstand, a wooden dresser drawer, and on top of it a picture frame of her and Lisa in their rocker outfits.

Roxy enters the room in her human form with a cup of coffee. Roxy gives Sherry the cup.

Sherry drinks the coffee.

> SHERRY
>
> I had the strangest night-
> mare, Roxy. You and Ricky
> and Nick Napalm were vam-
> pires trying to kill me.

Sherry puts the coffee on her nightstand.
Sherry's eyes are wide awake.
Nicholas and Ricky enter the room, in their human form.

> NICHOLAS
>
> It wasn't a dream, honey. We
> are vampires.

Sherry screams hysterically.
Roxy bitch slaps Sherry across the face.

> ROXY
>
> Oh, shut up!

Sherry calms down but is still frightened, with her left hand rubbing her stinging left cheek.

> SHERRY
>
> Are you going to kill me?

ROXY

If we were going to kill
you, we would have done it
already.

NICHOLAS

We don't kill innocent
people. We only kill people
who try to take advantage
of us or physically hurt us,
or to protect ourselves in
self-defense.

RICKY

What he means is we only
kill and feed off evil people...
a better word would be "ass-
holes and scumbags"

SHERRY

This can't be real.

ROXY

Yes, it is. We are what we are,
but we are still very human,
Sherry. Much like you.

Sherry lays on her bed.

SHERRY

W-w-what do you want?

Nicholas crosses his arms together, feeling slightly annoyed but remaining
calm.

NICHOLAS

We want to help you, as your friends. If you would just calm yourself down for a minute, we can tell you what the hell is going on.

Sherry calms down on her bed slightly tilting her head. Roxy stands up.

ROXY

A year ago, we got ourselves in a tough fix. Nicholas is the one who saved us from getting killed. Unfortunately, there were some casualties involved. Switch is dead.

RICKY

We got turned this way by accident. We've been trying to live with this condition for about a year. It happened right before we graduated from college. Nicholas here has been showing us the ropes. He's been like this much longer than us. We've been playing shows like this as our cover for a while now.

SHERRY

What happened to Lisa? Why isn't she with you guys?

RICKY

Lisa was with us two days ago. We were driving to see you after we gave you the call. That is, until some dick-less sheriff stopped us on the highway and busted us for nothing.

ROXY

He killed Lisa. Now you know.

Sherry is surprised about the bad news of her former friends.

SHERRY

Guys, I don't really know what to say. I mean, this is just... I think I need a drink.

Sherry gets out of her bedroom and into the kitchen, where she takes a bottle of vodka from her kitchen shelf and pours herself a drink in a shot glass.

INT. SHERRY'S APARTMENT - KITCHEN - CONTINUOUS

The Midnight Freaks follow her into the kitchen.

Nicholas asks Sherry her situation.

NICHOLAS

So who is the guy that attacked you?

Sherry drinks down her shot and exhales.

SHERRY

(sighs)

I can't tell you.

RICKY

Why not? We're here now.

Sherry smokes another cigarette nervously.

Nicholas figures out who did this to Sherry, by looking at her body movements and face -- his reaction shows on his upset face.

NICHOLAS

It was the sheriff, wasn't it? What have you told the police?

SHERRY

I lied to them. I told them it was a migrant worker who did it. Barton told me if I told them the truth, he'd kill me and shut down my bar. The cops have a lot of head way with the biker gangs here in town.

RICKY

Man. That's messed up.

SHERRY

Tell me about it. A bunch of us business owners have been forced to pay protection money on a weekly basis.

ROXY

How have you been holding up?

SHERRY

I'm barely surviving right now. This whole town has gone to hell in a hand basket.

RICKY

What about the gangs?

SHERRY

The Cortez Cobras. They're real bad ass guys.

NICHOLAS

How bad?

SHERRY

Bad... they've beaten some of my girls up on account of they wouldn't put out for them. But, I can't close this place down. This is the only work they can get here in this little town.

NICHOLAS

Damn.

SHERRY

Most of the people here are going broke, or they are going into foreclosures. They're just walking away from their homes and businesses. If this keeps going on, we won't have a town left.

ROXY

Why did Barton rape you?

SHERRY

Lucas and I were protecting my girls from getting hurt.

The Cobras nearly killed Lucas, but Barton was the ringleader of them all. Most of the police are connected with them.

NICHOLAS

What other things are these guys doing?

SHERRY

They're drug trafficking and smuggling crystal meth I think.

RICKY

Aren't there any honest cops around here in this town?

SHERRY

(sighs)

Only a few, many have left though. But there is one in particular -- Dixon. Eric Dixon. My ex-boyfriend, nice guy, he's a family man now.

The group recognizes the name Dixon.

RICKY

Dixon... that was the guy that was called in by the sheriff. He didn't hurt us. Seemed like he was a good guy, just doing his job.

SHERRY
He probably didn't know what
really happened. Eric is a
good man and a good cop. He
believes in strongly upholding
the law as a police officer.

Nicholas is concerned.

NICHOLAS
I don't think he would believe
us if we told him. By now, I'm
sure the word is already out
on us.

INT. EL CORTEZ POLICE STATION - NIGHT
The police station is a modern day police station, with computers, desk
clerks in cop uniform, police dispatch station with radio operators. Officers are
walking down the hallway, and the jail is empty.
Sheriff Mitch Barton is in the squad room, talking to the thirty officers,
including Eric Dixon.

MITCH
Everybody, listen up! We
have ourselves a major problem here. Three punk kids
are on the loose in a dark van.
They tried to kill me when I
pulled them over.
OFFICER
When?

MITCH

Earlier tonight. They'll probably try to kill again. They
are armed, and they are very
dangerous. I want you all to
comb the town because it's
very likely that they will be
heading down this way.

FELLOW OFFICER

What do they look like?

MITCH

Head banger, rock and roll
type kids. Ages early to late
20s, dressed in black.

The fellow cops are listening.
Dixon stands up.

DIXON

Are they the same kids that I
helped you arrest?

MITCH

Yes, Dixon. They somehow
managed to break out of the
handcuffs. I killed one of
them in self-defense.

DIXON

You could have used pepper
spray.

MITCH

I had no choice. They would
have killed me.

Dixon has a suspicious look on his face.

> DIXON
> Why didn't you radio me back
> for help when this happened?
> MITCH
> Look, I don't have time for
> this! All of you get your butts
> in gear and start searching.
> I want those suspects found
> before sun up! You got that?

All of the officers answer in unison.

> ALL THE OFFICERS
> Yes sir!
> MITCH
> Wait up... I want seven of-
> ficers to remain here with
> me and keep watch over the
> station, while the rest of you
> guys go out searching.

Most of the officers quickly head out of the station. Dixon stays with Mitch.
Mitch ponders.

> MITCH (V.O.)
> What <u>were</u> those things?
> Fucking monsters.

INT. PISTOL WHIP BAR AND LOUNGE - NIGHT

Three VAMPIRE HUNTERS, all male, ages between late 30s to early 40s, wearing long black trench coats and cop style shades, enter the bar
simultaneously.

The Middle Hunter, short greased jet black hair, is the leader of the group. The Middle Hunter pulls out his .44 Magnum and fires three shots in the air.

MIDDLE HUNTER

Everyone, get out of here!

Now!

The crowd is screaming as they run out through the large side door.

The club empties out.

Lucas pulls out his double barrel shotgun.

The hunters pull out their single barreled sawed off shotguns and simultaneously blow him away -- causing Lucas to misfire in the air before falling down dead.

In SLOW MOTION, Lucas is shot to piece with chunks of blood and flesh flying over his chest. He falls down dead behind the bar.

INT. SHERRY'S APARTMENT - LIVING ROOM - NIGHT

The "Midnight Freaks" and Sherry hear the gunshots downstairs. They hear the lower door broken down by gunshots. Heavy footsteps bang up the stairs.

Nicholas senses danger.

NICHOLAS

Shit.

Nicholas grabs Sherry, and leaps through the window! Ricky and Roxy follow. The group lands in a shower of glass on the sidewalk below, unharmed.

EXT. PISTOL WHIP BAR AND LOUNGE - NIGHT

The Vampire Hunters run out of the bar and fire rounds at the Midnight Freaks.

The Midnight Freaks dodge the shots and flee the scene.

Two police squad cars carrying four officers surround the Vampire Hunters as they shield themselves from the gunfire behind their car doors armed with pistols and shotguns.

OFFICER
(pointing a shotgun)
Drop your weapons, now!

The Vampire Hunters ignore the cops. One of the vampire hunters throws a grenade like a baseball at one of the cop cars.

The Vampire Hunters load their guns.

The Middle Hunter pulls the pin of another grenade with his teeth, and under hands the grenade like a bowling ball. It rolls right under one of the police squad cars.

The police officer is just shocked.

OFFICER
Oh... fuck!

BOOM! The police car explodes killing all the cops.

One police car flips over. When it lands, it then blows up.

The other police squad car is destroyed and left a burning wreck with pitch black smoke burning up into the night sky.

EXT. EL CORTEZ - MOMENTS LATER

The Midnight Freaks and Sherry run and hide behind a Barbecue House, as they take a minute to catch their breath.

RICKY
Who the hell were those guys?
NICHOLAS
They have to be vampire
hunters. They must have been
following us.

Roxy surveys the scene.

It is hell on earth in El Cortez.

Police and Vampire Hunters are at war, while the rest of the townspeople attempt to escape. A riot breaks out in the town. The townspeople pull out their weapons to defend themselves and kill each other.

INT. EL CORTEZ POLICE STATION - NIGHT

One radio dispatcher listens to the radio. They hear mass chaos, screaming, people killing each other, with gunfire going off in the distance.

A radio dispatcher is trying to communicate.

> OFFICER (V.O.)
> Send backup! We got our-
> selves a riot here!

Suddenly, the radio lines are cut. The radio buzzes in and out.

> RADIO DISPATCHER
> Officer, come in. What's your
> status? Over.

Then, the radio completely goes out.

Mitch gets out of his chair from his desk. He is already on his phone.

> MITCH
> (into phone)
> Hello! Hello! Hello!
> (to Dixon)
> Dixon I got nothing, the
> phones are dead.
> DIXON
> I'll try my cell phone.

Dixon pulls out his cell phone and calls.

> MITCH
> Contact the national guard!
> We need riot control assis-
> tance, now!

Dixon attempts to call his cell phone but all signals are down.

SFX: Phone lines are busy.

EXT. EL CORTEZ - NIGHT

A local townsman cuts a power line with bolt cutters. The act electrocutes him, and sparks explode from the wires. We see him fall down and hit the ground dead. THUD!

INT. EL CORTEZ POLICE STATION - NIGHT

Dixon can't get anything on his cell phone.

> DIXON
> No signal.

Mitch checks his cell phone.

> MITCH
> Mine too. It's those damn
> kids. They did this, it has to
> be!

> DIXON
> Should we go out there and
> look for them sir? It's our
> duty to uphold the law.

Mitch pulls out his Magnum and points it at Dixon's face.

> MITCH
> This is the law. Every man
> for himself.

Mitch cocks his gun.

Dixon backs off... he doesn't want to argue.

> DIXON
>
> Okay! Okay!

Sheriff Mitch lowers his gun.

> MITCH
>
> We go under lock down, now!
>
> Prepare for anything.

Every window and door is barred shut and locked. The deputies arm themselves with shotguns and assault rifles.

EXT. BARBECUE HOUSE - NIGHT

The band is still catching their breath behind the Barbecue House, while Roxy return to the group.

> ROXY
>
> The whole town's gone crazy.
>
> We gotta get back to the van
>
> and get out of here.
>
> NICHOLAS
>
> Not until we finish what we
>
> came here to do.
>
> SHERRY
>
> What are you guys going to
>
> do?
>
> RICKY
>
> What do you think? We're
>
> going to kill that pig sheriff!

Sherry doesn't want to be a part of the chaos as she steps back.

SHERRY
You guys are crazy!

Roxy is angry, yet defends their actions, as she walks towards Sherry.

ROXY
That dickhead raped you and
killed Lisa. Do you want him
to get away with that?

Sherry thinks for a brief second. She shakes her head slightly.

ROXY
That's what we thought!
NICHOLAS
If we're going to do this, we
need to do it right. We need
weapons, now.

Nicholas sniffs with his keen sense of smell, just like a bloodhound in the air.

NICHOLAS
I smell something.
ROXY
Don't tell me the barbecue.
(sticks out her thumb)
Hello!
NICHOLAS
It's gunpowder.

Ricky uses his sharp vampire psychic vision...
RICKY'S POV

Through a purple-blue psychic haze, he sees a crystal clear vision -- a ransacked gun shop.

BACK TO SCENE

> RICKY
> There's a gun shop, two doors
> down.

The Midnight Freaks and Sherry run over and break into the gun shop.

INT. GUN SHOP - NIGHT

The store is a wooden ramshackle building, the windows and front door broken in. There are half empty rounds of ammunition scattered all over the floor. All the shotguns and rifles are gone, leaving only a few six-shooters and pistols. There are dead bodies lying on the floor.

The GUN SHOP OWNER, 70s, bearded, a typical hillbilly, armed with a long double barrel shotgun, crouches down behind his cash register stand, paranoid.

The Gun Shop Owner's eyes are wide open, with sweat running down on his face.

The Midnight Freaks and Sherry enter the store looking for guns. They walk over dead bodies.

Sherry follows the group but is frightened of what she has seen, so she hides behind a large wooden barrel.

The Gun Shop Owner pops up from behind the counter and tries to shoot them, but misses.

The Midnight Freaks scatter in three different directions.

Nicholas jumps out, fully vamped out, with long claws growing out, fangs showing, eyes glowing red -- and flies out at the Gun Shop Owner.

His left hand grabs the Gun Shop Owner by the throat -- his right hand grab the shotgun super fast, and pulls it away as it fires.

The Gun Shop Owner drops his gun and screams in terror, while Nicholas' right hand claws into his chest. Then, he takes his left hand and rips open his chest like a bag of potato chips. He feeds on the dead Gun Shop Owner's neck. Ricky and Roxy join Nicholas to feed on the fresh corpse.

Sherry is mortified by what she is seeing. She finds a pistol and box of bullets behind her in a smashed open gun display cabinet and runs off.

After they stop feeding, the Midnight Freaks sense Sherry is gone.

> RICKY
> Where's Sherry?
> NICHOLAS
> We must have scared her.

Roxy is concerned.

> ROXY
> Shit. She's going to get her-
> self killed out there. We have
> to find her, right now!

Then, a Vampire Hunter comes in the room blasting his sawed off shotgun and fires at the band.

The band jumps over behind the counter and hides.

Pistols lie on the floor with bullets scattered all over.

The Vampire Hunter ceases fire, thinking that they are dead. He walks a little bit closer to the counter.

The Midnight Freaks pop up from behind the counter -- all three simultaneously fire pistols, blowing away the Vampire Hunter to pieces.

The Vampire Hunter falls down, dead.

> NICHOLAS
> One down. Two to go.

The Midnight Freaks exit through the front door with their weapons to find Sherry, kill the hunters and go after the corrupt Sheriff.

EXT. EL CORTEZ - LATER

The entire town is a war zone.

The band returns to the back of the Barbecue House alleyway and finds Sherry hiding, as she has no place else to hide.

> ROXY
> Sherry, don't do that again, okay? You could have got yourself shot.
>
> NICHOLAS
> We better move fast, with that riot going on out there. Pss! Looks like all hell's broken loose.

Sherry is nervous about the thought of killing a cop.

> SHERRY
> Forget this, you guys... I can't do this, I am outta here.

Sherry takes off not wanting to be part of killing the sheriff.

> ROXY
> Damn it, she took off again.

Roxy is about to run off to find Sherry, but Nicholas grabs her shoulder as he speaks.

> NICHOLAS
> We need to stay together. No one runs off or splits up. Now come on!

The Midnight Freaks takes off down the alley to find Sherry again before she foolishly gets herself killed.

EXT. EL CORTEZ - NIGHT

The townspeople are running around town in panic. Some of the citizens are blowing up buildings with Molotov cocktails and looting stores, wild.

The Midnight Freaks exit from the alleyway, and try to get through the wild crowd.

INT. GENERAL STORE - NIGHT

There is mass looting in the general store, as the townspeople are ransacking for food and water. Inside the store is Sherry, hiding behind one of the aisles stocked with fruits and vegetables.

She is texting Eric Dixon with her cell phone for help. A CRAZY WOMAN tries to rob her -- Sherry runs to the back of the store. The crazy woman goes after her.

> CRAZY WOMAN
>
> Give me your wallet! Give it
> to me!

The crazy woman attacks Sherry, trying to strangle her, but Sherry kicks her in the stomach. Then whips out her gun and shoots the woman in the head, killing her.

INT. EL CORTEZ POLICE STATION - NIGHT

Eric Dixon, armed with an M16 assault rifle, receives a text message from Sherry. He reads it:

"It's Sherry. Help me. I'm trapped in the General Store!"

Eric Dixon goes to the back door next to his fellow deputies.

> DIXON
>
> Open the door.
>
> MITCH
>
> Dixon! Get back here! Stay at
> your post!

                    DIXON
          I can't -- my friend is out
          there and so is my family.
                    MITCH
          I need you! Get your ass back
          here!
                    DIXON
             (to Mitch)
          Fuck you!
             (to the officers)
          Open the door!
                    OFFICER
          Officer Dixon...

Dixon pulls out his assault rifle in front of the officer.

                    DIXON
          Do it!

Dixon points his assault rifle to the deputies. They obey Dixon's command, unlocking and opening the door. Dixon leaves the station.

EXT. EL CORTEZ - NIGHT

The Midnight Freaks are able to get through the crowd, but the two remaining Vampire Hunters are on their tail. They shoot up in the sky with their pistols to clear away the crowd. The townspeople scatter out of the town.

The empty town is scattered with dead bodies on the ground and destroyed burning cars, trucks and a few chopper motorcycles.

Now it is a stand off between the Midnight Freaks, the remaining police, and the two remaining Vampire Hunters, in a guerrilla warfare type style of fighting.

The Midnight Freaks, the Vampire Hunters and the police face off.

There are only eight cops left alive, the rest having been killed during the riot. The police attack the Vampire Hunters, while trying to shoot at the

Midnight Freaks who try to run to their van while the police officers hide themselves behind the corners of their cars for protection from the Vampire Hunters.

The Vampire Hunters waste two of the cops out in the open like they were nothing.

Officer #1 barricades himself in his car, under fire.

OFFICER #1
(to his radio)
Backup! We need backup now! Officers down! I repeat officers down!

Suddenly. BANG!

Officer #1's head explodes. At the same time remaining officers are looking in confusion.

The two remaining Vampire Hunters in the ground flee the scene.

OFFICER #2
What the hell!

BANG! Officer #2 loses his hands! He screams in agony as blood squirts out of the ragged stumps. He falls to the ground writhing in agony.

OFFICER #3
Up on the rooftops!

The remaining police officers look up at the sky.

Out of nowhere -- six female Vampire Hunter snipers appear on rooftops all over the town and fire in all directions.

The Midnight Freaks are able to barely get into the Metal Machine van and drive away from the war zone -- but a blonde female Vampire Hunter sniper manages to fire two shots at them. She misses, hitting the band's license plate number and description of the band's vehicle.

INT. CHEVY VAN - MOVING - NIGHT

Ricky, Roxy and Nicholas are safe but freaked out. Nicholas is now in the driver's seat, with Roxy in the front passenger seat and Ricky in the back seat.

>   RICKY
>   (panicking)
>   What the hell is going on?
>   Where did these guys come
>   from? What do they want?
>   ROXY
>   Ricky... will you please shut
>   the hell up!
>   RICKY
>   Well excuse me, Miss Bitch-
>   a-lot!
>   ROXY
>   What did you just say?

Nicholas jumps in the conversation.

>   NICHOLAS
>   Both of you... shut up and let
>   me think here.

Roxy grabs a cigarette from underneath the radio deck. She lights it with the car cigarette lighter.

Nicholas drives while explaining to the others.

>   NICHOLAS
>   There is something I for-
>   got to mention to you both.
>   While I was an indentured

slave with my old master's vampire crew, we had hunters stalk us for six months before I met you guys.

ROXY

What?!

RICKY

(panicking)

I told you we should have buried those other dead vamps we killed!

ROXY

Well, we can't do anything about it now!

NICHOLAS

It's kind of weird that there are so many of those hunters com- ing after us. It's almost like they are looking for others. Something doesn't feel right.

ROXY

Are there other vampires out there?

NICHOLAS

I'm not sure, but yeah, there could be.

RICKY

That might be the reason why they are here. Maybe, they're looking for others. It looks like we just showed up at the in the right place at the wrong time.

Ricky takes a cigarette and smokes to calm himself down.

INT. DIXON'S CAR - MOVING - LATER

Eric Dixon scans the empty town, looking for his family and Sherry.

Dixon finds nothing. Then, he sees a shadow running in front of him, passing by.

Dixon stops his car.

Dixon gets out with his assault rifle with a flashlight.

EXT. EL CORTEZ - CONTINUOUS

It is pitch black in the alleyway. Eric uses his flashlight to see. He's battle prepared, holding his rifle.

Dixon follows the shadow figure. It comes from behind a large garbage bin.

Dixon raises his assault rifle.

> DIXON
>
> I know you're out there! Drop
> your weapon!

The shadow figure's hands pop up with a gun.

> DIXON
>
> Put your hands up!

The shadow figure's hands drop the weapon.

> DIXON
>
> Now come on out slowly and
> show yourself! Nice and easy!

The shadow figure slowly rises up -- it's Sherry.

Eric Dixon lowers his gun.

                    DIXON
          Sherry? Thank God that
          you're alright.
                    SHERRY
          Eric.

Sherry hugs Eric Dixon tightly. She is relieved to see him.

                    DIXON
          Where's my wife and son?
                    SHERRY
          They're dead.
                    DIXON
              (shocked)
          How?
                    SHERRY
          I saw their bodies lying out in
          the streets.

Dixon is in disbelief.

                    DIXON
          Oh God. This is not happen-
          ing to me!

Eric Dixon shakes off his mourning and realizes that he and Sherry need to
escape from the danger in the town.

                    DIXON
          Barton told me that some
          punk kids tried to kill him --
          did they do this?

When Sherry hears the word about Barton, she cringes.

> SHERRY
> No, it wasn't them.
> DIXON
> Who did this?
> SHERRY
> A group of guys in trench coats walked into my bar and shot up the place while I was talking to my friends upstairs. My friends saved my life.
> DIXON
> Come on. Let's take you back to the station where it's safe.

Dixon grabs Sherry hand, but she resists.

> SHERRY
> I can't go there.
> DIXON
> Why not?
> SHERRY
> It's complicated.
> DIXON
> Are you in trouble with the law or something?
> SHERRY
> No.
> DIXON
> Sherry, we've been friends for a long time. Tell me

what happened. You can
trust me!

SHERRY

I can't go to the station with
you. Barton will kill me.

Dixon is confused.

DIXON

What the hell are you talking
about?

Sherry lets out the truth in frustration.

SHERRY

Barton was the one who really raped me, okay! He'd said
if I talked, he'd kill me.

Eric Dixon thinks about what it means to be a police officer. He realizes that
the system is corrupt.

Dixon is disgusted.

DIXON

Son... of... a... bitch. I knew
it. Is there anyone I can take
you to?

SHERRY

Help me find my friends. We
got separated in the riot.

DIXON

Where can we find them?

SHERRY

I don't know. Can you help
me look for them? I think
they're still in town.

DIXON

Get in the car.

Eric Dixon and Sherry enter Dixon's police squad car.

EXT. CHEVY VAN - MOVING - NIGHT

It is 11:00PM in the now deserted town of El Cortez. The Metal Machine
van drives behind the building of an empty Cigar Lounge. Nicholas parks the
van. Roxy, Ricky and Nicholas exit the van and enter the Cigar Lounge.

INT. CIGAR LOUNGE - NIGHT

It is a clean wooden building filled with tobacco, cigars, cigarettes, wood-
en pipes on wooden shelves, and a couple of leather chairs around some small
spare lounge tables. There is a large leather couch in the room and glass shelves
stocked with hard liquor bottles behind a bar.

Nicholas and Roxy find a light hardware toolbox on the cashier's corner.
The two open the toolbox, and find a few hammers, a box of nails, a box of
screws, a couple of screwdrivers, a couple of wrenches and a battery powered
drill with accessories.

He group barricades the front door and windows with wooden shelves and
some wooden 2x4s.

Nicholas and Roxy get working.

Ricky sits on the couch relaxing, being lazy.

RICKY

Why are we here?
Roxy turns her head to face
Ricky, while she and Nicholas
is work.

ROXY

Cops and Vampire Hunters
out there! Hello! How about
pulling your weight for once?

Ricky points a finger.

RICKY

Hey, I pull my weight!

Nicholas is all by himself boarding up the Cigar Lounge window. He turns
around and looks at Ricky.

NICHOLAS

Then, get your stoner, bong-
loving ass over here and help us.

Nicholas continues boarding up the window.

RICKY

(sarcastically)
Okay.

Ricky gets up from the couch and grabs a spare hammer with some nails
from the toolbox and begins to help the others board up the window.

RICKY

Man, this sucks!

Roxy turns to Ricky.

ROXY

Ricky.

Roxy kisses Ricky by surprise.

Ricky decides to go with the flow and continues kissing Roxy.

Nicholas turns his head and sees Roxy and Ricky making out.

Nicholas is surprised and pissed off.

                    NICHOLAS
              (angry and annoyed)
              You guys!

Roxy and Ricky are startled.

Roxy leans against Ricky's right shoulder.

                    ROXY
              Hey, I just wanted to give him
              the proper motivation.

Roxy winks.

All three of the Midnight Freaks chuckle a little bit.

Roxy and Ricky get to work and help Nicholas finish boarding up the windows.

                    RICKY
              I could kill right now for an
              ice cold cherry slurpee, you
              guys.
                    NICHOLAS
              (to Ricky)
              Forget it bro -- the only red-
              colored thing you'll be suck-
              ing on is blood, my friend.
              Vamps to the end.

The Midnight Freaks laugh a little.

MIDNIGHT FREAKS
(in unison)
Vamps to the end.

They are interrupted by the band's cell phone beeping. Roxy picks it up and checks it. It's a text message:
"Where r u? -Sherry."

ROXY
You guys, it's Sherry!

Ricky and Nicholas are happy that she is alright. Roxy texts her back:
"We are at a boarded up Cigar Lounge. Come in the back. - Roxy."
INT. DIXON'S CAR - MOVING - NIGHT
Sherry looks up from her cell phone.

SHERRY
I found them. They're at the
Cigar Lounge.

Dixon drives his car to the Cigar Lounge.
INT. EL CORTEZ POLICE STATION - NIGHT
It is 11:30PM. Sheriff Mitch Barton is waiting for the inevitable to happen as he operates a CB radio. He is trying to send a signal for help in nearby cities around fifty miles away.

Then, SAM, 23, a rookie deputy, informs Mitch about the riot incident.

SAM
Sheriff, there is one of our
boys outside.

Mitch joins Sam at the window. Mitch looks through the blinds and sees a bloody, wounded, injured police officer.

MITCH

Let him in.

Sam walks down the hall to open the main front door and carry the wounded officer into the station, while another officer locks the door.

SAM

Bill, hang on buddy.

Sam grabs a first aid kit and pulls out rubbing alcohol and bandage wraps.

SAM

(to Bill)

Take your shirt off so we can
dress this wound.

Bill takes his shirt off and the deputies begin to clean the gunshot wound on the shoulder.

Mitch arrives on the scene to talk to Bill.

MITCH

Bill, what the hell happened
to you out there?

Bill can barely speak because he has lost a lot of blood. He's breathing heavy while in a lot of pain.

BILL

We are out there... trying to
break up the riot... when these
people in trench coats... pulled
out shotguns at us... snipers
also... they were everywhere...

they killed everyone else... it
was a war zone... they must've
been... they must...

Bill is unable to finish because of his wound as his eyes roll up. Mitch grabs his arms and shakes him out of frustration.

MITCH
Damn it! Tell me! Who did
this!

Bill is in pain as he coughs out blood on Mitch's shirt.

SAM
Sir, you're hurting him.

Mitch pulls out his Magnum and points it to Sam.

MITCH
Back off, boy. Or I'll blow
your head off.

Sam takes a few steps back, knows he doesn't want to get shot.
Bill starts to pass out as his eyes roll down.
Mitch and Sam argue over Bill's fate.

SAM
Sir, he needs medical attention.

MITCH
He's near dead anyway. Put
the poor bastard out of his
misery. Shoot 'em.

Sam is shocked.

>   SAM
>   Sir, we can't do that.
>   MITCH
>   The hell you say.
>   (points his gun at Sam)
>   Shoot him, or I'll shoot you.

Deputy TOM, late-twenties, glasses, curly hair, skinny, comes in and watches Mitch pull his gun on Sam to kill Deputy Bill.

Tom pulls out his gun and points it to Mitch.

>   TOM
>   What is going on, sir?

Tom points out his gun at Mitch on the right side.

>   MITCH
>   Just doing what I have to do.
>   TOM
>   (aiming his gun at Mitch)
>   You going to shoot your own
>   men?

Mitch starts to intimidate Tom.

>   MITCH
>   You going to shoot your own
>   superior officer? Or how
>   would you like to hear on
>   the news that a fellow dep-
>   uty officer killed me in cold

blood? No one would believe your side of the story. Think about it what it would do your career.

Bill is barely moving and breathing heavily.

                    TOM
              (looks at Bill)
              I'm sorry, Bill.

Tom cowardly points the gun directly at Bill's head -- BANG! --shoots him and kills him.
Mitch smirks.

                    MITCH
              Now mop this mess up and
              bury his body outside of
              town.

INT. EL CORTEZ - NIGHT
The Vampire Hunters walk down the empty street of El Cortez.
The Vampire Hunters search every block and building to find the Midnight Freaks. They are armed with sniper rifles and shotguns.
EXT. CIGAR LOUNGE - NIGHT
Sherry and Dixon arrive at the back door of the building.
Dixon holds his assault rifle, and surveys the scene to make sure they have not been followed.
Dixon sees nothing but an empty town.
Sherry knocks on the door.

                    NICHOLAS (O.S.)
              Who is it?

                    SHERRY
          It's Sherry, open the door.
                NICHOLAS (O.S.)
          Were you followed?
                    SHERRY
          No, just my friend came with
          me.

Nicholas opens the door.

                    NICHOLAS
          Get in here.

Sherry and Dixon quickly enter the back entrance of the Cigar Lounge and Nicholas quickly closes and locks the back door.

INT. CIGAR LOUNGE - NIGHT

Nicholas leads Sherry and Dixon into the lounge. Roxy hugs Sherry like a sister.

                     ROXY
          Thank   god,   you're   okay.
          Don't you ever run off like
          that again.

Dixon jumps in the conversation.

                    DIXON
          Can someone please tell me
          what the hell is going on
          here?

Ricky looks at Eric Dixon's face -- astonished to see the same cop who cuffed him.

RICKY

Holy shit, it's him!

Ricky pulls out his pistol.
Roxy pulls out her pistol in front of Dixon.
Dixon raises his rifle in front of Roxy and Ricky.
It's a Mexican standoff.

DIXON

Put the guns down now!

From behind a six shooter is pressed into the back of Dixon's head.

NICHOLAS
(to Dixon)
I don't think so. Stop right
there, or I'll pull this trigger.

Nicholas cocks his gun behind Dixon's head. Dixon freezes.

NICHOLAS

Ricky, take his rifle.

Ricky takes the assault rifle from Dixon. Then, Sherry jumps in between the standoff.

SHERRY

Wait! Wait! Don't shoot him!
He's a friend of mine!

Sherry shields Dixon.
Ricky and Roxy point their guns at Dixon.

RICKY

This jackass was the one who
helped bust us, and we didn't
even do anything wrong!

ROXY

I don't trust him!

Nicholas tries to command his troops. He senses with a gut hunch that
Dixon is okay.

NICHOLAS

Lower your guns! I'm not going to kill a good cop!

RICKY

But he works with Barton!
He's just as no good as him!

Dixon pleads his case.

DIXON

No, I'm not! I didn't know
what he did. Sherry told me
what happened to her.

RICKY

Did she also tell you that
Barton killed our friend Lisa,
after you left the scene?

Dixon is even more confused.

DIXON

Did he?

Roxy and Ricky are still pointing their guns.

> RICKY
>
> We were there, we saw it
> happen!

Nicholas is still pointing the gun at Dixon.

> NICHOLAS
>
> Whatever the sheriff told you
> about us is a lie.
>
> DIXON
>
> Who are you guys, really?

> NICHOLAS
>
> Just a band.
>
> ROXY
>
> We came here to play a few
> gigs at Sherry's place. That's
> when all the trouble started.
>
> DIXON
>
> I want to believe you, but
> who started the riot?

Sherry turns around, faces Dixon and to tries to reason with him.

> SHERRY
>
> Eric, I trust them. They are
> not going to hurt you or me.
>
> NICHOLAS
>
> (to Dixon)

Listen, I'm going to lower my
gun to prove to you that we're
not going to kill you.

Nicholas lowers his gun. Then, Roxy and Ricky lower their guns. Dixon
sighs with relief. Sherry gives her friends a look of gratitude. Ricky tosses Dixon
his rifle, Dixon catches it.

DIXON

I can take you to the station.
I'm going to bust that lying
son of bitch!

Dixon tries to walk out of the lounge.

RICKY

Hey man. I don't think we
should go out there.

Dixon turns around and faces the group.

DIXON

Why not?

NICHOLAS

There is a group of people in
trench coats out there that
want to kill us. They are the
ones who started the riot.

DIXON

Well who are they? Ex-friends
of yours?

ROXY

Pssh... hardly.

NICHOLAS

Let's just say they're trigger
happy psychos.

DIXON

How many did you see out
there?

NICHOLAS

We only saw two. But there
are probably more.

RICKY

I say we go out there and finish them off.

NICHOLAS

Don't be stupid. We don't
know how many are out
there, and we don't know
what else they're armed with.

Roxy goes up to the main boarded-up windows to look the cracked peep
holes.

Roxy sees through the cracks of the boarded windows and sees eight hunters
walking around town armed with rifles and shotguns.

ROXY

Guys, this is not good.

DIXON

What's wrong?

ROXY

They're out there, in front of
the building.

NICHOLAS

How many?

ROXY

Eight and armed. Looks like
they can't see us in here.

The Midnight Freaks, Sherry and Dixon try to come up with a plan of
attack.

DIXON

The only way we can take
them all out at once is to get
on the rooftop and shoot
them from up there. We'll
have a better chance if we
take them by surprise.

RICKY

How can we take them out,
with only a few pistols and
one assault rifle?

SHERRY

One thing about, El Cortez --
almost everyone in this town
owns a gun.

DIXON

She's right, let's search this
place. Look everywhere.

The Midnight Freaks, Sherry and Dixon search the Cigar Lounge to find
any guns, rifling every counter and drawer.

They fail to find any weapons.

They bust into the back office and turn the place upside down.

Ricky finds a large locker full of coats.

RICKY
Nothing. Damn it!

Ricky kicks the locker -- accidentally revealing a large trunk.
Ricky looks down and pulls up the trunk. It's a large steel trunk locked with a combination lock.

RICKY
(to everyone)
Hey guys! I found something!

Everybody gathers around to look at the trunk that Ricky found.

NICHOLAS
I got the combination...

Nicholas smashes off the lock with the bottom of the gun, which unlocks it.

DIXON
What are you?
NICHOLAS
I work out a lot.

Nicholas opens the trunk, revealing bad ass weapons -- a hunting rifle with a scope, an AK-47 machine gun rifle, two MAC-10 Uzi machine guns, three standard military grenades, a Desert Eagle pistol and plenty of ammunition.

ROXY
Now, it's time for us to do the
hunting.

The Midnight Freaks arm themselves. Nicholas grabs the AK 47. Roxy grabs the MAC 10 Uzis. Ricky grabs the hunting rifle. Sherry grabs the military grenades and the Desert Eagle Pistol.

Nicholas and Roxy load their guns with clips, while Ricky and Sherry load their guns with bullets one by one.

The Midnight Freaks, Sherry and Dixon are ready to fight and take the bad guys down.

DIXON

I guess whoever owned this
place, also was dealing illegal
weapons on the side.

ROXY

Shoot to thrill.

EXT. CIGAR LOUNGE - ALLEYWAY - NIGHT

It's 12:00AM Midnight. The Midnight Freaks, Sherry and Dixon exit the Cigar Lounge from the back, find a ladder that leads to the roof top and quietly go up the ladder.

EXT. CIGAR LOUNGE - ROOF - NIGHT

The Midnight Freaks, Sherry and Dixon emerge on the roof. The block is surrounded by Vampire Hunters spreading out.

The group hides behind the sign of the rooftop to survey the scene. There are eight Vampire Hunters looking for the vampires and other survivors of the town.

The Midnight Freaks, Sherry and Dixon hide below the rooftop's parapet.

Sherry is having second thoughts about killing people.

SHERRY

I don't think this is a good
idea.

Nicholas reasons with Sherry.

NICHOLAS
We have no choice. They're
not going to stop trying to kill
us unless we kill them first.

Sherry agrees with him with a nod.

RICKY
Let's jam.

Sherry throws each grenade at different corners of the street to create a diversion.

EXT. EL CORTEZ - NIGHT

A grenade falls down on the ground, right next to a female Vampire Hunter sniper. She looks down and...

BOOM!

She's blown to pieces. The Vampire Hunters scatter.

Sherry throws another grenade.

BOOM!

The second grenade explodes several feet in front of the Vampire Hunters which causes them to run to the right.

BOOM!

The third and final grenade explodes on the back of the street, blocking the Hunters' only chance of escape.

The Vampire Hunters scatter around the block to take cover.

This gives the Midnight Freaks a chance to attack.

The Midnight Freaks attack the Vampire Hunters from on top of the roof in a western shoot out.

Nicholas manages to kill a male Vampire Hunter with his Ak-47, while the final male Vampire Hunter (the Middle Hunter) takes cover behind a destroyed truck.

Nicholas jumps down out in the open street. He focuses at the Middle Hunter.

They both exchange gun shots, but simultaneously run out of ammo. Nicholas hides behind a destroyed Police Squad Car, to reload his AK-47.

Roxy gracefully jumps down to the ground, out in the open, and runs to a hiding spot in the corner of the Cigar Lounge, while being shot at by the Vampire Hunter Snipers.

Roxy fires her MAC 10 Uzis at the Hunters, wasting two female Vampire Hunter snipers, while standing up in a position like being on a surfboard.

Dixon and Sherry find cover on top of the Cigar Lounge rooftop and cover Nicholas and Roxy.

Ricky, on the roof, aims his rifle to fire at the fourth female Vampire Hunter sniper.

The blonde female Vampire Hunter sniper manages to shoot Roxy two times in the upper thighs with her USP 45 Tracer Pistol.

Roxy falls down out in the open street. She is unable to walk, making her vulnerable.

Ricky gets upset when he sees Roxy being shot at. He is enraged gritting his teeth.

RICKY
Nobody hurts my girl!

Ricky fires at the last two remaining female Vampire Hunter snipers, who dodge his bullets, hiding inside a three-story ruined building for cover. They fire at Nicholas and Roxy. The blonde is on the rooftop, while the other is on the middle window of the third floor.

Unable to find the snipers, Ricky moves from the tip of the rooftop to behind the air ducts to try and spot the snipers in the destroyed building.

SHERRY
Roxy!

Sherry tries to go out in the open to rescue Roxy, but Dixon holds her back because she might get caught in the crossfire.

DIXON

(to Sherry)

Stay down!

Bullets are flying everywhere on the rooftop of the Cigar Lounge, as Dixon and Sherry withstand sniper fire. It's only luck they don't get shot.

Ricky aims his sniper rifle at the building trying to find the female snipers.

Dixon climbs down the ladder behind the Cigar Lounge. He goes through an alley and into the open street and attempts to save Roxy.

Sherry is hiding behind the ventilation ducts.

The female Vampire Hunter snipers rapidly reload their weapons.

Dixon fires his assault rifle while trying to rescue Roxy.

Suddenly, a military jeep, armed with a mounted .50 Cal machine gun, drives by, manned by five male Vampire Hunters. They open fire at Dixon, missing him.

Dixon goes back up the alley to the back of the Cigar Lounge.

The Jeep Vampire Hunters sweep the area, firing at everything.

This gives the female Hunter Snipers the advantage.

Roxy crawls to the two wooden barrels for cover. Then, she tries to fire her MAC 10s but runs out of ammo. She reloads, using spare clips she's tucked in her boots.

Sherry, tired of running from her fears, pops up from the rooftop and fires her Desert Eagle pistol at the jeep Vampire Hunters, hitting the jeep's gunner in the head.

This gives Roxy the advantage. She rolls into the street -- kneeling like a knight, she fires at the jeep Vampire Hunters, killing one.

Dixon returns to the street and opens fire at two jeep Vampire Hunters, killing them.

The jeep driver tries to escape but is surrounded.

The blonde sniper aims her gun at Roxy's heart, ready to make the kill.

SCOPE POV

The crosshairs settle directly on Roxy's heart.

BACK TO SCENE

The blonde sniper smirks as her right index finger is about to squeeze the hair trigger.

> BLONDE SNIPER
>
> (to Roxy)
>
> That's it, baby. Come to mama!

Then all of a sudden...

BANG!

The blonde sniper is shot right between the eyes, causing her sunglasses to split in half.

Ricky, across the street, lifts his hunting rifle and smiles.

The last female sniper spots Ricky, and tries to get a beard on him.

Cool, calm, Ricky aims the hunting rifle at her, and squeezes off one single fatal shot. BANG!

The last female sniper falls back, headshot.

Ricky moves from the air duct to the top of the rooftop.

> RICKY
>
> (to everybody)
>
> All the snipers are dead!

Roxy, hiding on the corner behind two wooden barrels, fires her MAC 10 UZI's at the jeep's gas line, causing it to leak and pour on the street.

Sherry sees the jeep's leaking gas spreading around. She shoots the gas. Fire rushes up to the jeep --

KABOOM! The jeep explodes in a big fireball. Killing the gunner and the driver.

All that's left now -- the Middle Hunter and Nicholas, who are still reloading their guns. They take cover behind the wreckage and large debris in the street.

> MIDDLE HUNTER
> (to Nicholas)
> I've been tracking you and
> your friends for a whole year.
> We've had to kill so many of
> your kind, traveling all over
> just to find you're sorry ass,
> but it was worth it.

Nicholas is confused.

> NICHOLAS
> Others?
> MIDDLE HUNTER
> Not that it matters now!
> Cobra scum!

Nicholas and the Middle Hunter finish reloading. They both jump out of their hiding spots and take aim. It's like a quick draw western shootout -- Nicholas with his AK-47 and the Middle Hunter with his sawed-off Shotgun.

BANG! BANG!

The Middle Hunter dies.

Nicholas stands tall, in a cloud of smoke.

The Cigar Lounge street is full of dead Vampire Hunters. The coast is clear.

Nicholas goes to Roxy and helps her to her feet. Dixon helps Nicholas carry Roxy to the Metal Machine van. Ricky jumps down on the ground floor to check on Roxy, while Sherry climbs down on the ladder, and runs to the open street.

The Midnight Freaks, Sherry and Dixon regroup on the empty street.

> SHERRY
>
> Roxy, are you alright?
>
> ROXY
>
> I'll be fine.

Dixon looks at Roxy's gory wounds.
Dixon checks Roxy's wounds. He has blood all over his hand.

> DIXON
>
> We need to get her medical
> attention right away.

Dixon pulls out his clean handkerchief to cover Roxy's wound and ties it.

> NICHOLAS
>
> (to Dixon)
>
> We'll take care of it.

Nicholas is about to use his powers to heal her, but Roxy stops him.

> ROXY
>
> No.

Nicholas realizes that they can't reveal themselves as supernatural vampires. He turns to Sherry and Dixon.

> NICHOLAS
>
> Where is the nearest hospital?
>
> SHERRY
>
> We have a small medical clin-
> ic at the east side of town. I'll
> lead you there. Follow me.

The Midnight Freaks enter the Metal Machine van. Sherry and Dixon enter the squad car.

Dixon's squad car leads the Metal Machine van to the clinic.

INT. CHEVY VAN - MOVING - NIGHT

Nicholas drives the car, while Ricky is by Roxy's side.

> RICKY
> (to Nicholas)
> Why do you want us to go to a hospital when you could have easily healed Roxy?
>
> ROXY
> (to Ricky)
> We can't show Dixon our secret, idiot.
>
> NICHOLAS
> She's right. If he finds out, he might try to kill us. The guy won't understand what we are. Let's do this, and just get in and out.

INT. EL CORTEZ MEDICAL CLINIC - NIGHT

A small modern day hospital clinic, with a table, x-rays, a mirror, cabinets, medication bottles and some tools.

Roxy is lying down on the table, with Ricky and Nicholas standing by. Sherry and Dixon talk in the hallway.

> SHERRY
> Eric, can you check around town to find if there are any more of those trench coat people?

DIXON

Sure, but are you going to be
okay?

SHERRY

I'll be fine.

Dixon leaves the clinic, while Sherry enters the medical room.
Sherry watches Nicholas heal Roxy's wounds with his powers.
Nicholas removes the handkerchief, pulls the bullets out of her upper
thighs.

ROXY

(grunting)
God! That hurts!

Ricky finds a blood pack in small steel medical refrigerator. He steals it and
he gives it to Roxy.
Roxy slightly tears into the blood pack with her fangs and drinks from it
really fast.
Roxy's wounds fully heal on their own.
Roxy is fully healed and she can walk again.

SHERRY

Unbelievable.

Nicholas talks to Sherry.

NICHOLAS

Sherry, I want to know what
the Hunters want with the
Cobras. Who are these guys,
really?

SHERRY

I told you, they are bad ass biker type kind of guys. I don't know what they want with them. Maybe, hired guns. I don't know.

RICKY

Come on, Sherry. The Cobras come into your club all the time. Now what do they do exactly? You must have over-heard them talking about their business from time to time.

Sherry comes clean with the Cobras' business.

SHERRY

Okay, okay... the Cortez Cobras are not just your average rene-gade biker gang. They're in the business of arms dealing, drug smuggling and prostitution.

ROXY

That explains why your girls were being beaten by them for not putting out.

SHERRY

Exactly. I also have seen them only ride in and out of town at night.

NICHOLAS

Have you ever seen them in the day?

SHERRY

No. No one has ever seen them during the day or early afternoon.

NICHOLAS

That could explain that there are others out there like us.

ROXY

How do you know?

NICHOLAS

The Vampire Hunter that I fought with told me that they have been hunting down others like us for a year. Is it possible that the Cobras are like us?

RICKY

(interrupts)

No, that's impossible!

NICHOLAS

These hunters have been tracking us from state to state.

RICKY

Fuck! Every town we ever go to. There's going to be trench coat psychos waiting to stick a shotgun up our asses! We're up to our balls in deep shit.

> ROXY
>
> I'm a girl, Ricky.
>
> RICKY
>
> Sorry. Whatever! The point
> is--
>
> NICHOLAS
>
> (interrupts)
>
> Let's not talk about this right
> now.

Meanwhile, Dixon returns to the clinic. Nicholas senses his presence. Roxy grabs a bandage wrap and wraps her upper thighs to cover her wounds, in order to hide their secret.

Dixon enters into the room.

> DIXON
>
> I checked all over town.
> You don't have to worry
> about those trench coat guys
> anymore.
>
> SHERRY
>
> They're all dead?
>
> DIXON
>
> Yeah.
>
> NICHOLAS
>
> Then let's finish what we
> started. Time to take out the
> Sheriff.
>
> (to Dixon)
>
> Where is the station?
>
> DIXON
>
> A mile away from town,
> good luck trying to get in.

It's locked up tight and heavily guarded. Don't worry
though, I can get us in with
my key.
> (to Nicholas)

I'll take you all there on one
condition -- I bust Barton,
you guys don't kill him.

Nicholas reluctantly agrees.

NICHOLAS
Deal.

EXT. EL CORTEZ MEDICAL CLINIC - NIGHT
Dixon leads the Midnight Freaks out to the parking lot and instructs them.
Sherry loads the weapons into the back of the Metal Machine van.

DIXON
You three will ride with me
in the back of my squad car.
Sherry will drive your van behind us and park it but keep
it out of sight. I'll put you all
in handcuffs, but I won't fully
lock them.

RICKY
Say what?

DIXON
You'll be able to get out of
them easily if something goes
wrong.

Dixon cuffs Ricky, but he resists.

>   RICKY
> No! Wait wait wait! You're
> not putting me back in cuffs.
>   DIXON
> I have to make it look real!
> Otherwise, the other offi-
> cers will think something's
> suspicious.

Dixon gets a few spare sets of cuffs out of his car trunk. The Midnight
Freaks allow Dixon to temporary handcuff them.

>   SHERRY
> Everything is loaded.
>   NICHOLAS
> Are you sure about this?
>   DIXON
> Trust me.

Nicholas looks at Sherry.

>   NICHOLAS
> Sherry.

Nicholas tosses his car keys in one hand.
Sherry catches the keys.
Dixon cuffs Nicholas.
The Midnight Freaks enter the back of the squad car. Dixon closes the door,
and goes in the front driver seat of his car. He starts up the engine and drives to
the police station. Sherry goes to the Metal Machine van and follows him.

Dixon's car drives out of the ruined town of El Cortez, while the Metal Machine van follows.

INT. DIXON'S CAR - MOVING - NIGHT

It is 1:00AM. Dixon drives his car, while calling the station on his radio.

> DIXON
> This is Dixon, over.
> MITCH (V.O.)
> Dixon, where the hell are you?
> DIXON
> I've apprehended the sus-
> pects. They're in custody
> with me, right now.
> MITCH (V.O.)
> Well done deputy, bring them
> in.

INT. EL CORTEZ POLICE STATION - NIGHT

Mitch talks on the dispatcher radio.

After he gets off the radio, he informs his fellow officers.

Mitch rallies the troops.

> MITCH
> (to everyone)
> Alright you maggots! Listen
> up! Dixon brought the sus-
> pects in. Once they come in,
> we're going to kill them all!
> TOM
> But sir...
> MITCH
> What did I just say? Dipshit!

Tom does not say a word.

MITCH
That boy scout left his post.
The asshole deserves it.

Mitch and the police officers surround the station to get ready to kill the Midnight Freaks.

EXT. EL CORTEZ POLICE STATION - NIGHT

Dixon parks his squad car in front of the station.

The Metal Machine van parks next to the hardware store.

INT. EL CORTEZ POLICE STATION - NIGHT

Sam looks through the window blinds and spots Dixon's Car.

SAM
That's them.
MITCH
Get ready.

All six deputies cock their shotguns and assault rifles.

The deputies hide their weapons from the incoming visitors to ensure a sneak attack.

Tom sweats nervously.

One of the deputies opens the door. Dixon brings the Midnight Freaks inside the station.

Each of the Midnight Freaks walks in with their handcuffs in front of them. Out comes Mitch Barton. The moment the band sees Barton, they know something is not right.

Sheriff Barton talks to his deputies.

                    MITCH
        Boys, we got us some
        Hollywood street trash,
        here.

The Midnight Freaks smirk.

                    RICKY
        What a dumbass!
            (to Mitch)
        We're from New Orleans,
        douchebag!

Mitch looks at Ricky.

                    MITCH
        You're really pissing me off,
        boy!

Ricky just smiles at the sheriff.

                    MITCH
        What's so damn funny?

Dixon draws his pistol. He points it at the sheriff.

                    DIXON
        I'm taking you in, Sheriff.

Dixon cocks his gun.

MITCH

What the hell are you doing?

DIXON

Mitch, you ran this town for
too long.

Sherry enters into the building and stands next to Dixon.

MITCH

(to Sherry)

You damn little bitch!

DIXON

She told me everything and
how you killed these peoples'
friend. This is for every person you ever hurt. You're
coming with me.

The deputies come in pulling out their assault rifles and shotguns.
Tom points his assault rifle at Dixon.

TOM

Drop it, Dixon!

MITCH

(to officers)

Don't just stand there, do
something!

DIXON

(to Mitch)

Tell them about how many
girls you've raped and killed
in this town and about your
dirty work with the Cobras.

Mitch doesn't say a word -- he's caught red-handed. The deputies listen. Some of the Deputies stand back.

> MITCH
> (to Tom)
> Who are you going to be-
> lieve? Him or me?

Tom's sweat comes down his brow. His eyes are frightened like a scared puppy.
Dixon reasons with Tom.

> DIXON
> (to Tom)
> Barton is a liar. He played
> us all for suckers. Well aren't
> you going to stand up for
> yourself? Or are you going
> to choke your chicken in the
> bathroom like you always do?

Tom nervously shakes his gun in embarrassment.

> TOM
> Shut... up!

Mitch grows impatient and gets pissed off.

> MITCH
> Aw, fuck this!

Mitch quickly draws his gun, points it at Sherry and shoots her in the stomach.

BANG! Sherry's stomach blasts open and she falls down.

Dixon turns his focus on Sherry. Mitch escapes and jumps for cover behind a steel frame desk.

The Midnight Freaks break the cuffs, vamp out and pull out their pistols in unison. They duck and cover behind the other desk in the office.

The shootout between the Midnight Freaks and the corrupt police officers begins.

Deputy Sam dies in the crossfire with gunshots spraying bullets that cut through his body -- blood and smoke shoot out of his wounds as he falls down dead.

The band separates and crawls around on the ground, finding cover around scattered shot-up desks and file cabinets.

The Deputies and the Midnight Freaks exchange gunfire.

Computers are being blown up, radios are being shot to pieces, papers fly out in the air, glass windows explode from the gunfire from the deputies' assault rifles.

Barton hides behind a desk while Dixon fires his assault rifle.

Dixon and Barton exchange gunfire.

Nicholas has two pistols -- his modified civil war pistol and the other pistol he stole from the gun shop.

Nicholas shoots at the two deputies in the chest. The deputies drop their assault rifles and fall down.

Nicholas goes to Dixon to aid him. At the same time, Nicholas and Dixon are shooting at the sheriff behind their desk, the Sheriff is shooting at them from behind his desk.

Nicholas vampire face with glowing red eyes is revealed the moment Dixon sees Nicholas' vampire appearance.

DIXON
(surprised)
What the fuck?
NICHOLAS
Shoot now, talk later!

INT. EL CORTEZ POLICE STATION - RADIO DISPATCH - NIGHT

Roxy and Ricky crawl on the ground to avoid getting shot. They see some of the dead deputies' left over assault rifles on the ground. They grab the assault rifles for their own. Roxy and Ricky go out and crawl to fire at the deputies.

One deputy comes out of the closet and attempts to fire at Ricky and Roxy with his assault rifle, but misses and runs out of ammo.

Roxy shoots the deputy with the assault rifle. The deputy falls back into the closet dead. His feet kick the door closed.

Ricky sniffs for more deputies with his sharp vampiric sense of smell.

RICKY
(points the door)
He's in there.

The door says "Evidence Locker"

INT. EL CORTEZ POLICE STATION - EVIDENCE LOCKER - NIGHT

Ricky and Roxy enter the Evidence Locker room. It is an empty room with a bunch of bookshelves.

They find Tom squatting down like a scared child -- pissing in his pants and wetting the floor.

Ricky and Roxy surround him to make sure he is trapped.

Tom puts his assault rifle in his mouth. He pulls the trigger trying to commit suicide.

CLICK! CLICK! CLICK!

The gun clicks empty.

The two vampires smile evilly at each other. They both enjoy this moment of bloodlust.

Tom is trapped like a chicken in a cage waiting to be slaughtered.

TOM
Oh... shit!

Ricky and Roxy waste no time as they rip Tom apart in gruesome fashion. Tom screams a blood-curdling scream.

Blood splatters against the walls.

INT. EL CORTEZ POLICE STATION - NIGHT

The Sheriff crawls his way to the Radio Dispatch room.

Then he gets shot in the lower right thigh by Dixon's assault rifle. He struggles to crawl into the Radio Dispatch room.

Mitch's right hand tries to pull out his .44 Magnum.

Then Dixon blasts off the Sheriff's right hand! Blood spatters his face and chest. Fingers fly everywhere.

Barton's screams in agony.

> MITCH
> AHHHHH! You fuckers!
> Shit!

Dixon walks to Barton and points the assault rifle at him.

> DIXON
> It's over.

Behind his back, Mitch pulls out a small Derringer -- quick as a flash, he whips it up and fires -- shooting Dixon through the neck!

Dixon's blood splatters onto the wall behind his neck, and he drops like a rock.

At the same time, Nicholas pops out from behind the corner with two pistols in his hands -- and blows Sheriff Mitch Barton away! Shot after shot, overkill -- blood and guts splatter all over.

Nicholas fires until both his guns click empty. Finally his bloodlust subsides. The Sheriff's mutilated body is unrecognizable. Nicholas lowers his guns and breathes heavily.

Nicholas goes to Dixon, who is bleeding out, choking on his own blood. Nicholas kneels down and tries to heal Dixon putting his hand over Dixon's wound... but it is too late. Dixon dies, slouched on the floor dead.

Nicholas joins Ricky and Roxy. Their revenge is complete and Lisa's death is avenged.

> ROXY
>
> Is he dead?
>
> NICHOLAS
>
> Yes.
>
> RICKY
>
> Dixon?
>
> NICHOLAS
>
> Barton killed him.
>
> RICKY
>
> Damn it.

The Midnight Freaks are about to leave. Until...
...they hear Sherry screaming.
Sherry is dying.

> ROXY
>
> Sherry!

Nicholas, Ricky and Roxy go to a dying Sherry lying on the floor.
Sherry lays flat on the floor in a pool of her own blood, covering her wounds and agonizing in pain. She is very near death.

> NICHOLAS
>
> She's alive...

Nicholas examines Sherry's wound.
Sherry's feeling dizzy as she begins to fade away.

                    RICKY
She's bleeding all over the
place.
                    ROXY
Oh God. Nicholas, do
something!
                    NICHOLAS
I can't heal her like this.
She's lost too much blood.
If we don't help her, she's a
gonner.
                    ROXY
You can't let her die.
                    NICHOLAS
I'm not.
                    ROXY
What are you going to do?
                    NICHOLAS
We have to turn her into one
of us. It's the only way to save
her.

                    ROXY
Lisa would have wanted it
this way. Do it!
                    NICHOLAS
    (to Ricky)
Ricky, hold her up. I'm going
to make her one of us.

Ricky kneels down and cradles Sherry's arms.

Nicholas bites into Sherry's neck gently. He drinks a little bit of her blood in a split second. He pulls himself off.

Nicholas raises his right claws and slits open his left wrist. Blood starts to seep out.

> NICHOLAS
> (to Sherry)
> Drink this.
> SHERRY
> (whispering)
> I don't want to die...
> NICHOLAS
> (in a louder voice)
> Drink!!!

Sherry drinks Nicholas' blood from his left wrist. She continues to drink with an unquenchable thirst. While she's feeding her irises change to a dark blood-red.

Nicholas yanks his left arm away from her.

Sherry starts to go into convulsions as her transformation begins. She pants and trembles with great force. She is experiencing incredible pain -- her entire body is basically dying.

Ricky's unable to control her, so he lets go. Then Sherry stops shaking and lies still.

Sherry's tan skin turns pale. She lies flat on her back in a crucifixion position. Her fangs begin to come out of her teeth and her bridge comes out of her forehead. Her gunshot wounds automatically heal up. Her transformation into a newborn vampire is complete.

Sherry's face transforms back to her human appearance.

The Midnight Freaks transform back to their human appearances as well.

Sherry is dazed.

> SHERRY
> What happened?

                    NICHOLAS
We had no choice but to turn
you.
                    SHERRY
Am I dead?
                    NICHOLAS
Far from it. Your immortal,
angel cakes. You'll always stay
young and you never die.
                    RICKY
Are you okay?
                    SHERRY
What happened to the Sheriff?
                    RICKY
We killed him with his male
ass - deputy groupies.

The Midnight Freaks chuckle a bit.
Sherry gets up from them ground.

                    SHERRY
Where's Eric?
Nicholas brings the bad news
to Sherry.
                    NICHOLAS
I'm sorry, Sher. He didn't
make it.

Sherry walks to Eric's dead body. She takes her right hand and closes Eric's
open eyes on his dead face so that he may rest in peace.

ROXY

Come on, let's go. We did
what we came here to do.

RICKY

Wait a minute, I saw something back in the evidence
room. I'll be back.

Ricky goes to the evidence locker, and comes back with two large black
leather suitcases.

They open the cases, and find them loaded full of cash.

NICHOLAS

(excited)

Oh baby! We just hit the jack-
pot! Whoo!

RICKY

Now we can pay off our college debts, and this time we'll
make sure that we don't get
ripped off.

The Midnight Freaks celebrate their victory.

NICHOLAS

Damn, there must be three
million dollars in here! Sweet!

(sarcastically)

Good, now we got one less
problem.

(cheering up)
But this is still cool anyway.
How often do you find a suit-
case stuffed with cash? Not
often.

RICKY
(excited)
Hell yeah. We're freaking
rich! Fucking party time.

Ricky closes the cases and carries them with the others.

NICHOLAS
It's time to hit the road. Let's
go.

SHERRY
What's going to happen to
me now?

NICHOLAS
We need a bassist and a new
lead singer. You in?

SHERRY
Absolutely.

NICHOLAS
Welcome to the band.

Sherry transforms her human face into a vampire.

SHERRY
I think I'm going to like this.

RICKY
Let's burn.

NICHOLAS

First... let's send out a message to anyone who wants to
fuck with us. Vlad Dracula
style.

EXT. EL CORTEZ - NIGHT

It is 2:00AM in the morning. The Midnight Freaks drag Sheriff Barton's
dead corpse out of the station.

With a gruesome SQUISH, the Midnight Freaks impale the Sheriff's dead
corpse on the branch of a dead tree out near the open road as a symbol of justice.

Sheriff Mitch Barton hangs on the dead tree, with blood oozing out of the
impaled wound. The deceased Sheriff's body looks like stuffed poultry on a
stick.

Nicholas and Sherry stand side by side.

SHERRY

Let the vultures feed on his
worthless ass.

Sherry kicks Mitch Barton's corpse in the crotch.

SHERRY

Prick.

The Midnight Freaks take the money, hop in the Metal Machine van and
drive off.

INT. CHEVY VAN - MOVING - NIGHT

Heavy metal plays. Nicholas is driving. Sherry sits in the front passenger
seat. Ricky and Roxy are in the back seat.

SHERRY

(to Nicholas)

So where do we go from here?

NICHOLAS

I don't know. Let's just ride.

EXT. DESERTED HIGHWAY - NIGHT

The Metal Machine van drives out into the deserted moonlight highway passing a sign.

The sign says: "You are now leaving El Cortez. Come Again Soon!"

FADE OUT.

FADE IN:

INT. EL CORTEZ - DUSK

SUPER: "The Next Day"

The dark sky is filled with an orange sun, setting on the blood-red horizon.

It is sunset at the ghost town of El Cortez. A pack of vultures fly around the dead tree.

The vultures surround the sheriff's rotting corpse, pecking and eating him, ripping his eyes out and eating them.

We hear motorcycle engines burning.

A group of bikers rides into the outskirts of town.

The Biker Gang rides on the desert highway.

The Biker Gang rides into the abandoned town of El Cortez.

The Biker Gang arrives into town and parks their bikes.

The Cortez Cobras have arrived in town to pick up their cut of the protection money from the cops. They are a group of bad ass Hell's Angels/Vago type bikers. The group is a mix of white, blacks and Latinos. There are twenty members, all male.

Three of the Cobra Members enter the station, when they see the massacre before them. We don't see them. Then, they quickly exit the station when they realize that their money has been stolen.

One of the Cobra Members approaches their leader.

COBRA MEMBER
(to Cobra Leader)
It's gone.

The COBRA LEADER, a big, buff Latino, with black sunglasses, slick black hair, wears a black biker leather sleeveless vest, black leather pants and black biker boots. His fingers sport cut off black leather biker gloves. A gold crucifix gleams on his muscled chest.

The Cobra Leader investigates the scene. He sniffs out the Midnight Freaks' scent like a dog.

COBRA LEADER
We're not alone. Somebody
has stolen our cash.

The Cobra Leader raises his sunglasses -- his eyes glow red. His fangs glisten. He's a vampire!

COBRA LEADER
And when we find them,
they're gonna find out --
there'll be hell to pay.

The Cortez Cobras, all vampires, rev up their chopper bikes. The Cobra Leader gets on up his custom-made chopper bike. He leads his bikers into the sunset on the long strip highway road.

FADE OUT.

NIGHT OF THE FREAKS
3

Sanctuary

DOMINIC R. DANIELS

WGA Registered.
Dominic Rocky Daniels
Email: dominicdaniels777@gmail.com

FADE IN:

Instrumental Heavy Metal music plays.

A quote appears in red on screen.

"The gates of hell are open, night and day; Smooth the descent, and easy the way. - Virgil (70-19 BC)"

EXT. NEW MEXICO HIGHWAY - DAY

The band's new ride is a 1952 Ford Short Dinky Bus, custom restored, painted black, with a high horsepower engine complete with a decor of gothic designs and highly custom decals of monsters and vampires.

The roof is custom made like a rock concert stage with strong square metal steel railing on the center roof. The back end of the bus has a small chrome ladder attached to the rear end. Lettering is detailed on the back of the bus saying "Metal Forever".

The bus is newly christened as the "THE METAL MACHINE III" custom detailed with writing on the left side of the bus.

The Metal machine iii drives on the open secluded highway filled with brown and red sands, cactuses and black asphalt with yellow stripes.

On the roof of the van is RICKY, 24. The funny man, the joker, laid back stoner, hard partier and lead guitarist of The Midnight Freaks metal band.

Ricky is rocking on his guitar playing and singing a cover song, while the bus is cruising.

INT. THE METAL MACHINE III - DAY

The gang's all here:

NICHOLAS, 47, looks 28, drives the bus. A strong and collected leader, he's the kind of guy you don't want to mess with but still admire and like to have as friend for his bravery and good heart.

SHERRY, 24, sits in the passenger seat, singing. The new lead singer and bass guitarist of The Midnight Freaks, Sherry is half-Irish and half-Latina.

She's a lush fallen angel of a girl rebuilding her life with a new identity -- as a newly-sired vampire. Reborn as a new being, still recovering from the shellshock of her old human life, she's slowly growing into a strong woman.

ROXY, 25, sits in the back of the bus, singing along. A goth girl, a free spirit, beautiful and deadly, wild and fun to be around, she's book smart in dealings with the supernatural and paranormal.

Inside the back of the bus is a large drum set, two brand new Fender lead guitars, two brand new fender bass guitars, a new KORG keyboard, two medium amps, a microphone set, a fog machine, a medium strobe light, strung black lights hanging all around the walls inside the bus for decoration, a small couch to crash on, a boom box and a battery-operated mini freezer to store blood packs and glass cola bottles to sustain the band's vampiric needs.

After the song ends, Roxy calls out to Ricky, poking her head outside her window.

ROXY
(knocking on the side window)
Hey Van Halen, get down here!

EXT. THE METAL MACHINE III - DAY

Ricky is still on the roof of the bus.

RICKY

Hang on, I'm coming!

Ricky comes down from the roof and slides into the bus through the right hand side of the middle open window with his guitar.

INT. THE METAL MACHINE III - DAY

The Midnight Freaks celebrate their victory as it seems their troubles have finally ended and life is starting to turn out for the better.

RICKY

(excited)

We made it! We're free, you guys!

ROXY

Hell yeah!

RICKY

No more debt! No more cops and best of all, no more fuck-ing problems! It's time to PARTYYYY!

Roxy playfully grabs Ricky by the waist.

ROXY

Come here, hot stuff!

She kisses him.

Sherry looks at the couple smiling while lightly chuckling.

SHERRY

You two are such dorks!

Ricky smiles and flips the bird at Sherry.
Sherry laughs.

> SHERRY
> (joking)
> Oh go get a room and get it
> on. You know you want to.
> ROXY
> (smiling back at Sherry)
> Hey, I love him.
> SHERRY
> (points at Roxy; smiles)
> No, you want to fuck him.
> RICKY
> (being coy but funny)
> Hey, I don't mind volunteer-
> ing. But can I have you both?

Sherry throws a small pillow from her passenger seat at Ricky. Ricky blocks the throw, knocking the pillow down to the floor.

> SHERRY
> (playfully smiling)
> You horny asshole!
> RICKY
> (sarcastically smiling)
> Yes, I am.

Ricky and Roxy pull out a few cola bottles and toss one to Sherry. The three twist off the bottle caps with their hands and drink their cola bottles.

Everybody is having a good time and laughing... except Nicholas.

NICHOLAS

Hey, we're not out of the woods yet. You guys forget that we need to take care of our business and get things rolling.

RICKY

And what's that, man? Lighten up. It's time to party!

ROXY

Come on, Nicky. We've been through hell the past week. Let's try to have some fun.

NICHOLAS

It's easy for you guys to say. Lisa is dead.

(beat)

I miss her.

RICKY

(down to earth)

Hey buddy listen to me... I know what you're going through. How do you think I feel about it? I cared for her too, we all did, man. She was a good friend, but she's gone now... it sad but that's the way things are.

ROXY

Ricky's right. She didn't deserve what happened to her,

she was a kind and loving person. But as much as we miss her we can't stop living in the now. If we don't move on, we'll never be able to live or be happy. I hate that she is gone, she was family. But we can't help that. That's just how life is. It's not fair at times, but I mean... come on, it's not like we can bring her back. We're vampires Nicky, not gods.

NICHOLAS

I know. It's just... everything is changing so fast.

RICKY

What are you saying?

NICHOLAS

First we didn't have any money, now we're rich... We still haven't cut our first album, and we still don't know if the cops are looking for us. It's like we don't know where we are all going. You know what I mean?

ROXY

(annoyed)

Piss on the cops, pssh. I eat cops for breakfast.

Sherry feels sympathy towards Nicholas.

> SHERRY
>
> He's right you know. It's great that now we have a lot of cash, but we don't have a plan for the band's future. I mean, what do you do to kill the time when you're immortal and you live forever?

Nicholas, pondering, seems unsure of himself.

> NICHOLAS
>
> I don't know about you guys but it's been bothering me ever since I got turned into this thing by Kane. The question is this -- what do you do when you have an endless lifetime to live? It kind of sucks.

> RICKY
>
> (optimistic)
>
> Come on, it's not that bad, man.

> NICHOLAS
>
> Face it, we can't see our families anymore and we will sooner or later have to change our identities as time goes on.

Ricky thinks.

> RICKY
>
> I don't know... try to think positive bro. Wait I got it! Why don't we go out to Hollywood? We could buy a condo or a loft out there and start playing shows again.
>
> NICHOLAS
> (sarcastic)
> And do what? Go back to playing in shitty clubs to get our name out?

> ROXY
> (casually)
> So what, we're immortal anyway. Besides we'll all have fun when were jamming on stage and the people love us.

Nicholas pauses for a second, reflecting. He changes his mind, turns positive.

> NICHOLAS
> You know what. Fuck it. You guys are right.
>
> RICKY
> Exactly.
>
> NICHOLAS
> You got to admit maybe life is better. Maybe we should go higher. Get to the top.

Roxy is confident and laid back.

>   ROXY
> Oh, stop worrying so much,
> you'll see... once we hit it big
> in Hollywood, Tinseltown
> will never let us go. We
> wanted to be rock stars,
> well... this is our big chance.
> We got all the benefits that
> everyone else wants and
> doesn't have.
>   NICHOLAS
> So what's your point?
>   ROXY
> Look at us, we live forever,
> we got supernatural powers,
> and we have all the opportu-
> nity that normal people don't
> ever have in their lifetimes.
> Now that is being lucky, if
> you ask me.

Nicholas stops thinking and worrying. He is trying to stay positive.

>   NICHOLAS
> Maybe you're right. We got
> the world by the balls and
> don't even realize it.
>   SHERRY
> Hey, speaking of Hollywood...
> my manager Ronnie lives out

in Beverly Hills. Let's give
him a call sometime.
                NICHOLAS
That's great and everything,
but can you sing the same
style as good as Lisa did? If
you can't, we are going to
sound like shit.

Sherry thinks about the band's style. She starts to get nervous but gathers the
strength she has and speaks up.

                SHERRY
Yeah.
                NICHOLAS
Are you sure?
                SHERRY
        (sarcastic)
Are you good at charming la-
dies and playing drums?
                NICHOLAS
Yeah.
                SHERRY
        (calmly, smiling)
Then there's your answer.
Relax, everything is going to
be fine.

Nicholas commands his band.

                NICHOLAS
Then, here's the plan. We
head out to Hollywood, set

up a little studio and start
pumping out some fresh
tracks for our first album...
get it mastered, start a band
website then do the audition
thing and finally get a con-
tract deal with a record label.
In any case we could always
start our own with the money
we got.

Sherry gets up from her seat and massages Nicholas' shoulders to relieve his tension.

Nicholas looks at Sherry and smiles.

> SHERRY
> Better now?
> NICHOLAS
> Yeah. Thanks.
> RICKY
> I'm down with that.
> ROXY
> Same here.
> NICHOLAS
> (to Sherry)
> What about you?

Sherry likes the idea.

> SHERRY
> Why not? It's not like we got
> anything else going on in our
> lives.

Suddenly, the bus's back window shatters with a sound of a shotgun blast.

The band ducks down dropping their cola bottles on the floor. The soda spills all over the rug. Nicholas swerves down the road.

Nicholas looks in his center driver mirror.

> NICHOLAS
>
> Oh, shit! Look who's followed
> us!

Ricky looks out the side window, and sees a group of bikers behind their bus.

> RICKY
>
> It's those damn hunters again!

EXT. NEW MEXICO HIGHWAY - DAY

The Metal Machine III is being tailed not by Hunters, but by a motorcyclist on a Harley-Davidson.

INT. THE METAL MACHINE III - DAY

Roxy runs to the left side windows to see who's out there. Ricky is freaking out.

> RICKY
>
> Hunters! Why is it always
> hunters?!!
>
> ROXY
> (surprised)
> It can't be.

Nicholas looks at his center driver mirror.

> NICHOLAS
>
> It's not.
>
> RICKY

(freaking out)
It's them I tell you.
NICHOLAS
(commanding)
Get the guns!

Nicholas points his right thumb at the back seat.
Ricky looks at the left side.

RICKY

Get down!

A biker pulls out his double-barrel shotgun and fires. BANG!

Ricky and Roxy duck before they get hit. Glass shatters around them. They open up the footlocker and pulls out their weapons. A Desert Eagle Pistol, two MAC-10 Uzis, a hunting sniper rifle, and an AK-47 fully automatic machine gun.

Each band member frantically grabs a weapon while being shot at by the bikers.

Meanwhile all the glass windows are being blown out and the sides of the bus taking heavy damage from the enemy gunfire. Bullets hit the sides of the bus and sparks fly everywhere.

Roxy grabs her MAC-10 Uzis. She blasts through the left side windows, using the side of the bus as an armored shield.

Ricky grabs his hunting rifle, nervously loading the rifle. He uses the right side windows to shoot at the bikers.

Sherry grabs her Desert Eagle Pistol. She shoots two of the bikers on the right side of the bus. One in the head and one through the heart.

It is a classic Western stagecoach style shoot out.

EXT. NEW MEXICO HIGHWAY - DAY

A biker rides towards to the left side of the bus.

Nicholas swerves toward the biker and knocks him off the road.

The biker falls down on the red dirt.

INT. THE METAL MACHINE III - DAY
Nicholas continues to drive, while the rest of the band squats for cover.

RICKY
Did we lose them?

Suddenly, The Midnight Freaks hear more motorcycle engines revving up.
Sherry looks out the middle right side window to see how many attackers are after them.

SHERRY
We got company! Nicky get
us out of here!
NICHOLAS
Hang on!

Nicholas increases the bus's speed to 80 -- the vehicle's top speed.

RICKY
(nervously)
Faster man! Faster! Lose
them!
NICHOLAS
I'm hitting full speed!
SHERRY
(to the band)
I told you guys not to buy this
thing!
NICHOLAS
Too late now!

EXT. NEW MEXICO HIGHWAY - DAY

A group of twenty motorcyclists rides towards The Metal Machine III. They ride in on Harley-Davidson motorcycles. The bikers ride on all sides of the road surrounding the bus. Two of the bikers jump on top of the roof with the ramp bars.

RICKY

They're on the roof!

ROXY

Get them!

The Midnight Freaks vamp out and transform into their vampiric forms. They are fueled with adrenaline and blood pumping inside, ready to go to work and start killing.

BACKGROUND HEAVY METAL MUSIC:

EXT. NEW MEXICO HIGHWAY - DAY

One of the bikers pulls out his .45 Magnum and fires at Nicholas only to shoot at the glass, shattering it.

INT. THE METAL MACHINE III - DAY

Nicholas fully ducks while the rest fire at all sides of the bus. Nicholas is covered by pieces of glass. He pulls out his modified-civil war pistol from the left side of his jacket and fires at the biker who shot at him.

The shot hits the biker in the forehead killing him, and the dead biker flips over his motorcycle.

EXT. NEW MEXICO HIGHWAY - DAY

The two bikers who Sherry shot at flip their bikes over the side of the road and their motorcycles explode. BOOM!

INT. THE METAL MACHINE III - DAY

Suddenly, the two bikers on the roof claw a big hole in the metal sheathing of the rooftop and rip a part of the roof right off! They jump inside the bus.

Roxy and Ricky shoot the two bikers in the chest killing them.

Then, Roxy goes to the left side of the bus and fires at two more bikers on their motorcycles -- knocking them off the road.

The two bikers on the floor inside the bus recover from their wounds. These bikers turn out to be vampires. They vamp out and fight.

Sherry and Nicholas are shocked at what they see, while they fire at the bikers on road.

NICHOLAS

They're like us!

The two biker vampires disarm Ricky and Roxy. One of the bikers destroys Ricky's hunting rifle by bending the barrel with his hands. The other cross kicks the Uzis out of Roxy's hands, the MAC-10s flying out the window.

He punches Roxy hard in the stomach, knocking her down to the floor in a daze.

Nicholas is unable to help because he is driving. Sherry is shooting at the other bikers on the road.

One of the bikers manages to strangle Nicholas with both his hands, causing Nicholas to lose control of the bus.

Nicholas tries to remove the biker's hands but his opponent's grip is too strong.

Ricky claws one of the vampire bikers through the neck but ends up ripping off his head and tosses it out to Roxy, just like a hot potato. Blood splatters like a fountain from the headless vampire, spraying on Ricky's face and clothes.

Roxy catches the decapitated head by reflex and is grossed out.

ROXY

Aw, shit!

Roxy tosses it back to Ricky.

RICKY

(spooked)

Don't give it to me!

Ricky tosses the head to Sherry.

Sherry is holding her gun with both hands, arms extended out in a shape of a basketball hoop. She freaks out when the head flies through her arms and to her lap.

Sherry accidentally loses her Desert Eagle pistol out the window.

RICKY

Hey, two points.

SHERRY

Jack ass! You made me lose
my gun!

Meanwhile, The vampire biker in the front of the bus is still strangling Nicholas. Nicholas grunts.

NICHOLAS

Guys, a little help here!

Sherry manages to pick up the decapitated biker's head and throws it, hitting the other biker in the back of his head while he is attacking Nicholas.

Nicholas is still struggling to drive and swerving all over the road.

The vampire biker turns around, focuses on Sherry and growls like a beast in anger.

Meanwhile, Nicholas grabs his revolver and blows the back of the vampire biker's head clean off. Blood and brains splatter all over against the bus's entrance doors and on Nicholas's face and clothes.

Nicholas releases the dead headless biker's grip from his throat, and the corpse falls to the ground. Nicholas regains control of the bus.

Ricky goes to the back side of the van and grabs the AK-47 and fires at the remaining bikers on the road.

EXT. NEW MEXICO HIGHWAY - DAY

Some of the bikers get hit and fall off their bikes, while others bikes explode on the highway.

The road becomes clear of the bikers.

The Metal Machine III continues to drive, then turns off the road.

INT. THE METAL MACHINE III - DAY

The Midnight Freaks are all relieved that the bikers are all gone, for now. However, The Metal machine iii has taken heavy damage from the gun battle.

Sherry looks at the dead biker to find out who he is. The patch on the back of his vest says: "Cortez Cobras". The logo has a snake with vampire fangs.

SHERRY

Nicholas, pull over!

EXT. THE METAL MACHINE III - DAY

The Metal Machine III pulls over to the right side of the road and stops.

Ricky pulls the side switch lever by his driver seat and opens the main swing doors. He drags one of the bodies out the door and throws it on to the dusty ground.

Roxy drags the decapitated body by the arms and tosses it out the door on to the highway road.

Sherry throws the decapitated head out the window.

RICKY

Let's get out of here before
someone sees us.

The band gets back in the bus and drives off the road.

INT. THE METAL MACHINE III - DAY

Ricky starts to freak out when his sees his damaged bus.

RICKY

Son-of-a-bitch! Those creeps
wrecked our ride. Mother-
fuckers! I just finished rebuilding this sucker.

ROXY

You mean "we" built it.

RICKY

Yeah I know, alright? I'm pissed off, okay? Can somebody please tell me what the hell is going on?

NICHOLAS

Stay cool man... don't be such a hot head.

RICKY

(angry and sarcastic)

Oh real funny, first we got voodoo zombies and a ghoul shaman bugging us. Then, we got crooked cops and whack job hunters! And now this shit! Reject vampire bikers from planet nine?

SHERRY

It's the Cobras. They must have found out that we killed Barton back at the station in El Cortez. But why would they want to come after us?

ROXY

Because we got their protection money, that's why.

RICKY

Let's just get out of here before the pigs show up! I'm not

spending the rest of my life in
a damn cell with Bubba.

Roxy cracks a joke to lighten up Ricky.

>   ROXY
> Ricky, what are you worried
> for? You would rip Bubba
> a new asshole in less than a
> minute.
>   RICKY
> Oh God. That's gay!

Everybody starts laughing.

EXT. NEW MEXICO HIGHWAY - DAY

The Metal Machine III drives on the road.

INT. THE METAL MACHINE III - DAY

It is 5:00PM. The sun has not yet set. Nicholas is driving, while Roxy, Ricky
and Sherry wipe the bloodstains with rags and their dirty shirts.

Roxy and Sherry are wearing their black bras as they clean the walls of the
bus.

Ricky is bare-chested, cleaning the floor of the bus.

>   RICKY
> So what do we do now? We
> lost most of the guns and
> we're low on ammo.
>   NICHOLAS
> We'll have to use our heads,
> then.
>   ROXY
> Yeah, but what about those
> Hell's Angels rejects?

RICKY

Man! This is really fucked up! Why is it that when we try to start fresh we always get into a bloodbath and get screwed over? Fuck this road trip crap, let's just go back home.

Nicholas stays tough while he wipes the blood off his face with his handkerchief.

NICHOLAS

Ricky, we can't, these guys are cold-blooded killers. These bastards are not going to stop till they get us. We'll have to kill them all. If we don't, we're dead. You understand? Dead!

RICKY

I hate this.

NICHOLAS

Yeah, well, that's too bad. We got ourselves into this mess and now we gotta get ourselves out of it.

SHERRY

(timid)

Isn't that a little much?

NICHOLAS

(annoyed)

No it isn't. You want to rot in
a pine box with a bunch of
maggots?

SHERRY

(intimidated)

No.

NICHOLAS

There's something you're not
telling us. I want to know
right now. You're holding out
on us.

SHERRY

The hell I'm not. You get
your ass down here and clean
this crap up!

NICHOLAS

Hey I'm driving. Don't mess
with me, just tell me the
truth. Please.

Sherry, Roxy and Ricky finish cleaning the inside of the bus. They put their
dirty rags in a black trash bag.

SHERRY

I've told you guys everything
I know about them already.
Honest.

NICHOLAS

But you didn't tell us that
they were like us.

Sherry, Roxy and Ricky opens the footlocker, then pick up and put on clean
black shirts. Two black tank tops for the girls and one black muscle shirt for Ricky.

SHERRY

Forget the finger pointing and he said she said crap. How the hell was I supposed to know? I'm not a damn fortune teller. If I knew I would have already told you.

ROXY

Would you two shut up! This is not going to solve our problem.

Nicholas gets pissed at Roxy.

NICHOLAS

Hey fuck you!

Sherry calms everyone down.

SHERRY

Look... right now the most important thing is that we find a place where we can hide to be safe. They're not going to stop until they get back their money that we stole from them.

Lighting strikes Ricky's brain with an idea.

RICKY

Why don't we head to Phoenix or Vegas? If we go

there, those idiots won't be able to find us.

Roxy, calculating, lays it out.

> ROXY
>
> That's a good idea... but we have a problem. How are we going to get into those cities without anyone seeing us carrying almost three million dollars in cash while walking on the street? It's not like we can just walk into a bank, pull out the money bags and set up an account. They'd think something was suspicious... then the cops would get involved.

Nicholas takes charge.

> NICHOLAS
>
> The hell with that idea. We're going to the next town we find and ditch this bus and split.
>
> SHERRY
>
> Why?
>
> NICHOLAS
>
> We got to get us a new set of wheels and get out of here. If we don't, the cops will be on us quicker than flies on shit.

SHERRY

He's right, let's go.

RICKY

(worried)

But what about those bikers who attacked us? What are we going to do?

NICHOLAS

We got to find a place to hide until everything cools down. If those guys find us they'll kill us all.

RICKY

We are outnumbered then.

NICHOLAS

Not if I can help it. Ricky, can you find a place for us to hide out at? There has to be some place at all where we can hide.

RICKY

I'll try. Give me a second.

Ricky psychically searches for the area.

RICKY

Head three miles north. There is a small mining town with an abandoned power plant nearby.

NICHOLAS

Cool, let's go.

Nicholas floors the gas pedal to gain speed on the open road while rushing to find the mining town.

> ROXY
> Sherry, do you know who's in charge of the Cobras?
>
> SHERRY
> Yeah, I've seen him a few times before. He rarely comes into El Cortez. His name's been mentioned by the other bikers around town but I've never talked to him in person.
>
> NICHOLAS
> Who is he?
>
> SHERRY
> The founder of the Cortez Cobras Motorcycle Club. I've heard from different people that the guy is so rotten that he ripped a man's throat out with his bare hands. They call him... Barabbas, I think.
>
> RICKY
> What kind of a name is that?
>
> NICHOLAS
> Look it up, it's in the bible.
>
> RICKY
> Screw that -- I'd rather rock, man.

Ricky turns on the radio that picks up a rock station already starting to play a song.

Everyone smiles a little and begins to cheer up as they jam with the music and head to the mining town.

EXT. NEW MEXICO HIGHWAY - DAY

It is 5:30PM. The highway is scattered with dead vampire bikers.

Eight more Cobra bikers arrive in the scene. One of the bikers is Barabbas the COBRA LEADER, a big, buff, Latino, with black sunglasses, slick black hair, dressed in a black biker leather cut off sleeved vest and black leather pants. He wears black biker boots, cut off black leather biker gloves and a gold crucifix around his shirtless neck.

He gets off his custom Chopper bike, and walks over to investigate the scene. He sniffs out The Midnight Freaks' vampiric scent, catching the smell in the air like a bloodhound.

One of the Lieutenants is LIPS, a 30 year old vampire in appearance. 5'8". He has a Southern redneck accent. Slim but in good shape, his body is like a professional lightweight boxer.

> LIPS
> Barabbas!
>
> BARABBAS
> Lips. What do you got for me?
>
> LIPS
> Dio said that those burn-outs' bus is headed towards Manuela. It's a mining town north from here.

Barabbas raises his sunglasses.

> LIPS
> Those bastards took out a lot of our guys.

> BARABBAS
> Make 'em bleed. Head north
> and ride like hell. Let's go.

The Cortez Cobras, all now in their true vampiric form, rev up their chopper bikes. Barabbas gets on his custom-made chopper bike and leads his biker comrades to the mining town.

EXT. MINING TOWN - NIGHT

It is dusk at 5:30PM at the small mining town of MANUELA, NEW MEXICO. Population: 100 People.

The Metal Machine III creeps into the town. Then, out of nowhere it breaks down with the front engine smoking like a chimney. BANG! The bus stops dead.

INT. THE METAL MACHINE III - NIGHT

Nicholas tries to turn on the ignition switch to restart the bus, but the engine will not start and stalls out. He hits the dashboard in frustration.

> NICHOLAS
> Damn this old piece of junk!
> (beat)
> Ricky, go out and check un-
> derneath the hood.
> RICKY
> I got it.

Ricky grabs a rag and a portable flashlight lantern from the footlocker, gets up and leaves the bus.

EXT. THE METAL MACHINE III - NIGHT

Ricky goes to the front hood of the bus. He uses the rag to open up the hood and waves his hand as smoke spews out.

> RICKY
> Whoa!

Ricky continues to wave the smoke out of the engine. He starts to cough and sputter.

Nicholas, Sherry and Roxy get out of the bus with their flashlights to assist Ricky.

NICHOLAS

What's wrong with the motor?

Nicholas looks at the engine. The radiator is leaking water from several gunshot holes and one of the engine's rods has been damaged.

RICKY

The engine is shot. We must have blown out a rod.

NICHOLAS

Can you fix it?

RICKY

It's going to take me some time to change it out. Plus I also need some tools for this type of repair work.

ROXY

We don't have any tools on us.

SHERRY

Then, we'll have to search around the town then. Maybe we can find someone who can help us.

NICHOLAS

Let's split up then. Be back here in half an hour.

Nicholas, Roxy, Ricky and Sherry scatter around town to find tools.

EXT. MANUELA - NIGHT

The town is pitch black. The only light is moonlight and the light from the band's flashlights. The band members split up.

Sherry searches the town's Hardware Store and enters the unlocked store.

INT. HARRY'S HARDWARE STORE - NIGHT

Sherry tries to turn on the lights in the store, but nothing is on. She calls out for help.

SHERRY

Hello, is anyone there?

She searches the store with her flashlight only to find the entire store ransacked.

SHERRY

What happened here?

UNKNOWN POV

Someone... or some<u>thing</u>... watches Sherry from the shadows...

BACK TO SCENE

Sherry enters the large storage room of the hardware store.

INT. STORAGE ROOM - NIGHT

Sherry searches the storage room. She finds wooden bookshelves torn up and broken to pieces. Giant claw marks are embedded in the broken shelves. Open spilled paint cans are on the ground.

A rat startles her. She steps back, knocking a paint can out with her back foot by accident. She falls down and lands on her rear end. She slowly points her flashlight on the ceiling, only to find long bloody animal style claw paw prints.

Sherry points her flashlight in another direction. Only to find a dead rotten mutilated human corpse filled with maggots and cockroaches coming out of the head's rotted out eye sockets.

The right arm is ripped off -- as if it were bitten off by a large strange creature. The legs are completely gone, and rotten intestines ooze out of the ripped section left over of the corpse's stomach.

There is a giant bite mark on the corpse's neck, like something ripped out a large chunk of neck meat. The bite indentations show that whatever did this had large sharp teeth and was not human.

Sherry freaks out and runs out of the hardware store, and frantically runs and screams in shock back to the Metal Machine III.

EXT. MANUELA - NIGHT

Roxy looks for a place that has tools. She sees a garage and walks toward to the location. Then, she runs into Ricky from behind.

> ROXY
>
> Hell, you scared the shit out
> of me.
>
> RICKY
>
> Did you find anything?
>
> ROXY
>
> No. Everywhere in this town
> is empty. What happened to
> everyone?
>
> RICKY
>
> I don't know, but I don't like
> it. Let's just find what we
> need and get out of here.

Roxy points her flashlight at the garage.

> ROXY
>
> Look, it's an old auto garage.
>
> RICKY
>
> Let's check it out. Maybe we
> can find some tools.

Roxy and Ricky walk to the garage. The service door is locked. Roxy breaks the padlock with her right hand. They enter the garage.

INT. BLAZING JACK'S AUTO GARAGE AND REPAIR - NIGHT

Roxy searches for the light switch. She finds it and turns it on.

Ceiling fluorescent lights turn on. The garage is a spacious medium sized car garage with a high ceiling.

The place is filled with a few tool boxes, two car lifts, wiring, a couple welding torches, some rims, a row of tires, two gasoline cans, some air canisters, a box of road flares and a pack of cigarettes sitting on a wooden work shelf. There are dry oil stains on the cement floor.

There are two customized hot rod vehicles sitting in the garage:

One is a black 1960 Morris Minor Pickup truck detailed with hot flames and a psychobilly illustration of a devil head. Emblazoned on the side: "Speed Demon".

The other vehicle is a black 1951 Mercury Eight Lead Sled with zombie and skeleton decals. A painted logo identifies it as the "Ghoul Mobile".

RICKY

Whoa! Check it out.

Ricky goes to the Ghoul Mobile, while Roxy pulls the keys of each car from the key rack.

RICKY

It's a 1951 Mercury Eight Lead
Sled. Flathead V8 engine with
an F-R layout. Sweet!

Roxy gives the keys to Ricky. Then, she goes to the Speed Demon truck. Roxy is impressed by the ride.

ROXY

Look at this one. It's a 1960
Morris Minor Pickup. Fully
modified. My dad used to own
one of these when I was little.

Ricky opens the hood on the Mercury Eight.

RICKY

The engine looks like it's in
good condition.

Roxy opens the hood on the Morris Minor Pickup.

ROXY

Same here on this one. Both
of these cars must have been
restored by the shop owner.

Roxy goes inside her car to turn on the ignition. The truck starts. The engine
roars like a tiger. The gas gauge is full.

ROXY

The gas gauge is up. We got a
full tank.

Ricky starts his car. The engine roars like a bat out of hell. The gas gauge is
full.

RICKY

So is this one. Forget the
tools. This is better. Let's go.

Shit keys are even on the dash
board. We can just drive off.

EXT. BLAZING JACK'S AUTO GARAGE AND REPAIR - NIGHT

The Speed Demon and the Ghoul Mobile crash through the wooden garage
doors and drive back to the Metal Machine III.

EXT. THE METAL MACHINE III - MOMENTS LATER

Nicholas walks back to the Metal Machine III with a gas can and a toolbox
he has found in one of the empty buildings in the town.

Then, all of a sudden Sherry runs into Nicholas. She is in shock after what
she has just seen.

> SHERRY
>
> Nicky, let's get out of here!
>
> NICHOLAS
>
> What's wrong?
>
> SHERRY
>
> We're not alone. I just saw
> a human body ripped up in
> the hardware store. It looked
> like something literally ate it.
> Something not human and I
> don't mean like us.
>
> NICHOLAS
>
> Calm down! You're freaking
> out!
>
> SHERRY
>
> No, I'm not! Let's go.
>
> NICHOLAS
>
> Look, we're stuck here. Until
> Ricky and Roxy come back to
> fix the engine, there's noth-
> ing we can do.

Then, Sherry and Nicholas hear the hot rod cars' engines roar. The vehicles pull up, revealing Ricky and Roxy doing a tripping figure eight turn and slide on the dirt road.

Ricky is psyched up and loving it.

> RICKY
>
> Hey guys! Check it out. We got us some new toys to play with.
>
> NICHOLAS
>
> Cool! We're back in business. Let's roll.

Nicholas and Sherry go back to The Metal Machine III to get their equipment.

Ricky and Roxy turns off their engines on their vehicles to assist loading the band's equipment and instruments.

Then, suddenly they hear the motorcycle engines of the Cortez Cobras.

> RICKY
>
> Hey Rox, you hear that?
>
> ROXY
>
> Shit. It's them.

They go back to their cars and fire up the engines.

Nicholas grabs two of the guitars out of the bus, While Sherry grabs Roxy's keyboard and puts it in the back seat of the Mercury Eight.

In the distance Roxy sees the Cortez Cobras' headlights on the road.

> ROXY
>
> They're coming!

The Cortez Cobras are now twenty members strong. The sounds and echoes get louder as they ride into town.

NICHOLAS

That's our cue. Let's go!

RICKY

What about the rest of the
gear?!

NICHOLAS

Screw the gear.

RICKY

Forget that! Grab the cash!

NICHOLAS

Crap!

Nicholas quickly runs back to the bus.

INT. THE METAL MACHINE III - NIGHT

Nicholas runs into the bus to grab the two duffel bags of cash from the
footlocker. He quickly zips the bags open to make sure is that the money is still
there and quickly zips them both back up and runs out of the bus with them.

EXT. THE METAL MACHINE III - CONTINUOUS

Ricky opens the back trunk of the Ghoul Mobile.

Nicholas quickly runs to the Ghoul Mobile and puts the duffel bags in the
trunk.

Ricky shuts the trunk and locks it.

ROXY

Come on guys! Hurry!

Nicholas and Ricky hop into the Ghoul Mobile. Ricky is the driver. Sherry
hops into the passenger seat of the Speed Demon with Roxy driving.

The Cortez Cobras' motorcycle engines are getting louder and louder.

Ricky and Roxy starts up their vehicles. Their wheels screech, burning rubber. Flames shoot out of the tailpipe of the Mercury Eight Lead Sled and also
the Morris Minor Pick Up.

The two hot rod vehicles speed off to the open road with Ricky leading the way heading toward the power plant.

EXT. MANUELA - NIGHT

The Cortez Cobras arrive in town with Barabbas leading. They see the band's fresh tire tracks in their front motorcycle lights.

Barabbas and DIO, 29, lean, half-Spanish and half-white, smell the scent of the tire tracks. Dio has a mullet and a clean shaven face.

> BARABBAS
> These tire tracks are fresh.
> They're heading to the old
> power plant on route 82.
>
> DIO
> (to Barabbas; points)
> That way.
>
> BARABBAS
> (to the Cobras)
> Come on!

Barabbas leads the Cortez Cobras to the power plant. They are all speeding like hell.

EXT. ABANDONED PLANT - NIGHT

The Midnight Freaks drive towards a massive abandoned fossil fuel propane power plant. The only lights around are the headlights of their vehicles and the moonlight.

The architecture of this power plant goes back to the 1950s. It is a giant 100-foot building connected with three 50-foot warehouse style building, storage houses, a giant outdoor cargo yard, possibly for storing oversize and overlarge service equipment, and a huge junkyard filled with rusted scrap metal.

It also contains high rusted steel gates, giant pipe lines, giant vents, generator silos, and circular rusted metal chimney stacks.

The plant is located in the open countryside with dead grass and brick red dirt.

The Midnight Freaks pull over. The main entrance gate says with a large sign, "CONDEMNED - DO NOT ENTER - TRESPASSERS WILL BE PROSECUTED." The sign is tagged with lots of graffiti. The gate is heavily chained up with a large rusty padlock.

Nicholas gets out of the car from the passenger's side door, pulls out his revolver and shoots the old lock off. He pulls the chains off and opens the gate and enters the power plant yard. The Midnight Freaks drive through the gate to enter the main yard of the plant and stop to wait for Nicholas. Nicholas closes and re-chains the gate, tying the chain in a knot.

He catches up and hops back in the Ghoul Mobile leaving the shattered padlock on the ground.

The Midnight Freaks park their vehicles in the scrap yard behind a pile of scrap metal, debris, flatbed trailers. There are also a few rundown fuel trucks, and an old vintage 1950s rusted steel bungalow trailer office.

The Midnight Freaks run to the main building which has been severely damaged, with years of rust. They use their flashlights as they come to the entrance door.

They look up and see rows of huge massive dusty glass windows, many of them broken or shattered from previous acts of vandalism. The roof is covered up by old thick sheet metal.

The outside of the main power plant is battered and heavily rusted, covered with dirt and grime from years of neglect. There are also dried water stains on the windows from every rainstorm that has fallen on this metallic mausoleum.

There are two huge rusted sliding doors at the main entrance door leading into the main section of the plant. Ricky and Nicholas each grab a door handle and open the huge rusted sliding doors.

The doors creak open due to their bearings not being oiled for years. Both young men struggle to open a small gap to squeeze everyone in.

NICHOLAS
Get inside, quick.

Roxy and Sherry enter the main work floor quickly. Then, Ricky and Nicholas enter. Finally they close the door.

INT. ABANDONED PLANT - NIGHT

The room is pitch black and silent. The Midnight Freaks turn on their flashlights.

> NICHOLAS
> Everybody stick together!
> SHERRY
> What's the plan?
> NICHOLAS
> First, let's find a power switch
> to get some light in here.
> SHERRY
> What about the cobras?
> They'll see us.
> NICHOLAS
> We can't stay here in the dark.
> If they want their money,
> they're going to have to come
> and get it.

Ricky uses his psychic abilities to find the power switch. He finds a massive steel stairway leading up to a catwalk.

He finds a medium-sized power switch at the bottom of the stairway that lights up the main work floor.

> RICKY
> Found it!

Ricky turns on the power switch, but sparks fly off. Some of the hanging ceiling lights from the high rafters turn on, but two of them pop and explode. The girls are startled by this.

INT. ABANDONED PLANT - MAIN WORK FLOOR - NIGHT

The main work floor is surrounded with a network of two-story level cat-walks. There are multiple railings and massive rusty copper piping that runs from the ceiling down the walls.

The piping on the walls connects to an enormous propane tank sphere, with "Flammable" and "Danger" on it. Next to the tank sphere is a large set of gas-powered water heater boilers.

The work floor is layered with ladders all over from top to bottom. The room looks like a highway maze of metal and steel. The skylight above consists of dusty windows covered by steel bars. The main work floor is full of dust and cobwebs, which hang in the stale musty air.

The ground floor is layered with trash and scrap debris of burnt metal. Mice and roaches crawl on the floor of this dilapidated dump.

> RICKY
>
> Whoa! This place is huge.
>
> NICHOLAS
>
> We should hide out here to be safe, then we can get back on the road in the morning.
>
> ROXY
>
> What is this place?
>
> RICKY
>
> I think it's an old power plant. Looks like it's been abandoned for years.
>
> SHERRY
>
> So what now?
>
> ROXY
>
> Anyone have a pistol on them... besides Nicholas?
>
> RICKY
>
> (sarcastic)

We left them in the trunk
back in the bus. Hauling ass
without a plan as usual.

NICHOLAS
(annoyed)
Ricky, shut up.
(checks his pistol)
I still got mine... but I only
have a few shots left.

ROXY
Do you think they'll find us?

Nicholas keeps his cool.

NICHOLAS
I don't know, but we bet-
ter lay low for a few hours.
Maybe they'll go away.

The group hears strange scratching coming beneath the floor.

SHERRY
What was that?

NICHOLAS
I don't know. Just keep quiet
so no one will know we're
here. Hide.

EXT. ABANDONED PLANT - MOMENTS LATER

The Cortez Cobras arrive in front of the power plant.

KUDOS, 35 year old, a shortish and very muscular Mexican, with a long goatee, stands there. He wears a skull bandanna wrapped around his head. He has rows of different types of tattoos on his arms.

Underneath Kudos' biker vest is a black t-shirt. He pulls out a double-barreled sawed-off shotgun and fires at the chains, blowing them to pieces. He kicks the doors of the gate open.

The Cortez Cobras drive their bikes through the front entrance yard. They park their bikes in front of the main entrance and cock their sawed-off shotguns and pistols.

They go to entrance door and open it. When they look inside, the Midnight Freaks are nowhere to be found.

Barabbas leads the other bikers into the large work floor.

INT. ABANDONED PLANT - MAIN WORK FLOOR - NIGHT

Barabbas and the Cortez Cobras walk as a group fearlessly.

> BARABBAS
>
> Come on out putos!

The Midnight Freaks hide behind the large spherical propane tank, layered with pipes, valves, and mid-sized pressure knobs.

Nothing happens. The work floor remains silent.

The Cortez Cobras move closer into the heart of the work floor, while the main entrance door is left open.

> LIPS
>
> Maybe they took off.

Barabbas looks back and forth.

> BARABBAS
>
> No, they're still here.

An eerie strange breeze blows quickly through the room. Bizarre echoes hum through the dreary place, taking the Cobras by surprise.

KUDOS

What was that?

LIPS

They're pulling something.

All the lights on work floor start to flicker rapidly. The remaining non-damaged glass windows begin to shatter on their own.

DIO

What the hell?!

The pressure gauges on the water heaters begin to go out of control with steam blasting out and whistling. The valve knobs start twisting and turning on their own, until they blast off.

The Cobras duck the flying objects, while in fear they fire their guns in different areas of the plant to destroy this unseen force.

Tons of sparks begin to short circuit off the electric generator equipment. Flying bullets from the Cobra's guns hit random pipes, equipment.

Suddenly the large propane gas tank gets hit, shooting out a yellow flammable gas. The gas has the look and color of mustard gas.

The Midnight Freaks super jump out from behind the large methane gas tank to the side to avoid being shot.

Barabbas sees the gas and immediately commands his troops to cease fire to prevent an explosion from happening... but it is too late.

BARABBAS

Stop shooting!! You'll hit a...

At the exact same moment a Cobra member fires his single barreled shot gun in the air -- the muzzle flash ignites the yellow flammable gas from the large gas sphere tank causing it to EXPLODE!!!

The raging fireball blast kills two of the Cobra members who are near the tank but not too close.

The explosion sets them on fire -- the two Cobra members burn and scream in agony running around while they cook, then they fall to the ground dead from the intense pain. Their bodies are burnt to a crisp.

At the same time, when the blast occurs the other Cobras, the Midnight Freaks, and Barabbas leap to the ground for cover. The fire dies down though still burning from the leftover methane gas.

No time for confrontation, both groups immediately run to the entrance door to get out before the entire plant is set ablaze.

Suddenly, the main entrance doors slide shut and lock on their own.

The Midnight Freaks and the Cortez Cobras back up surprised.

Barabbas struggles with all his great strength to open the door but it is sealed shut and does not even budge.

> NICHOLAS
> What are you waiting for?!
> Open the door!

Barabbas grunts.

> BARABBAS
> I can't!

All of a sudden the high panel windows steel shade guards slam down one after another, fast like a set of falling dominos, until the whole work floor room is locked down.

The only remaining light comes from the ceiling lights that are flickering.

> ROXY
> We're trapped!

The sounds of demonic and demented evil laughter, like from an insane asylum, pierce the room taking everyone off their guard in shock and fear. Then, the evil stops for a brief minute and dies.

LIPS
What the fuck is happening?!

The room starts to hum with the sounds of generators starting on their own by invisible demon spirits, and insane wicked evil laughing.

RICKY
It's Kane man! He's back!
NICHOLAS
Bullshit!
RICKY
Then, what the fuck is that?!

The ceiling and wall pipes burst open like a broken fire hydrant, gushing out dark red blood everywhere, spraying down the Midnight Freaks and the Cortez Cobras and knocking them to the floor.

The blast spraying power of the multiple broken pipes is like a fire hose -- blood sprays everywhere: the walls, floors, machinery, the stairways, and the heater tanks. Everyone is soaked to the bone, drenched in blood.

The ceiling fire sprinklers go off supernaturally, spraying out slightly thick black blood, that rains down on the victims. Then blood puts out the burning gas tank and the fire is quenched.

The Midnight Freaks and the Cortez Cobras scramble to their feet in the chaos as the gushing blood from all the pipes and the sprinkler system dies down and stops. The evil laughing pauses for a beat... a second of silence.

The Cobras and the Midnight Freaks are totally freaked out.

Ricky, overcome by the smell, vomits on the ground.

Everywhere gets away from Ricky and his vomit.

LIPS
Oh shit, man!

Barabbas spots the biker who caused the explosion and blows his head off with his pistol in anger. He wipes the blood off his face and hair.

> RICKY
> What is this?!
> BARABBAS
> Blood.

Barabbas points his gun directly at Ricky's head -- Nicholas points his pistol at Barabbas' skull.

Several of the remaining Cobras point their weapons at Nicholas and Ricky. Lips and Kudos hold Sherry and Roxy with their strong arms while pointing their guns at them. Lips holds Sherry, while Kudos holds Roxy.

The Cobras have the Midnight Freaks in their mercy. Then, all of a sudden, Lips and Kudos' guns start to supernaturally melt like wax burning off a hot candle. They drop the guns to one side, away from their captors.

> BARABBAS
> You're the one who doing
> this!
> NICHOLAS
> No, you are!

Roxy's sixth sense kicks in and her eyes glow yellow. She senses a strong dark spiritual presence.

> ROXY
> There's something else here
> besides us.
> KUDOS
> (looks at Roxy)
> Oh shit, look at her eyes man.
> Es Diabla!

NICHOLAS
(to Kudos)
No it's a gift she's recently
developed.
KUDOS
How do you know?
NICHOLAS
Because I made them all,
idiot!

Kudos vamps out.

KUDOS
Fuck you!

Kudos runs to attack Nicholas but Nicholas punches him in the face knocking him down.

Kudos gets up to attack but Barabbas restrains him.

BARABBAS
The girl is right. Something
else is causing this.
KUDOS
Hey, I'm on your side!

BARABBAS
Back off!

Barabbas lets Kudos go. Kudos backs off knowing his place.

Barabbas and Nicholas lower their pistols as they know that something else is here that wants to get them.

BARABBAS
There's something here, that
shouldn't be.
RICKY
Maybe we're seeing things.
BARABBAS
No.

Suddenly, an invisible DEMON SPIRIT speaks.

DEMON SPIRIT (V.O.)
Trapped, trapped... trapped
like rats.

The Demon Spirit laughs insanely with unholy madness.

Barabbas and Nicholas' pistols supernaturally melt halfway in their hands.
The two men drop the guns on the floor, while watching them melt in puddles
of black tar. Then, the all of the Cobras' guns melt into tar. Each drops their gun
to the ground.

Roxy and Sherry break away from Lips and Kudos and rejoin Nicholas and
Ricky.

The Demon Spirit stops laughing.

The Cobras and The Midnight Freaks have no weapons to fight or defend
themselves with.

LIPS
What the fuck was that!
ROXY
Demons.
SHERRY
You mean ghosts right?

ROXY

No, when a human dies their souls or spirits will go straight into the afterlife. Demons are different -- these are evil spirits. Some call them fallen angels, others, disembodied spirits.

NICHOLAS

This place must be haunted.

ROXY

It's not haunted. Listen to me. All of you. These things are not ghosts. Demons are creatures made up as spirits. Ghosts are people who have died. If a living person tries to bring a dead person's spirit back by occult means, a demon will come in disguise to fool the summoner in the form of a ghost.

BARABBAS

Why?

ROXY

To possess and kill the person for their soul. It gives them their power.

KUDOS

She's lying.

ROXY

No I'm not. I can spiritually sense things like this.

BARABBAS
(to his men)
They're vamps like us. She's
on the level.

ROXY
I had a girlfriend I knew back
in school who accidentally
got involved into devil shit
like this.

RICKY
(to Roxy)
Didn't you tell us that she
died? I thought it was because
of drugs.

ROXY
I heard rumors it was because
of this. I didn't want to believe it. But now... I do.

NICHOLAS
(to the group)
How the hell do we stop
these things?

DEMON SPIRIT (V.O.)
You don't....DIIIIEEEEE!!!!!!

Suddenly, random members of the Cortez Cobras levitate into the air. Two
of the members get thrown like rag dolls to different walls of the room -- their
heads are smashed open, their brains splattering against the walls.

The other members of the Cobras are levitated, then ripped to pieces by
invisible demon spirits. Their legs and arms are torn right off and the torsos are
ripped in half, their organs and intestines falling to the ground with their dead
bodies, bathing the floor with a giant pond of red crimson and blood.

The walls bleed with blood flowing down them like a water fall, increasing the terror.

SHERRY

Let's get out of here!

The Midnight Freaks stick together as a group with the survivor Cortez Cobras, Barabbas, Lips, Kudos and Dio.

The earth shakes violently with a powerful earthquake, caused by the demon spirits. Part of the work floor collapses right underneath their feet. The survivors fall through the hole in the floor.

INT. BASEMENT LEVEL - BONE PIT - MOMENTS LATER

The group lands in a dark room on top of different piles of festering human corpses and bones that have been torn to pieces. The floor is drenched in pools of blood.

Everyone is dazed from the fall, but otherwise okay and not injured. However, none of them can see anything.

KUDOS

Uggh! What the hell?

NICHOLAS

Is everyone alright?

ROXY

I think so. Hey, do you guys feel that.

SHERRY

I can't see anything.

LIPS

Anyone smell that?

DIO

It smells like rotten eggs.

BARABBAS

Anyone got a light?

> RICKY

I do.

Everyone gets up in the dark as Ricky flicks on his Zippo cigarette lighter for everyone to see. The lighter reveals the horror before them of the countless human victims who have been slaughtered in this cursed place.

> NICHOLAS

Jesus!!!

Sherry's spooked.

> SHERRY
> There is no way a vampire could have done this. No way.
> ROXY
> Looks like our hosts' handi-work.
> KUDOS
> Did those things do this?
> ROXY
> You all saw what they did back up there.

Kudos looks down at the piles of dead flesh.

> KUDOS
> These poor bastards look like something ate them. Damn.
> NICHOLAS
> Bet these were the same things that ate that corpse back in Manuela.

SHERRY

Couldn't something else have done this? How can a demon eat someone if it has no body?

ROXY

Demons can kill people, being what they are, but they can also take physical form, through magical rites. Certain ceremonial spells and incantations can make it happen.

Barabbas checks the area out.

BARABBAS

Forget the school lesson. We have to find a way to fight these things before they try to attack us again.

(points)

But that does not let you fuckers off the hook.

Barabbas in his vampiric form grabs Roxy holding her in a tight head lock about to break her neck.

NICHOLAS

Let her go!

BARABBAS

I want my money back!

               NICHOLAS
         You'll get it back. I promise.
               BARABBAS
         I don't trust you.
               NICHOLAS
         You have my word. Just let us
         go.

The lights on the wall go on, flickering, while some pop and shatter. Showing the demonic infestation.

               DIO
         Shit!
               LIPS
         Forget the money! Let's get
         the hell out of here.
               BARABBAS
         Shut up.

Barabbas thinks for a second then makes his move.

               BARABBAS
         Alright. Here's the deal, I get
         the money back, you all go
         free. I don't, you're all dead.
         Get it.
               NICHOLAS
         Deal.

               BARABBAS
         Good.

Barabbas lets Roxy go. She backs up to where Sherry is standing. Barabbas changes back to his human form.

The Midnight Freaks and the other Cortez Cobras revert back to their human form with the tension going down.

The group starts walking down the dim-lit hall following Barabbas. The light fades in and out.

> SHERRY
>
> So how do we get out of here?

> BARABBAS
>
> We make our own way out,
> that's how. Come on. What's
> your names?
>> NICHOLAS
>> I'm Nicholas.
>> ROXY
>> Roxy.
>> RICKY
>> Ricky.
>> SHERRY
>> And I'm Sherry.

Barabbas turns his head to the side to point out his biker comrades.

> BARABBAS
>
> I'm Barabbas. This is Lips,
> Kudos, and that's Dio.

The Midnight Freaks nod in greeting.

> BARABBAS
>
> If we want to get out of here
> in one piece, we are going to

have to work together wheth-
er we like it or not.

NICHOLAS

For now, anyway.

BARABBAS

You're smart. Keep it that
way.

(to the other Midnight Freaks)
All of you.

SHERRY

Fine.

RICKY

No problem.

ROXY

Okay, just don't touch me
again.

BARABBAS

Promise.

ROXY

We'll see.

BARABBAS

When we get out of here,
everyone goes their separate
ways. Until then, listen to me
if you all want to survive.

RICKY

And what are you going
to teach us? You special or
something?

BARABBAS

Yeah. I've lived this way for
more years than all you have.

A hundred and fifty-five. Been
in worse scrapes than this.
I used to be a captain in the
army. The Spanish-American
War. Long time ago.
> ROXY

You're kidding.
> BARABBAS

No I'm not. Know this -- a
vampire gets stronger as they
age. Just like fine wine. Some,
though, get their powers faster than others, like your chick
friend there.
> SHERRY

Meaning?
BARABBAS
You're all new meat. I can
smell it.

Barabbas turns to Nicholas.

> BARABBAS

Except you pretty boy.
> NICHOLAS

Fine. You know us, want a
medal tough guy?
> BARABBAS

Watch it kid, or--

Out of nowhere an eerie ghostly voice echoes through the hallway.

WOMAN'S VOICE (V.O.)

Help me...

The group sees a spirit of a young blonde woman dressed in rocker clothes run through from the left wall into the right side of the hallway.

BARABBAS

(spooked)

You see that?

Above them, unseen by the group, two lean gangly reptilian ITSUTHA DEMONS materialize. Quadruped and long-legged, they have ominous glowing yellow eyes and razor-sharp teeth.

The creatures silently crawl right above our heroes' heads with their hideous snake-like tongues coming out. One of the creatures drips saliva on Dio, walking behind the others.

Dio wipes the saliva from his face. Surprised, he slowly looks up.

DIO

What the fuck?

The twin demons spring down like hunting spiders from their webs on Dio, pulling him right up in the air.

DIO

AHHHHHHHHH!!!

Nicholas quickly turns around along with the others -- all witness the horror as the demon rips Dio apart and eats him alive.

NICHOLAS

RUN!!!

INT. HALLWAY BASEMENT LEVEL - NIGHT

The group takes off running through the halls around intersecting corners and turns. The two demons chase after them on the floor, running on all fours like rampaging animals gone wild.

The humans lose them... but not for long. Nicholas finds a heavy steel door on the right side of the hallway. He opens the steel door revealing a large office room.

NICHOLAS

This way, hurry.

Everyone follows Nicholas' command as they rush to get in.

Sherry and Roxy enter first. Ricky, Lips and Kudos enter second. Nicholas and Barabbas enter last. They shut the steel door and bolt the locks.

The two Itsutha Demons arrive outside and commence trying to break through the door.

INT. OLD DILAPIDATED LARGE OFFICE - NIGHT

Nicholas and Barabbas hold the steel door to make sure that the Itsutha Demons don't break through. The rest of the group stands there watching.

The office has rusty metal desks and file cabinets. The walls are moldy and dirty. A broken typewriter sits on the desk. There are old papers on the floor everywhere. The lights are dimly-lit.

The Itsutha Demons relentless try to break down the door.

NICHOLAS

Wait a minute! What are we
running for?

BARABBAS

(agreeing)

Right. Let's fuck them up!

NICHOLAS

We need a plan.

BARABBAS

Stand back. I can take them.

> NICHOLAS
>
> No, all of us can. Everyone, spread out to the sides of the room. When we open that door, we're going to dog pile those things and tear them apart.

The group splits up on the sides of the wall, vamps out and readies to attack.

Nicholas gives out the command.

> NICHOLAS
>
> Get ready! One... two... THREE!!!

Nicholas and Barabbas open the door wide open. The Itsutha Demons ram right into the walls. One of the demons' heads gets stuck right in the wall. It struggle to get out.

The other demon tries to attack Barabbas, but Barabbas knocks the demon out cold. Barabbas stomps and crushes the demon's head with his right foot.

The other members of the group rips the other demon apart as it screams in agony until it's killed. Green blood spurts on the floor and walls.

Everyone is panting and breathing heavily from the running and killing.

> SHERRY
>
> Piece of shit!

Sherry rips the back of the spine of the dead Itsutha demon's head stuck in the wall.

Sherry claws through the wall.

SHERRY

How do you like that!

Ricky grabs her shoulders to calm her down.

RICKY

Sherry! It's dead! Cool it!

Sherry calms down, though still pissed off.

BARABBAS

What's wrong with her?

Nicholas speaks calmly.

NICHOLAS

Sherry got raped by a crooked
cop a week ago. She's been a
wreck ever since.

LIPS

That sucks.

NICHOLAS

We took care of that bastard
but good. Killed his sorry ass
and stuck him on a pike.

BARABBAS

You mean Mitch Barton,
right? That hillbilly fuck? ...
So you're the ones who killed
the sheriff?

NICHOLAS

Yeah... you got something to
say about it?!

BARABBAS

You all got balls. I'll give you
that. You did me a favor.

RICKY

How?

BARABBAS

Barton always was an asshole.
The redneck never wanted to
play the game of crime, the
right way. Not a team player,
you could say.

NICHOLAS

You're welcome.

Then, a young woman's voice cries for help.

WOMAN'S VOICE (V.O.)

Is anyone there?! Help me!

The group hears the woman screaming from the ground air conditioning
vent.

ROXY

Where are you?

WOMAN'S VOICE (V.O.)

I'm trapped in the boiler
room. Help me!

ROXY

Where is the boiler room?

WOMAN'S VOICE (V.O.)

Right beneath you. I can hear
you from down here. Hurry.

> ROXY
>
> Hold on, we'll get you out of
> there.

> BARABBAS
>
> (to Roxy)
> It's another one of those
> things' tricks.

Sherry speaks up.

> SHERRY
>
> No it's not. Someone's down
> there.

> LIPS
>
> B., you can't let that girl die
> down there.

> BARABBAS
>
> How can we be sure?

> NICHOLAS
>
> That's the chance we are go-
> ing to have to take.

Barabbas goes next to the air vent gate on the floor.

> BARABBAS
>
> Alright... stand back, let's get
> her out.

Calm now, the group reverts back to their human forms.

Barabbas then grabs the air vent gate and rips it out.

One-by-one the group enters through the air vent and drops into the boiler room.

INT. BOILER ROOM - NIGHT

The boiler room is dimly-lit and cold. There are large pipes, small pipes, valves, a broken boiler tank, a ramp and chains.

The group drops down on the floor. Only to find out that the room is cold as death's icy touch.

Ricky wraps his body with his arms and rubs his arms repeatedly to keep himself warm. The others begin to shiver, breathing out mist as they take each breath. The room is so cold that it might as well be frozen.

> RICKY
>
> Damn! Why is it so cold in here?
>
> ROXY
>
> It's the demons. They're doing this.
>
> RICKY
>
> Man it's cold! I'm freezing.

Roxy is annoyed by Ricky's complaining.

> ROXY
>
> Shut up, Ricky.

Barabbas is hardcore. Built like a machine, he's able to take the cold like it's nothing.

> BARABBAS
>
> Both of you, shut up.
>
> WOMAN'S VOICE (V.O.)
>
> Help me! I am over here by the pipes!

The group finds a young woman, BETH, mid-20s, shoulder-length blonde hair, wearing bell-bottom blue jeans, light blue jeans jacket, a button up white long sleeve shirt, tennis shoes and a ruby ring on her right ring finger. She is the innocent girl next door.

Her arms and legs are tied up with electrical wires. She is lying on the ground next to the railings.

ROXY

Hang on.

Roxy unties the bindings on the young woman's wrist.
Sherry goes over to Roxy to aid her as she unties the young woman's bound legs.

SHERRY

I'll help you.

BETH

Thank you all so much!

Nicholas and Ricky go over to help her to her feet.

NICHOLAS

Steady, easy there. You alright?

BETH

I'm okay.

RICKY

What happened to you? How
did you get here?

BETH

My name is Beth Madison. I
was driving out to Manuela
to see my uncle for a few days
to help him with repainting
his business. The night I got

there, I found the whole town deserted.

NICHOLAS

How did you end up here?

BETH

I went to my uncle's hardware store to see if he was there. When I got inside I saw that his body was ripped to pieces. Then this monster -- I don't how to describe it -- attacked me. I must have passed out from being so scared and when I woke up I found my-self tied up down here.

ROXY

What did this thing look like?

BETH

Like something out of a nightmare, the kind of crea-ture you see in horror mov-ies. It had these horns coming out of its head, burning red eyes that looked like fire... it looked almost goat-like, it was taller than anything I have ever seen before. Scared the hell out of me.

SHERRY

We saw the town the same as you did. Monsters we didn't see, but when we got here,

we've seen just about every
creepy thing.

> BETH
> How did you all get here?

> BARABBAS
> It's complicated.

> ROXY
> The important thing is to
> find a way to get out of here.

Lips and Kudos speaks up.

> LIPS
> Can we get the hell out of
> here now, before those things
> come back?!

> KUDOS
> (in Spanish)
> Barabbas, homes. Let's go!

The group is about to leave, but Beth speaks up.

> BETH
> Wait! I heard other people
> screaming down here.

Barabbas gets aggravated.

> BARABBAS
> And what the hell do you
> want us to do about it? We
> already had one of our own

get torn up by two of those
things.
                NICHOLAS
Hey! Your guys. Not ours.

Barabbas and Nicholas have an eye-to-eye confrontation.

                BARABBAS
Want to do something about
it?
                NICHOLAS
Yeah. The right thing.
                BARABBAS
You kids want to play hero?
Fine! Be my guest then.
That's not my problem.
        (to Lips and Kudos)
Let's go, boys.

The Cortez Cobras leave the Midnight Freaks and Beth to find another
way out on their own. They find a steel door, open it and walk out of the boiler
room.

                ROXY
Where the hell do you think
you're going?!
                BARABBAS (O.S.)
I only look out for two types
of people. Me and my boys.
And you ain't them.
                ROXY
Bastard!

SHERRY
Well fuck you, then!

The Midnight Freaks and Beth head to the steel door.

Suddenly, pools of steaming black blood and tar ooze out of the floor. The pools starts to bubble and transform into blood, bone and flesh, forming four demonic beasts.

The creatures are a cross between goats and horses. Their appearances are disfigured. They have anthropomorphic humanoid bodies with seven goat horns on their heads, six human-like eyes on their heads and chests.

They have human-like faces with razor sharp fangs, multiple human-like arms and claws for limbs, and have furry large satyr-like legs with giant hoofs and small bushy tails.

These unholy demons are ten feet tall. They are called YORUBA DEMONS.

Beth turns around and sees the Yoruba Demons. She screams.

Ricky turns around and sees them.

RICKY
What the...?
NICHOLAS
Run!

The Midnight Freaks and Beth run to the steel door but it slams shut on its own.

The lights buzz in and out.

Nicholas tries to open the steel door but it won't budge.

BETH
Open the door! Hurry!
NICHOLAS
I'm trying!
RICKY
Come on! Come on!

Nicholas tries to knock down the door with his rage and strength, but it's no use.

The Yoruba Demons attack the band members and Beth. Beth runs to hide behind one of the pipes, terrified of what she is seeing.

One of the demons grabs and picks up Sherry by her waist and bites into her shoulder. She screams in agony.

At the same time the three other demons close in and try to claw at Ricky, Roxy, and Nicholas, blocking their path from helping Sherry.

NICHOLAS

Sherry!

Nicholas is helpless to help Sherry.

In a last-ditch effort, Sherry vamps out in anger, eyes burning with rage like hell. She slugs the Yoruba demon in the face, dazing it.

Then, using both of her hands despite being in pain and wounded, she rips out the demon's two main front horns on its head.

Blood gushes out of the creature's head. It screams in rage, dropping Sherry to the ground. The creature holds its hands over its bleeding head while in pain.

Sherry gets up and slashes open the creature's stomach, gutting the demon's intestines, pulling them out. Then she kicks the demon in the stomach as it falls to the floor dead.

Roxy vamps out. With her super speed, she zips around two of the other Yoruba demons to distract them -- Ricky and Nicholas vamp out and jump on the demons' backs and force the demons to fall on the floor.

They rip off the demons limbs, blood splattering on the floor, and kill them.

The last demon backs off and opens a portal on the wall as red blood flows around it. It flees through the portal, and the portal closes up.

The dead demons lie on the floor and the battle is over for now. Or so they think.

Behind the wall, the bandmembers hear the demon scream.

CRASH! The last Yoruba demon crashes through the granite concrete wall of the boiler room. Creating a large hole.

Emerging from the hole in the wall are the Cortez Cobras, all vamped out. Barabbas with Lips and Kudos by his side.

Barabbas uses a long, thin, sharp broken metal pipe and impales the demon through the middle eye on its forehead -- killing it instantly.

Then, they see the dead demons on the floor that the band members killed. All of the dead demon corpses melt into black tar ooze, and evaporate into black mist.

> NICHOLAS
> What the hell?
> BARABBAS
> I thought you little pukes
> could use a hand after all.
> SHERRY
> You left us! Why come back?
> BARABBAS
> Because I felt like it.

Beth is still hiding behind the pipe, horrified.
The group turns their attention to Beth.

> BETH
> Get away from me!!!
> BARABBAS
> Hey kid, do us a favor... shut
> up! We're not going to kill
> you, alright?

Nicholas pushes Barabbas in disgust and goes to Beth.
The Cortez Cobras laugh at Beth. Kudos gives Barabbas a high five.
Nicholas morphs into his human form, trying to reason with Beth.

NICHOLAS
Are you hurt?

Beth is still in shock at what she has just seen. The band members morph into their human forms. Sherry's wound heals up on its own, and she and Ricky try to assist Nicholas.

BETH
What are you?
NICHOLAS
What do you think?
BETH
You're vampires.
SHERRY
(to Nicholas)
Nicky, ease off!
(to Beth)
We're not the type you think.
Don't worry, we're not going
to hurt you.
BETH
This is not happening!

Roxy assists her band mates to help Beth.

ROXY
Yes it is. Just don't ask! It
would take too long to
explain.
BETH
What about them?

Beth points at the Cortez Cobras.

RICKY
(to Beth)
They're just a bunch of ass-
holes. Don't worry about
them.
Lips and Kudos answer
Beth's question.
LIPS
We're just messing with you.
KUDOS
Lighten up chica!

Lips and Kudos laugh.
Nicholas offers Beth his hand to help her up.

NICHOLAS
Come on, let's get you out of
here.

Beth reluctantly grabs Nicholas' hand and gets up. She hugs Nicholas and
stays by his side, while Sherry looks at them together with jealously.

NICHOLAS
(to Barabbas)
Why did you jerks come
back?!
BARABBAS
Because, I keep my word. It
was wrong to ditch you.
NICHOLAS
You just want your money
back.

BARABBAS
Maybe, but you all handled
those things pretty good by
yourselves. For that, you get
my respect.

The Midnight Freaks and the Cortez Cobras have officially formed an alliance.

NICHOLAS
Let's move before something
else jumps us.

INT. HALLWAY BASEMENT LEVEL - NIGHT
The surviving group walks in the piped hallways.

NICHOLAS
Roxy, do you feel anything?
Can you sense anything
around us?

Roxy pauses for a second and closes her eyes.

ROXY
No, nothing. There's nothing
here.
NICHOLAS
Ricky, what do you see?

Ricky pauses and psychically senses for a way to get out of the basement level.

> RICKY
>
> There is a generator room,
> two flights up. I can see
> where the stairs are at. Follow
> me, quickly.

The surviving group quickly runs to the stairway leading to the generator room.

INT. STAIRWAY LEVEL - NIGHT

Ricky leads the survivors to the stairway area. They go upstairs. Sherry and Roxy are behind Ricky. Barabbas, Lips and Kudos are behind them. The last of the group behind them is Nicholas and Beth.

> NICHOLAS
>
> Sorry for not introducing
> ourselves. I'm Nicholas, but
> my friends call me Nicky.
>   (motions to the others)
> That is Ricky, Roxy and Sherry.
>
> BETH
>
> What about you're other
> friends there?

Barabbas turns to Beth.

> BARABBAS
>
> Friends wouldn't necessarily
> be the right word. More like...
> associates gone sour.

Nicholas turns to Beth.

> NICHOLAS
> Beth, how long have you
> been here?
>
> BETH
> I don't remember. It could
> have been days for all I know.

Sherry, listening in, has a suspicious look on her face. She doesn't quite trust this innocent-seeming girl.

> SHERRY
> How did you survive being
> down here, while everyone
> else was killed?

Before Beth can answer Sherry's question, Ricky finds a doorway.

> RICKY
> This is it.

Ricky tries to open the door but it is too rusted.

> RICKY
> Damn it! It's locked!

Lips cracks his knuckles and comes to aid Ricky.

> LIPS
> Relax kid, let me show you
> how a real man does it.

Lips kicks the steel door open. Then, he pats Ricky on the shoulder, smiles and enters.

Kudos looks at Ricky and chuckles at him. He enters the room.

KUDOS
(messing with Ricky)
Weak sauce.

Barabbas just silently enters the room.

RICKY
Weak sauce, my ass.

Ricky enters. Roxy shakes her head with an "Oh brother" look while the rest of them enter the room.

INT. GENERATOR ROOM - NIGHT

It is a giant work floor room filled with obsolete, run-down, old electrical generator equipment.

The survivors are finally at the ground floor.

LIPS
Thank God!

NICHOLAS
All we have to do is find another main door and we're
out of here.

Then by surprise, the power goes off in the entire plant. The lights go dark and the group is separated. The plant fades away, leaving only an invisible maze of darkness and pockets of light.

INT. MAZE OF DARKNESS (SHERRY'S FEAR) - NIGHT

Sherry tries to find her friends as she calls out their names.

> SHERRY
> Nicky?! Roxy?! Where are
> you?!

Sherry hears the voices of her friends calling back to her but she can't find them. Then, out of the shadows into the dim light comes a horrifying abomination -- her worst fear come to haunt her.

A strange figure emerges from the darkness. His face is hideous, bloated and partially rotted away with maggots coming out of his right eye socket.

His body is pecked to pieces from the vultures who tore it and ate from his flesh, with a see-through hole in the center of his chest. He is dressed in a blood-soaked brown police uniform.

This zombie from hell, awakened to life, is revealed to be SHERIFF MITCH BARTON (aka ZOMBIE MITCH).

> ZOMBIE MITCH
> Sherry, my little slut. How
> nice to see you.

Sherry slowly backs up, paralyzed by fear. She is so frightened that she wants to scream, but she can't. Tears of terror spring from her eyes.

> SHERRY
> No, not you.

Zombie Mitch licks his rotting mouth lustfully as he slowly advances towards her.

> ZOMBIE MITCH
> Come to Mitch.

Zombie Mitch continues to walk toward Sherry.
INT. MAZE OF DARKNESS (ROXY'S FEAR) - NIGHT

Roxy tries to find her friends by calling out their names.

> ROXY
> Ricky, where are you?!
> Suddenly, KANE LOUIS
> WILLIAMS, aka the
> VOODOO MAN, appears
> behind her. He holds a long,
> thin hand sickle in his right
> hand. He places his left
> hand on Roxy's shoulder,
> spooking her.
> KANE
> Your blood calls to me.
> ROXY
> You? We killed you!

She slowly walks back, while Kane walks towards her.

> ROXY
> It was you all along!
> KANE
> (ominously)
> No child. It is your own fear
> that has summoned us... or
> maybe you're just going mad
> from guilt. Your sister is dead
> and not coming back, she's
> burning in hell with us.

Roxy starts to feel terror and guilt at the same time.

                    ROXY
          Stop it!
                    KANE
          (evilly)
          Oh no child... we've just be-
          gun.

INT. MAZE OF DARKNESS (RICKY'S FEAR) - NIGHT
Ricky starts his own search for Roxy.

                    RICKY
          Roxy? Where are you?

Then, Ricky hears a masculine tough guy voice in the echo.

                    SWITCH (O.S.)
          She's not here.

Ricky turns around and sees SWITCH, his former best friend, before his untimely death.

He appears to be a normal-looking human, a hardcore buffed up metal head burnout with long black hair tied back in a ponytail. He wears a black t-shirt with the band's logo, a cut-out sleeveless denim vest jacket, torn up jeans and black shoes.

Ricky is in disbelief that his friend is alive.

                    SWITCH
          Hey, buddy.
                    RICKY
          Switch?
                    SWITCH
          In the flesh.

RICKY

It can't be you. You! You're
dead!

SWITCH

You left me there. Asshole.

Switch transforms in a dead mutilated corpse. He looks like he was mauled
by a lion. There are vampire bite and claw marks on his neck, arms, chest and
face. Blood drips down his face. His clothes are torn up by slash marks.

SWITCH

Now look at me!!!

Ricky runs away trying to get away from Switch in the darkness -- but everywhere he goes, Switch is there.

SWITCH

Trying to run again. Like
how you ran away when you
could have helped me!

Switch pushes Ricky to the floor. Ricky falls down. Switch strangles Ricky.

RICKY

(struggling)
I had no choice!

SWITCH

(aggressive)
No you chose to fuck her
instead!

Switch tightens his grip around Ricky's neck.

INT. MAZE OF DARKNESS (LIPS AND KUDOS' FEARS) - NIGHT
Lips and Kudos are already in their worst fear.
An OLD JUDGE slams his gavel repeatedly.

JUDGE
Guilty! Guilty! GUILTY!

Kudos is locked in a small room with steel metal bars screaming in agony. Kudos' fear is claustrophobia.

Lips is strapped in an electric chair, while the hooded EXECUTIONER pulls the switch. Lips' body starts to shiver and shake as his body fries.
INT. MAZE OF DARKNESS (NICHOLAS' FEAR) - NIGHT
Nicholas is all by himself. He cannot find Ricky, Roxy, Sherry or Beth. He sees a tombstone. It reads, "IN LOVING MEMORY - LISA CARLYLE - SISTER AND DEAR FRIEND".
Nicholas drops down on his knees.

NICHOLAS
I should have protected her.
It's my fault.

FLASHBACK - MONTAGE
Nicholas and Lisa together, happy and in love -- Nicholas teaches her how to use her new found powers and gifts while at the same time romantically teasing her. They start to kiss and make out
Nicholas proposes to Lisa in front of his bandmates at the Cobra Club on Halloween night before they go onstage. Lisa is surprised and elated as she says yes, and he puts the ring on her finger. The band congratulates the two lovers together.
Mitch Barton, grinning evilly, kills Lisa.
Nicholas grieves after Lisa is killed.
Enraged, Nicholas kills Barton.

INT. MAZE OF DARKNESS (NICHOLAS' FEAR) - NIGHT

Nicholas comes out of it filled with guilt and grief that he failed to save his fiancÈe who he deeply loved.

Nicholas starts to cry. Tears of sorrow run down his face.

> NICHOLAS
>
> It's all my fault.

The hand of a woman gently touches Nicholas. He turns around in shock of fear. He crawls back on the ground.

> NICHOLAS
>
> This isn't real.

LISA appears. She has long blonde straight hair with orange flames for highlights, wears a black leather vest with red and orange flames, a black tank top that exposes her belly button with a silver belly button ring, leather pants with chains, heart necklace, red lips, silver earrings, and black boots.

She has a bloody gunshot wound through her heart.

> NICHOLAS
>
> (faintly)
>
> Lisa?

Lisa kneels down to Nicholas.

> LISA
>
> I am real. I came back to help
> you all. Listen to me. I don't
> have much time.
>
> NICHOLAS
>
> How is this possible?

                    LISA

Don't ask questions. Just pay
attention. You've got to get
away from her.

                    NICHOLAS

Who?

                    LISA

She's the one who's causing
all this to happen. Get out of
here before she kills you all.

Nicholas is in disbelief and fear. He wraps his arms around his head, bury-
ing his face.

                    NICHOLAS

No, this is not real! I'm
dreaming.

MEMORY FLASH

Nicholas experiences a nightmare of Lisa haunting him as undead ghoul...
her corpse is soulless... her eyes are like black pearls... her lips are blue...

She walks to Nicholas like a zombie trying to grab him in anger for letting
her get killed... she digs her zombie claws on his face as blood runs down... then
kisses him...

BACK TO SCENE

                    NICHOLAS

You're dead! Go away! Stop
tormenting me!

Lisa looks at him sadly and her spirit dissolves.

LISA (V.O.)
Leave before it's too late.

Nicholas is still in fear. Then Beth comes out of the shadows and finds Nicholas. Strangely, she is completely unharmed.

BETH
Nicholas!

She runs to Nicholas to help him.

NICHOLAS
Leave me alone!
BETH
Nicholas, it's me Beth! It's
okay! It's okay!

Beth shakes his body. Nicholas opens his eyes and sees Beth.

NICHOLAS
(in a cold sweat)
Beth, what happened?
BETH
I tried finding the others. I
don't know what happened
to them.
NICHOLAS
We got to find them, now!

Nicholas gets up and tries to walk. Beth grabs his left shoulder tightly with both hands.

NICHOLAS

Ow! What are you doing?
That hurts!

She is desperate.

BETH

I'm not going to lose you again.

NICHOLAS

What the hell are you doing?!

Beth tightens her grip. Her nails are long, almost clawlike. Blood seeps through Nicholas' left shoulder, soaking his leather jacket.

NICHOLAS

Let go my arm!

Beth's closes her eyes. Then she opens her eyes revealing glowing blood red eyes, smooth as polished marble stone.

He is shocked beyond belief.

NICHOLAS

You're not human.

Beth transforms from her modern day appearance into a beautiful enchantress of desire, beyond what any man could dare to dream.

Her strawberry blonde hair is long and soft as silk. Her skin is fair as an innocent virgin's. Her lips are red as the darkest rose. She is dressed in a very sexy, revealing dark scarlet red gown.

BETH

No. I'm yours. As before.

Beth passionately kisses Nicholas.

> BETH
>
> I have searched for eternity to find you. Now nothing will ever take you away from me again. Nothing.

INT. DREAM BEDROOM FANTASY - NIGHT

The dark maze transforms into a dream illusion of a candlelit bedroom.

Beth seduces him, putting him in trance. She lays on top of him on the bed and kisses him. Overtaken by this siren's hypnotic seduction he willfully kisses her.

INT. MAZE OF DARKNESS - LATER

Barabbas is looking for the other survivors. Suddenly, Lisa's spirit arrives in front of him.

> LISA
>
> Barabbas.
>
> BARABBAS
>
> It's you.
>
> LISA
>
> Barabbas, you must help the others. They need you.
>
> BARABBAS
>
> Who are you?
>
> LISA
>
> I'm a friend. That is all you need to know. My soul is trapped within the walls of this cursed place.

> BARABBAS
> What the hell is happening?
> LISA
> Face your worst fears and you
> will be able to escape.
> BARABBAS
> I already have.
> LISA
> Then help the others face
> theirs.

Lisa opens the gateway portal.

> LISA
> Go through the gateway, be-
> fore it closes.

Barabbas enters the gateway.
INT. MAZE OF DARKNESS (SHERRY'S FEAR) - NIGHT
Sherry runs -- Zombie Mitch catches up with her. He pins Sherry to the ground, getting ready to rape her.
Sherry is in tears.

> ZOMBIE MITCH
> Just like old times.

Zombie Mitch laughs evilly. Suddenly -- Barabbas punches Mitch. Mitch falls to the ground and disappears.
Sherry is relieved that she is rescued.

> BARABBAS
> Wake up.

Barabbas picks Sherry up and helps her to her feet. Sherry looks around to see if Mitch is still there. He is not.

> SHERRY
> What happened?
> BARABBAS
> Your worst fear is trying to fuck with you. You have to fight it! He's not real!

Zombie Mitch reappears. Sherry vamps out as her powers begin to develop.

> SHERRY
> Go to hell!

She lunges at Zombie Mitch and attacks him. Zombie Mitch disappears for good. Sherry's worst fear has been conquered.

> BARABBAS
> Good girl.

Another portal opens up out of the darkness.

> BARABBAS
> Follow me.

Barabbas and Sherry enter the portal.
INT. MAZE OF DARKNESS (ROXY'S FEAR) - NIGHT
The Voodoo Man, Kane, wrestles Roxy on the ground, tries to cut her with his hand sickle. Roxy is putting up a good fight.
Barabbas and Sherry come through the portal.

SHERRY
He's not real. Face your fear.

Roxy intimidates Kane.

ROXY
Go ahead, do it. You don't
scare me anymore.

Roxy surrenders herself, fearlessly looking at him straight in the eyes. Kane tries to stab her but the sickle goes through her like a ghost, leaving her completely unharmed.

Kane lifts up the hand sickle. He sees his hands dissolve in front of his eyes.

KANE
NO!!!

Kane disappears and is no more.

Roxy gets up and another portal opens up. Barabbas, Sherry and Roxy exit through the portal.

INT. MAZE OF DARKNESS (RICKY'S FEAR) - NIGHT

Ricky continues to struggle -- Switch continues to beat the shit out of him.

Roxy and Sherry enter through the portal with Barabbas. They see Ricky actually hitting himself across the face.

RICKY
It's not my fault, Switch! It's
not my fault!

Roxy and Sherry each grab Ricky's arms to stop him from hurting himself.

> ROXY
> Ricky! Wake up! You're see-
> ing things.

Ricky is still in fear.

> RICKY
> I couldn't save him! Switch
> is dead; I should have helped
> him instead of running away.
> I'm a coward.
> ROXY
> No you're not. There was
> nothing you could have done
> for him.

Ricky snaps back to reality. Switch is gone. He sees Roxy, Sherry and Barabbas with him.

INT. MAZE OF DARKNESS - NIGHT

Lips and Kudos continue to live their worst fears, until the rooms begin to fade away. They see Barabbas, Sherry, Roxy and Ricky appear.

The darkness quickly shatters like a broken mirror as pieces of it scatter around the generator room and dissolve on the floor and fade away into nothing.

INT. GENERATOR ROOM - MOMENTS LATER

The survivors are all back into the generator room.

> LIPS
> What the hell just happened?
> BARABBAS
> Your worst fears came true.

                    SHERRY
How come your fear didn't
come to life?
                    BARABBAS
Because, I beat mine a long
time ago.

Lisa appears out of the shadows.

                    LISA
It's not over yet.
                    ROXY
Lisa! You're dead!
                    LISA
I'll explain everything. Just
follow me, quickly.

INT. DREAM BEDROOM FANTASY - NIGHT
Beth and Nicholas make love. They are partially naked, covered in the bed
sheets. Beth is on top of Nicholas.

                    BETH
Remember...

Nicholas's eyes glow blue.
FLASHBACK - INT. CASTLE BRUNESVICT - NIGHT
SUPER: "MEDIEVAL HUNGARY - 1241 A.D."
The wedding altar is in a castle with two burning torch sconces hanging
from the wall above them. The row of wedding flowers are in a garland hanging
from the ceiling.
The wedding of LADY BETHIA and NICOLAI is taking place with sev-
eral nobles and royal soldiers attending the ceremony.

Lady Bethia wears a royal medieval wedding gown and Nicolai wears his battle armor and a cape. They exchange vows and the rings.

> NICOLAI
>
> With this ring, I thee wed.

> BETHIA
>
> With this ring, I thee wed. My love, upon this night I pledge my heart is yours forever.
>
> NICOLAI
>
> As do I.

They exchange a kiss.

INT. CASTLE BRUNESVICT - BEDROOM CHAMBER - LATER

Bethia and Nicolai make love on their honeymoon in their bedroom chamber.

INT. CASTLE BRUNESVICT - BALCONY - DAY

The next afternoon. Nicolai has been summoned by the Hungarian King to leave for battle. Nicolai says goodbye to his wife, Lady Bethia.

> BETHIA
>
> Nicolai don't go on this campaign. I fear for your safety. What if you are killed or captured by the king's enemies?
>
> NICOLAI
>
> I will be alright. I must go. It's the king's command. Don't worry... I shall see you again.

Nicolai holds his love and wife in his arms and makes his vow to her as she embraces him with love and tenderness.

> BETHIA
>
> I just don't want to lose you. I
> love you so much.

Nicolai cradles Bethia in his arms. He's her protector, her angel, her love in this life and in the next.

> NICOLAI
>
> Nothing will ever separate
> us. As long as one of us lives,
> we'll always have each other
> in our hearts. I love you. As
> you do I.

The two kiss.

EXT. HUNGARIAN FIELDS - NIGHT

Nicolai rides his horse with his fellow soldiers. Nicolai fights bravely, killing many Mongols.

He gets shot by a hailstorm of flying arrows. Nicolai falls down, dead.

INT. CASTLE BRUNESVICT - NIGHT

A Hungarian soldier arrives and whispers to Lady Bethia the tragic news.

Lady Bethia falls down to her knees weeping.

INT. TUNNEL OF SOULS

Nicolai's immortal soul goes through the tunnel of light -- heading past ghostly forms -- headed to rebirth...

INT. DREAM BEDROOM FANTASY - NIGHT (BACK TO PRESENT)

Nicholas wakes up from his vision, astounded.

> NICHOLAS
>
> I remember.

Beth is now Bethia. Her American accent is gone, replaced with a Hungarian accent.

> BETHIA (BETH)

Nicolai.

> NICHOLAS

Bethia.

INT. HALLWAY - NIGHT

Lisa leads the survivors through a long pipe hallway out of the generator room. She stops walking.

> LISA

> The past and present now come full circle.

Roxy interrupts.

> ROXY

> Wait a sec. How do we know you're who you say you are?

> LISA

> Rox, I had to escape from hell to get here.

> RICKY

> Umm... it's her alright.

> SHERRY

> What happened to you?

> LISA

> I'll show you everything.

Lisa uses her spectral powers to show them a vision of the past, but is interrupted--

The lights begin to supernaturally flicker with an evil spiritual presence.

The group hears the sounds of scratching on the walls. Its rhythm grows louder and louder as if thousands upon thousands of critters are burrowing through the concrete wall.

The lights go dark and they turn back on dimly. There are thousands of creepy, crawling, leech-like demons crawling through the walls.

> BARABBAS
>
> Holy shit!

The demons are known as LEECHERS. Multiple leechers spring jump on Kudos, biting him repeatedly. Kudos is able to throw the leechers off him... but bleeds from many bites. He stumbles and falls.

> KUDOS
>
> Poison...

Kudos dies.

The rest try to kill the leechers by stomping and squishing them. Then, more leechers arrive.

Lisa takes charge. She transforms into a vortex of white mist that quickly spreads through the hallways. The white mist quickly exterminates the leechers. It has no effect on the vampires.

Lips goes to his dead friend's body.

> BARABBAS
>
> Forget him, he's dead.

The white mist turns back into the spirit form of Lisa.

> LISA
>
> Quickly.

Lisa leaves. The group follows her.

A monstrous creature cries out.

ROXY

What now?!

Out of the shadows comes a giant blob like centipede demon, disfigured and grotesque in appearance and size. It has large glowing eyes, and can clearly see in the dark. It hungry and its mad.

She is large but very slow in speed due to her massive weight as she materializes in front of them. This demon is the great MALOCKAR DEMON.

LISA

Shit, it's a Malockar Demon!

The Malockar Demon rushes to the group along with thousands of leechers on her side.

ROXY

(to Lisa)

I think you pissed off their mother.

The group races toward the steel metal door leading into the steam plant's storage warehouse.

Barabbas sees a portable propane tank hanging on the wall. He smashes open the glass case that it's in and grabs the tank off the wall. Thinking fast.

BARABBAS

Ricky, your lighter!

Ricky tosses the lighter to Barabbas. Barabbas catches it and opens the valve on the propane tank and ignites it.

Using the propane tank as a makeshift flamethrower, he roasts the Malockar Demon which screams in agony.

The Malockar Demon fries and explodes! The fireball shoots in front of the group down the hallway, killing all the demons at once.

The group finds the double doorway to the steam plant's storage warehouse. They open the doors, only to make a shocking discovery...

INT. DREAM BEDROOM FANTASY - NIGHT

Bethia has assumed her full demon succubus form -- her long strawberry hair covers her torso, her horns are long and sharp like a goat's horns, her claws are about a foot long, her teeth are razor sharp, her eyes are red as a blood moon and her skin is fair like snow.

She still wears the scarlet red gown along with ancient jewelry around her neck and left wrist.

While she makes love with Nicholas, she is feeding off him -- biting into his neck and drinking his blood.

Then, she looks up and sees the group standing there...

The dream bedroom illusion vanishes abruptly, revealing...

INT. STORAGE WAREHOUSE - NIGHT

... nothing more than a rundown storage room with Nicholas and Bethia covered in a pile of old blankets, sheets and rags.

The group is in shock.

ROXY

Beth!

LISA

She never was.

Bethia looks up at the group with her evil red eyes and her bloodstained lips.

BETHIA

HE'S MINE!!!

Bethia evilly laughs. Bethia and Nicholas vanish into red smoke. The pipes begin to rumble. Smoke comes out of the pipes. Fire blast out of the pipes, engulfing the whole room.

The survivors are trapped in the fire. Lisa psychically turns on the ceiling sprinkler system -- water jets out and douses the blaze.

The sprinkler system turns off.

Sherry goes to Lisa and confronts her.

> SHERRY
>
> Alright, no more games! Tell
> us what is going on!
>
> LISA
>
> This is not my fault. You want
> the truth. Here.
>
> (raises her right hand)
>
> See and believe!

Lisa creates a vision of the past before them to see.

FLASHBACK - INT. CASTLE BRUNESVICT - DAY

The castle is filled with sorrow and sadness. Dozens of people attending the funeral of Lady Bethia's deceased husband and Hungary's greatest warrior, Nicolai Estratos.

Lady Bethia Brunesvict stands with her sister ANGELICA, who bears an extremely close resemblance to Lisa. In attendance with the two royal women are their closest friends, two maidens who resemble the appearance of Roxy and Sherry, dressed in black gowns.

Two soldiers stand next to them, bowing their heads out of respect to their fallen comrade and friend. They bear a strong resemblance to Switch and Ricky.

> LISA (V.O.)
>
> Bethia was my sister at one
> time. I learned the truth
> about all of our former lives

in the past while I was in hell.
In the spirit world, the dead
can link psychically with one
another, sharing memories
of their former lives and past
ones. We were all reincarnat-
ed at one time or another.

ROXY (V.O.)

But how?

INT. TUNNEL OF SOULS

Lisa shows them another vision of the souls of mankind -- how they either go through the tunnel of light or are lost to hell.

Lisa is shown walking to a tunnel of light to be reborn a second time.

Out of the darkness comes a dark figure to take her away. The dark figure is revealed to be Bethia in her full demon form.

LISA (V.O.)

Some people, when they die
see a tunnel of white light and
come back to be reborn on
earth or go to a higher place,
some call this place, heaven.
Others, who are damned,
go to hell. When I died, as
I crossed over into the spirit
world, I saw the tunnel but
Bethia came for my soul and
kidnapped me, before I had
the chance to be reborn.

EXT. HELL - NIGHT

Hell is a dark inferno, with a cave-like atmosphere. There is a burning river of fire and lava that bubbles and spews surrounded by desolate rocks and canyons.

There are voodoo demon creatures of all types and size roaming all around the rock valleys and ridges of hell.

On charred and blackened scorched hilltops is a city of sorrow and torture, where Baron Samedi rules alongside with the other lords of hell.

Hell's design is based upon English romantic 19th century painter John Martin's paintings of hell.

INT. CASTLE BRUNESVICT - CHAMBER ROOM - DAY

Angelica is seven months pregnant. Her husband, GUSTAVO, a Hungarian soldier, consoles her.

Behind the door, Lady Bethia spies on them with burning envious eyes filled with jealously and hate.

INT. ANGELICA'S BEDROOM - NIGHT

Angelica is all by herself looking out in the window. Lady Bethia emerges from the shadows with a dagger.

> LISA (V.O.)
> In a fit of jealous rage. She
> killed me and my unborn son.

A silhouette of Lady Bethia stabbing Angelica in the back. Angelica falls down and dies.

EXT. COURTYARD - NIGHT

Several angry citizens and nobles have Lady Bethia executed in the kingdom's main city square.

> LISA (V.O.)
> For her crimes, the people
> cursed her and burned her at
> the stake.

As she burns, Lady Bethia shows no emotion but coldness.

INT. STORAGE WAREHOUSE - NIGHT (BACK TO PRESENT)

RICKY

But how did that bitch become...You know...

Ricky makes devil horns on his forehead.

LISA

He is the one who made
her. The god of hell. Baron
Samedi.

FLASHBACK - EXT. HELL - NIGHT

Bethia's naked body falls deep down into hell. Her body is unharmed in hell but in perfect condition. She lands on the rocky ground.

BARON SAMEDI, the god of death and hell, comes to a weak Bethia and offers her his hand.

Baron Samedi is the vodun god of death in the voodoo faith and mythology. He is also a sex spirit besides being a deity.

BARON SAMEDI

(deep and echoing voice)

I have waited for you to
come. No other woman has
pleased me. Your hate is like
pure fire. Your evil is beyond sweet. Serve me and be
spared from eternal death in
hell. Taste the pleasures of
immortal life. Be my consort

and you will live in boundless
pleasures, forever.

At first, Bethia wants to say no, but after seeing the pain and suffering of
the damned souls...

BETHIA
(weakly)
Yes.

Baron Samedi picks up Bethia's naked body in his arms.
INT. BLOOD POOL CHAMBER ROOM - NIGHT
In this ancient torch lit chamber room is a large bathing pool filled with
bubbling dark red and black blood that almost resembles pitch and tar.
Baron Samedi places the living dead Bethia, nude, into the blood pool and
fully submerges her underneath the burning liquid. Bethia screams in agony as
her body is savagely burned by the boiling substance in the pool. The liquid has
no effect on the Baron.
A human female demonic face in living fire burns in the pool as steam
comes up from the vat.
Bethia resurfaces out of the liquid fully restored and given dark powers by
the god. Her red eyes burn brightly. Her face has sensuous features and sharp-
fanged teeth. She emerges out of the blood pool naked.

BARON SAMEDI
Of lust and blood. Be my
queen, my bride.
BETHIA
Yes. My lord.

Bethia is reborn as a succubus demon. Beautiful but deadly.
Baron Samedi magically wraps energy around Bethia's body. The baron
gives Bethia a sexy scarlet red gown.

LISA (V.O.)

She became his temptress and love.

INT. STORAGE WAREHOUSE - NIGHT (BACK TO PRESENT)

The vision over, Lisa turns to the group.

LISA

Did she really love the baron? I don't know. But I do know from these things of the former memories that I have been given. I know that she loved Nicholas at one time.

SHERRY

How did you come back?

LISA

I managed to find a gateway portal that sent me back. She must have seen and followed me to get here to this place.

ROXY

Where did she take Nicky?

LISA

Back to hell.

RICKY

No way.

LISA

Yeah she did. Listen, I can lead you all there. We have to help him.

LIPS

(sarcastic)

Hey, sweetheart -- I hate to
rain on your parade... but we
got no weapons.

She calmly smiles.

LISA
Oh yes you do.

Lisa points to the wooden crates in the storage room. The members of the
group find weapons and ammunition in the crates.

Barabbas opens a top secret U.S. Army crate and finds a flamethrower.

Roxy finds an M79 40mm Grenade Launcher.

Lips finds an M-16 machine gun rifle.

Ricky finds a trench combat shotgun.

Sherry finds an S&W M76 "The Swedish K" sub-machine gun.

LIPS
Looks like some of our boys
did some previous gun run-
ning in this place.
BARABBAS
These are guns from 'Nam.
(to the Midnight Freaks)
Lips, lock and load.

Lips smiles wickedly.

LIPS
Gotcha.

Barabbas and Lips load all the guns.

LIPS

Ready.

The Midnight Freaks with Barabbas and Lips grabs their weapons.

SHERRY

Rock N' Roll!

EXT. HELL - NIGHT

The dark underworld city of Hell.

INT. BLOOD POOL CHAMBER ROOM - NIGHT

Nicholas, fully-dressed in his rocker outfit returns to the place that he was created.

NICHOLAS

This is the place where Kane made me.

(to Bethia)

Why did you bring me back here?

BETHIA

Because I still love you. I always have. I want us to be together again. You are the only one, who ever made me truly happy, when I was alive.

NICHOLAS

How do you know what I am?

BETHIA

I saw when Kane made you what you are. Serve me and I will make you more powerful

than you ever were before.
Love me again, and I will
yours forever. Devoted, faith-
ful and ever pleasing.

MEMORY FLASH

Nicholas is being made a vampire -- baptized in the blood pool by Kane, emerging as a vampire -- Bethia peeks behind the blood chamber door spying on them.

BACK TO SCENE

Bethia beckons to Nicholas.

BETHIA

Be my husband again. My angel, prince.

Bethia recreates the Hungarian wedding ceremony with her magic.

BETHIA

My former master, the Baron,
is no more. I killed him.

FLASHBACK - EXT. HELL - NIGHT

As Bethia serves Baron Samedi his drinking goblet one night, she slips a clear liquid into his wine.

Samedi nods to his wife and drinks from the goblet -- then begins to choke. The poison is really a magical potion.

Baron Samedi drops to the floor dying. Bethia kneels down beside him and pulls out a dagger that has been concealed in her solid blouse dress. She stabs him in the heart, finally killing him.

INT. CASTLE BRUNESVICT - NIGHT

Nicholas is back in his royal armor. Bethia is back in her medieval wedding dress. The attendees are dressed in noble clothing with golden masks covering their faces. The priest is wearing Catholic vestments and a platinum mask on his face.

EXT. HELL - NIGHT

A portal opens and Lisa, The Midnight Freaks, Barabbas and Lips comes out of the portal.

Lisa points out to the great city of hell.

> LISA
>
> There we must go. Hurry.

Lisa leads the group to Bethia's castle. These chosen warriors of Rock N' Roll are ready for battle.

EXT. BETHIA'S CASTLE - NIGHT

Several Yoruba Demons, Skeletons and GALENITE DEMONS (decapitated demonic heads with wings) guard the entrance.

Lisa stops and disappears.

> SHERRY
>
> Lisa! Where'd she go?!
>
> LISA (V.O.)
>
> This is far as I can take you.
>
> Good luck.
>
> BARABBAS
>
> Looks like, we're on our own
>
> now.

The group reaches the entrance to the castle and charges the demon guardians. The battle begins.

> LIPS
>
> (to the demons)
>
> Alright, you reject fuckwads!
>
> Come get some!

A Yoruba Demon points his left index claw to the group.

YORUBA DEMON
(in demon voice)
FUCK YOU!!!

MONTAGE - BATTLE
Heavy Metal Music Plays.
Roxy fires her M70 40mm Grenade Launcher and blasts a couple of Yoruba Demons.
Lips and Sherry blast the Galenite Demons with their machine guns.
Barabbas barbecues some skeletons with his flamethrower.
Ricky blasts the last of the skeletons with his trench combat shotgun.
The final Yoruba Demon rips open Lips' neck, killing him.

BARABBAS
Lips!

Barabbas goes to the Yoruba Demon, grabs it by the jaws and breaks it and body slams him. Killing the demon.
Barabbas super punches the door down. The group enters the courtyard.
INT. CASTLE BRUNESVICT - NIGHT
The priest brings a chalice filled with blood.

BETHIA
(to Nicholas)
Drink and be one of us.

Nicholas grabs the chalice. He seems to embrace Bethia's request as he closes his eyes and pretends to drink from the chalice. Then, he opens his eyes and spits the blood in her face.
He is filled with disgust

NICHOLAS

In your dreams.

He throws the chalice at the priest.

The illusion disappears and the room changes back to the blood chamber!

INT. BLOOD POOL CHAMBER ROOM - NIGHT

Nicholas returns to his rocker outfit appearance and confronts Bethia who has returned to her scarlet red dress.

NICHOLAS

I saw the past when you put
that trance on me. I saw what
you did.

MEMORY FLASH

As Nicholas makes love to Bethia, he sees in a vision her killing her own sister and unborn child.

BACK TO SCENE

BETHIA

What do you mean?

NICHOLAS

You killed your own sister.
Even if she had been reborn
to live in another time, she
was my dearest friend. I cared
about her. You evil bitch!
She's the only woman I truly
love.

Her heart is shattered inside.

BETHIA

It's not true!

Nicholas is filled with contempt and hate.

NICHOLAS

Why would I want to love
someone like you? You're
more of a monster I am.

Heartbroken and angry, Bethia transforms into her demon succubus form.

BETHIA

Then you will die. If I can't
have you -- no one will!

Bethia grabs Nicholas by the collar. She is super strong but sexy. Her claws grow about a foot long ready to strike.

Suddenly, BOOM! The wooden double door explodes. The Midnight Freaks and Barabbas arrive, blasting open the door.

Bethia looks at the heroes.

ROXY

Party's over.

BETHIA

(evilly)

You're too late!

Bethia impales Nicholas through the chest with her claws. Nicholas screams in pain. Bethia tosses Nicholas to the floor.

SHERRY

Nicholas!!!

Sherry goes to a wounded Nicholas. Nicholas is gushing out blood from both his chest wound and his mouth.

SHERRY

Heal! Come on, you can do it!

Nicholas tries to use his powers to heal himself but the wound is beyond repairing.

NICHOLAS

I can't!

SHERRY

Don't give me that!

Bethia tastes the blood on her claws, smiling victoriously.

Sherry turns her attention to Bethia, with furious anger. She charges Bethia, but Bethia knocks her down.

Barabbas and Ricky without hesitation try to shoot Bethia.

Bethia uses her magic to melt their guns right in front of them.

Barabbas and Ricky drop their guns.

Out of options, the group vamps out and tries to attack Bethia in hand to hand combat. But Bethia is too strong and knocks them all down.

BETHIA

I expected better.

She cracks her knuckles, mocking them.

BETHIA

Push overs.

BARABBAS

She's too strong! We got to
get out of here!!!

A blue portal strangely opens on its own.

LISA (V.O.)

Go quickly!

Barabbas gets up and picks up Nicholas in his arms -- then he the Midnight
Freaks rush through the portal.

BETHIA

(enraged)

NOOOOOOO!!!

INT. BOILER ROOM - NIGHT

The Midnight Freaks and Barabbas are back in the steam propane power
plant. They land in the boiler room where they first found Bethia.

Then Lisa appears.

ROXY

Lisa!

LISA

Where is he? I can heal him.

Barabbas lays Nicholas on the floor at Lisa's feet.

Lisa kneels down and uses her spectral powers, placing her hand on Nicholas'
chest to heal his wound.

Nicholas' wound closes up and he breathes deeply.

She is concerned but happy he is alive.

LISA

You almost died.

Nicholas opens his eye and looks up at Lisa.

NICHOLAS

Lisa, you are here. It is you.
But where's Bethia?

Bethia appears from the portal in her succubus form.

BETHIA

Right here.

Lisa turns to Sherry.

LISA

Let me use your body. You
have the power. Unleash your
hate!

Sherry shakes her head.

SHERRY

I can't.

LISA

(commanding voice)

Yes you can!!! Let me possess
you.

Bethia mocks Sherry.

> BETHIA
> (flipping her fingers)
> Come on, little girl. Show me
> what you got! I'll kill you like
> a fly.

> ROXY
> (to Sherry)
> Do it!

Sherry surrenders herself.

> SHERRY
> (to Lisa)
> Okay.

Lisa possesses Sherry's vampiric body.

Sherry levitates in the air, red lighting shooting out of her body. She instantly vamps out transforming to a more demonic version of her vampire self. Her transformation complete, she is evil beyond evil. Ready to kick some ass.

Bethia, eyes glowing red with malice ready to kill, uses her magic to transform the boiler room into a demonic dungeon-like battle arena. The rest of the group disappears as the room has changed.

> BETHIA
> (maniacally)
> HA! HA! HA!

INT. DEMONIC DUNGEON BATTLE ARENA - NIGHT
The fight begins.
Instrumental heavy metal music plays.

> SHERRY
> Let's go!

Sherry and Bethia leap in mid-air, lunging at one another, and fight in hand to hand combat with claws and hatred burning. Devil against devil.

Evil red energy surrounds Sherry as she unleashes her full primal fury. Her inner hate and pain from being raped lets loose like a bomb exploding violently -- the two fight with super speed, and move and clash like "THE FLASH".

The two supernatural women zip around the room dodging each other's strikes and attacks, until Sherry gets the upper hand and zaps Bethia with an evil energy attack --

Powering up, she shoots an energy blast at Bethia knocking her out cold to the ground. Bethia is defeated.

The demonic arena vanishes back to the boiler room and the fight is over.

INT. BOILER ROOM - NIGHT

Evil red lightning shoots out of Sherry's body as Lisa's spirit comes out of her host's body. Sherry reverts back to her human appearance. The rest of the group reappears along with the boiler room.

> SHERRY
> (to Lisa)
> Thanks, I needed that.
> LISA
> That's all the hate that you had in you after being raped. If I did not help you get rid of it, it would have killed you.
> SHERRY
> Is it still there?

> LISA
> Yes, but now you have the
> ability to control it as well as
> your powers.
> RICKY
> What just happened?
> SHERRY
> I kicked her ass!

Sherry kicks Bethia in the side of her belly.

> SHERRY
> (to Bethia)
> Bitchy Cunt.

Barabbas chuckles.

> NICHOLAS
> She's going to wake up any
> minute.
> BARABBAS
> Oh, no she's not.

Barabbas breaks the piping off the wall, and wraps it around Bethia's body tying her up.

Ricky brainstorms an idea.

> RICKY
> (spontaneously sarcastic)
> What are we standing around
> for? Let's send this bitch back
> to hell!

The rest of the group stares at Ricky.

> NICHOLAS
> (to Ricky)
> That's the best thing you've said all night.
>
> RICKY
> How are we going to blow this place?
>
> BARABBAS
> Like this.

Barabbas turns on the gas valves in the boiler room. The Midnight Freaks follow his lead, opening up the other gas valves in the boiler room. Methane gas starts to fill the room.

> NICHOLAS
> Let's get out of here!
>
> RICKY
> How can we? The main door is still locked! We'll be killed!
>
> LISA
> Bethia's power over this place is weakening. The main entrance door is unlocked. I'll bring you all there.

Lisa uses her power to teleport the Midnight Freaks and Barabbas to the main entrance work floor.

INT. ABANDONED PLANT - MAIN WORK FLOOR - NIGHT

Lisa, The Midnight Freaks and Barabbas arrive in the main work floor room. They rush to the main door and Barabbas opens it up. A light hits the horizon as dawn approaches. Everybody gets out of the plant, except for Lisa.

NICHOLAS
Lisa come on!
LISA
No! I have to finish this. Go
now!

Lisa psychically turns on all the methane gas valves in the blood-soaked work floor room.

Then out of nowhere, Bethia busts straight through the ground floor, in her full succubus form. She now has large demon wings, a prehensile long demonic tail and an evil red aura surrounds her. Her red gown is in shreds.

BETHIA
NO ONE ESCAPES ME!
NO ONE!!!

Roxy, who still has her grenade launcher on her, fires one last shot.

ROXY
(tough as nails)
Toast this, Bitch!

The grenade hit Bethia blowing her into smithereens with the explosion igniting the methane gas-filled plant.

The plant starts to explode and the Midnight Freaks run to the cars.

EXT. ABANDONED PLANT - NIGHT

The Midnight Freaks quickly get into their cars with Barabbas joining them and drive out of there, slamming through the main gate -- as the entire plant explodes in a fiery inferno ten times the size of fourth of July.

The Ghoul Mobile and the Speed Demon do a 180 on the dirt road -- the Midnight Freaks and Barabbas witness the plant blow up and collapse as it comes crashing down.

The cars turn to the long open highway and drive off into the morning dawn.

EXT. NEW MEXICO HIGHWAY - DAY

The sun rises as the Ghoul Mobile and the Speed Demon drive on the road.

INT. THE GHOUL MOBILE - DAY

Ricky drives the car. Nicholas is in the front passenger's seat. Barabbas is in the back seat.

> BARABBAS
>
> Head two miles up the road.
> There is an open all night
> biker bar that me and my
> buddies own.
>
> RICKY
> (worried)
> You still going to kill us?
>
> BARABBAS
>
> No.

EXT. COBRA BIKER BAR - DAY

The Ghoul Mobile and The Speed Demon pull into the parking lot of a small biker bar in the middle of nowhere.

The Midnight Freaks and Barabbas exit their vehicles. Nicholas opens the back trunk of the Ghoul Mobile and hands Barabbas the duffel bags filled with cash.

Barabbas opens one of the bags and finds that some of the money is missing.

> BARABBAS
>
> Hey. Some of the cash is
> missing.
>
> ROXY
>
> We kind of used some of it to
> pay off our college debts.

Barabbas grunts in disappointment. He looks up and slowly his frown turns into a smile and he chuckles.

>   BARABBAS
>   You guys are off the hook.
>   But don't ever stick your
>   face in my business again.
>   Got it?
>   NICHOLAS
>   (understanding)
>   Yeah.

The rest of the Midnight Freaks nod their heads in understanding.

>   RICKY
>   (wipes his forehead)
>   Thank God.

Barabbas just smiles.

>   BARABBAS
>   You guys aren't that bad
>   for being a bunch of metal
>   heads. Here... take half. My
>   way of saying thanks for
>   helping me get through the
>   night.
>   Barabbas gives the bag with
>   less money as a gift to thank
>   them, while he keeps the
>   other half in full amount.
>   He offers Nicholas a friendly
>   handshake.

NICHOLAS
Thanks Barabbas. You're not
so bad yourself.

Nicholas accepts the offer as they make a truce.

BARABBAS
If you guys ever have a chance
to head down to New Orleans,
stop in at "The Cobra Club"
and come see me.
NICHOLAS
Hey, Stevie ripped us off there.
BARABBAS
Who?
NICHOLAS
The manager of the club. He
screwed us out of our money.
Said he owed the mob.
BARABBAS
Yeah, the mob was my boys.
Don't worry about it. I'll take
care of him for you.
ROXY
Thanks.
BARABBAS
Do me one last favor before
you guys go -- let me have
that fine truck of yours and
we'll call this whole thing
even.

Barabbas points at the Speed Demon truck.

NICHOLAS
Done.

Roxy tosses Barabbas the keys. Barabbas catches the keys.

BARABBAS
Take care of yourselves out
there, you hear? And stay out
of trouble.

Barabbas smiles, picks up the money and walks inside the bar.
The Midnight Freaks walk back to their cars with their money bag.
Then, Lisa's spirit appears in her rocker clothes fully restored with no wounds. Her long hair is back to its normal blonde color. Her soul has been mended and healed.

NICHOLAS
(surprised)
Lisa.

Lisa walks to Nicholas and kisses him on the lips.

LISA
(smiles angelically)
I'll always be with you.
(beat)
Lover boy.

Then, she speaks to the Midnight Freaks.

                    LISA
Thanks all of you for freeing
me. My soul can now rest in
peace.

A portal of white light opens up.

                    LISA
          (smiling to them all)
I love you all.

Lisa starts to walk to it.

                    ROXY
          (to Lisa; smiling)
Hey sis. Don't forget about us
up there. Huh?
                    LISA
I won't. Keep rockin'.

Lisa goes into the light and her soul is set free as she has fully crossed over
into a higher place, a beautiful dream. The light disappears.
Nicholas smiles.

                    NICHOLAS
          (to the band)
Let's go.

EXT. NEW MEXICO HIGHWAY - DAY
The Ghoul Mobile drives on the open highway.
INT. THE GHOUL MOBILE CAR - DAY
Nicholas drives the car. Sherry is in the front passenger's seat. Roxy and
Ricky are in the back seat.

SHERRY
(wondering)
Hey Nicky, can I ask you
something?

NICHOLAS
What?
SHERRY
Do you regret that we killed
Beth? I mean Bethia?
NICHOLAS
No, you guys are more im-
portant to me. We are a fami-
ly. That what counts. Besides,
how could I ever love some-
one like that? The past is
dead. It's time to look to the
future.
RICKY
So where to now, bro?
NICHOLAS
(smiles a little)
I hear L.A. is a great place to
visit this time of year. How
about Hollywood.
ROXY
(smiles)
Let's rock and roll.

Nicholas smiles and turns on the radio. The Midnight Freaks heavy metal
theme song plays.

The circle is complete for the Midnight Freaks.

EXT. NEW MEXICO HIGHWAY - DAY

The Ghoul Mobile with the Midnight Freaks drives on the open highway into the morning sunrise to an uncertain but hopeful future.

FADE OUT.

...To Be Concluded

www.ingramcontent.com/pod-product-compliance
Lightning Source LLC
Chambersburg PA
CBHW061304170626
46817CB00001B/42